LOVING Leopold

AMOUR TOUJOURS

Diane Coia-Ramsay

ARCHWAY
PUBLISHING

Archway Publishing books may be ordered through booksellers or by contacting:

Archway Publishing
1663 Liberty Drive
Bloomington, IN 47403
www.archwaypublishing.com
844-669-3957

ISBN: 978-1-6657-2272-8 (sc)
ISBN: 978-1-6657-2271-1 (hc)
ISBN: 978-1-6657-2273-5 (e)

Library of Congress Control Number: 2022907874

Print information available on the last page.

Archway Publishing rev. date: 05/10/2022

CONTENTS

CHAPTER 1
Fathers and Daughters, Mothers and Sons

The year was 1904, and it was finally summer. The winter had been bitter cold and the spring even wetter than was usual for London. This had somewhat delayed the Blakeleys' return to Blakefield Castle, in addition to Amalie's now flourishing design business, Madame Bouchard's Interior Designs.

There was to be a grand dinner at the home of Lady Agatha Pengallon, to see the Blakeleys off on their annual retreat to the country. Amalie had remained close to the duchess and, through the complete modernization of her London residence, had a waiting list of customers seeking the services of her much-sought-after design team. Amalie now had three female designers, headed by Maryia Smith and all lured away from Harrods Department Store. Harrods had easily forgiven her transgressions, due to the money spent in the establishment by these designers, who had considerable budgets at their disposal. In addition, Amalie's exquisite taste in clothing was now extended to her baby daughter, Cosette.

Leopold Blakeley kept a tight rein on the financial side of Madame Bouchard's Interior Designs, and he was still a man who would never give another a bargain. The Blakeleys were, by now, very rich, and Leopold's passion for automobiles was reaching its zenith with his purchase of a brand-new shiny red Daimler. It seemed every year, motorcars and fashions were changing, at least for those with the money to fully exploit these new ideas and concepts. Leopold had had an extensive garage built at Blakefield Castle to house his new Daimler and the old Wolseley. He had every intention of adding to his collection as motorcars became faster and more efficient and was even learning the mechanics from McBride, who it seemed was a natural.

Amalie had spent the summer of 1903 mostly in London, and although she had stayed very busy with a new baby and her business, that summer had paled in comparison to the previous year—the year of Malcolm McFadden's adulation and Leopold's extreme jealousy. Amalie looked back on that summer with sentimentality. She knew she should have been completely taken up in caring for her new baby, so sweet and angelic, in that summer of 1903; however, Leopold was completely besotted with his new baby girl, causing a jealousy within Amalie's heart that she had dared not admit, even to herself, as she recalled her own father's devotion to her.

Cosette Fleur Blakeley had been born in the early hours of Christmas Day, 1902, following a long and arduous labor that had put a tortuous end to her mother's Christmas Eve celebration. That particular Christmas Eve had been special since Amalie and her husband were retaking their vows in the small village church.

Amalie had been dressed in sumptuous mink and sapphire blue velvet, and little Leon, dressed as a replica of his father in a morning suit and top hat, was the best man. This special apparel had been purchased by Leopold in New York that December as a peace offering, during an emergency trip taken with Amalie's uncle, Edward March, to fix an almost disastrous speculation that could have brought ruin to both the Blakeleys and the Marches— at least, that is how Amalie and her aunt, Henrietta March, saw it since neither man had ever spoken to them about what truly had occurred that winter.

That was also the time during which Leopold had eavesdropped on Bridgette and Amalie's conversation regarding his parents and childhood. Bridgette had pieced together much of the sad story, which turned out to be the truth of it and which explained all of the half-truths that Amalie's husband had previously told her. He was humiliated to hear it so revealed to his wife, who had been so adored and treasured as a child, whereas he was the product of hate and humiliation. When he left that December for New York, Amalie had feared not so much financial ruin as the ruination of her marriage. She was ashamed and grieved so badly for her handsome and proud husband, who was so disappointed in her listening to Bridgette's rendition of the servants' gossip.

Amalie Bouchard had fallen hopelessly in love with Leopold Blakeley from the moment she first laid eyes on him in the spring of 1898.

After Amalie's parents' untimely death in the summer of 1897, when she was just nineteen, she had been forced to leave her beloved Paris for a new life with her aunt and uncle, Henrietta and Edward March, in London.

Initially, her plans had been to return to Paris the moment she came of age, and she had been fortunate enough to be financially independent, which would have enabled her to do so. However, she wasn't yet in London a year when she first met Leopold Blakeley at her aunt's dinner party, and for all his bad manners and unpleasantness toward her, she was completely lost to him that very first evening. She might not have fully known that at the time, but she had assuredly known it ever since.

Since that spring, Leopold had essentially become Amalie's life, which she had, in essence, given to him freely. There were times when she questioned her haste in doing so, but for all that, she wouldn't have changed a thing, even in her moments of resentment about their life, which along with their very different childhoods resulted in a tumultuous and passionate union between them, since upon that first night, Leopold had found himself no less smitten than she.

Leopold Blakeley, at the age of thirty-two, had been well aware of the attraction he held for the ladies. Although conceited enough regarding his good looks, he was not so ingenuous as to believe that his reputed fortune did not also play a role in his prodigious eligibility, most especially since his reputation of moodiness and surly disposition had done little to temper these ladies in their pursuit of him.

By the time he first laid his eyes on Amalie Bouchard, he had ceased to spend very much time in London society, instead preferring his country estate, Blakefield Castle, and was in the pursuit of enlarging upon his already considerable wealth. He had little intention of ever marrying, coming as he did from an unloving and dysfunctional home. However, he was intrigued enough to make discreet inquiries about the mysterious French beauty, following a curious dinner invitation to the Marches' family home in Belgravia. At the time, he had little acquaintance with the Marches, and he knew enough to realize he was being set up, especially when Freddie Allsop, who had begged his attendance, said so little about her.

He had ascertained that she had thoroughly entranced the young men in London society when first she appeared on the scene, only to disappear shortly thereafter, attending very few social events. He was told she was a young woman of fortune, whose beauty was beyond compare. However, he was also warned that she was very vain and aloof and was reputed to be secretly engaged to a Russian prince. He put the last part down as idle gossip but found himself intrigued to meet this proud, vain Venus. His inquiries, however discreet, caused much speculation in society, even as he assured himself that he was destined to be disappointed.

He had, in the end, reluctantly attended the Marches' dinner party that evening in May 1898, more out of curiosity than out of any concern for Freddie, who was courting the younger March daughter, Judith, with the intention of a proposal of marriage— and disappointment was hardly the emotion he felt upon seeing Amalie. Nor was he disappointed when she, with her French air of aloofness and superiority he had heard so much about, attempted quite adorably to insult him—she so petite, at almost a foot shorter than he, and so very beautiful. She had glared up at him, and he had known quite instantly that she was the very woman he had been seeking, without knowing that he had been seeking out any woman. Essentially, he knew there and then that he would marry her and would allow no other man to touch her. His heart was gladdened as he was well aware of her secretly assessing his manly attributes the entire evening, since he never took his eyes off her and could almost swear that he heard her heart beat faster when he kissed her gloved hand.

Since Cosette's birth, Leopold Blakeley had declared many times that she was the best Christmas present a man ever could have been given. However, on the night of her birth, Amalie had feared for her life. Her confinement during pregnancy, unlike her previous experience with her son, had not been a pleasant one. She had fallen ill with pneumonia and had even fallen down the grand staircase at Blakefield Castle, and it seemed that she was continually prescribed bed rest by Dr. Matthews. However, her baby girl was tiny and as quiet and as sweet-tempered as her brother Leon was boisterous and loud. To some extent this made up for her manner of entering the world.

Amalie did not bounce back as quickly after her daughter's birth as she had after her son's, and she was glad when Dr. Matthews told her there would be no future additions to her family. Leopold also was glad because he too had feared for her life the night she gave birth to Cosette. He already had a perfect son and a beautiful baby daughter. He had no inclination to watch his wife go through such agony ever again.

Leopold had recently employed a governess for Leon, who was by then almost five—Miss Jean Buchanan. She was Scottish and had been recommended to Leopold by Lady Agatha Pengallon, who saw the need for some structure in the boy's home. The nanny, Eloise, doted on the boy and spoiled him completely, and Amalie was no better at disciplining him. Lady Agatha loved Amalie as if she were her own daughter, but she was less than impressed by her mothering skills. She agreed entirely with Leopold's princess theory and was busily securing a surprise knighthood for him for no greater reason than to bestow the title of Lady Blakeley on her dearest little friend, who could make her laugh as no others could, with her airs and idiosyncrasies.

Amalie, in her fondness for the grand dame, had taken to reading aloud to her most afternoons from her scandalous French novels. She translated each paragraph as she read it, and the duchess was much impressed by her intelligence in being able to do so and with such drama.

She had once remarked that dearest Amalie would have made a superb actress on the stage, and Leopold, slightly shocked by the absurdity of this notion, stated that she was already quite the dramatic actress in his home.

Lady Agatha sensed something a bit strange in his response; however, it also gave her an idea. Amalie had told Lady Agatha of the impending arrival of her American guests that summer, a visit that was as yet a secret from Leopold, and Lady Agatha thought what a jolly idea it would be for them to stage a play at Blakefield Castle—private and just for the household. When the grand dame shared this suggestion with Amalie, she too thought it an inspired idea, but as usual, neither of them had yet mentioned it to "Leopold dear," as Lady Agatha always referred to Leopold Blakeley.

Bridgette was now fully occupied with the nursery, the household, and of course, her mistress. Amalie, being Amalie, was setting her mind onto new pursuits, the Women's Social and Political Union, or WSPU, for one thing, which was headed by Emmeline Pankhurst.

Blanche and Cordelia were coming for the whole summer. Amalie was so looking forward to their visit and fully intended to take them to several meetings, since they too were very passionate about the rights of women, and nothing would ever be much achieved without the vote.

Amalie had written to them of Leopold's lack of attention. Of course, he was still kind and generous, but she feared, after six years, that his passion might be waning—for her at least— amid his preoccupation with Cosette and his motorcars. She had included this as an aside among other updates and gossip, but the meaning was clear enough. Trouble was again brewing in the Blakeley household, and she wanted them to come to England.

The letter set the ladies' plans in full motion, and this time they would be accompanied by the newly married Annabelle Havemeyer, née March—the elder of the March sisters—and her husband Harvey, a wealthy industrialist and a widower with two grown sons. He was quite a number of years older than Annabelle, but she was happy to be finally settled and financially secure. In addition, her home was in Long Island, and she was practically neighbors with Blanche and Cordelia.

The ladies also had heard the happy news of Malcolm McFadden's recent nuptials with a local Texas gal. During his long absence from the ranch in 1902, his brothers had managed to keep things running beautifully without him, so he once again had planned his escape and would be taking his bride on an extended honeymoon to Scotland and England. He would be sailing with Blanche, Cordelia, and Annabelle and her husband. Malcolm had never once heard from Amalie but had kept in touch with Cordelia after they all had returned home following that bittersweet summer of 1902. He therefore knew much about her life. He had never stopped loving her, and her huge portrait dominated his dining room wall. He had not explained the painting to his family or to his bride, and it was generally believed that it was some extravagant purchase he had made when he was in Europe. He didn't ever speak about the emotions that had never left his heart.

Blanche ventured to say to Cordelia, "Well, he will be on his honeymoon after all, so hopefully no more wistful gazing at Amie, who still appears to be jealous of her own daughter. It will be interesting to see how our favorite old married couple are making out these days, most especially with Amie's latest passion, women's suffrage. Although it is a subject close to our hearts, Leo's concept of the modern world seems to extend no further than the opportunity to collect the latest automobiles."

The letter containing the news from Cordelia arrived, and although ecstatic, Amalie decided not to mention it quite yet to Leopold, at least not until after Lady Agatha's dinner party. They were leaving for Blakefield Castle the following day, and she was longing to return there. Henrietta March knew of the planned visit, and although somewhat concerned about the age difference in her daughter Annabelle's marriage, she was also happy to have her finally settled. She had kept the matter from her husband too, for the present time at least, since he tended to blurt everything out to Leopold, even when positively told not to do so!

Leopold had noticed Amalie's quiet and distracted behavior, which was remarkably evident one particular night at dinner in their London home. He felt that she was a woman who had everything, yet she sat with little or no conversation for him, playing with her food.

He finally could take it no more. "Okay, Amalie, what have I done now? Clearly, something is bothering you. By the way, have you spent any time with Cosette today? She is walking now and has quite a little vocabulary, and it was Eloise who spoke with me about it. You never mentioned it to me. Did you even know?"

Amalie responded uninterestedly, "Well, she is sixteen months, Leo. One would hope she would be walking and talking a little. Leon was walking before his first birthday."

Leopold stared quite harshly at his beautiful yet distant wife and stated flatly, "You appear to spend more time with Lady Agatha and your new militant friends than you do with our daughter. I am glad we are leaving for Blakefield after this damn dinner party, and I think it's time I put an end to your relationship with the Women's Social and Political Union. I should have nipped it in the bud right away. I am, however, doing so now!"

Amalie knew he was right; she was deliberately holding back from Cosette, simply because her father doted on her. Guilt washed over her because, indeed, she had been too busy to see her daughter for more than a few moments that very day. Leon still rushed into her room every morning, and now at five years of age, he was completely incorrigible, and he would frequently hide in her bedroom to escape his governess. Amalie did not like

Miss Buchanan and felt she could hardly blame her son for hiding from her. She hadn't been consulted when Leo employed her, and she never would have done so. This was yet another issue she currently had with her husband.

Amalie was aware of her husband staring angrily at her, as if waiting for a response, but she had already forgotten what he had said. "I'm sorry," she responded unapologetically. "What did you say? I wasn't really listening."

Leopold stood up. In truth he didn't really know what he was saying. He wanted to say, "Come back to me, Amalie." And perhaps he should have done so. Instead, he walked over to her and told her to come with him to the nursery. Suddenly, she was her mother, and he her father, instructing her on how she should behave. Amalie had worshipped her father without a thought about his disdain of her mother, since Amalie was clearly his pet. She regretted that bitterly now and imagined that this turn of events would be her punishment.

Amalie could not understand that Leopold's love for his daughter was very much related to his love for his wife, who had given him his daughter. So she answered, "I think not," and stood up to walk away, but Leopold grabbed her arm. Surprised, she tried to pull away and heard her dress rip at the shoulder, the fine silk too delicate for such roughness.

He let go, embarrassed by his sudden reaction, and she proceeded on her way, afraid to turn around and see what was in his eyes.

She held back her tears until she reached her bedroom, only to find Bridgette already there with baby Cosette, climbing on her bed. Bridgette, of course, noticed the dress but said nothing as she helped her take it off and assisted her into her night attire.

The baby seemed happy rolling around amid the fluffy blankets and soft pillows. Finally, Bridgette spoke. "You are not Marcia, and the monsieur is not Georges Bouchard. I know what this is about, but he doesn't. You have hardly seen your daughter today. She says '*maman*,' but I'm not sure she knows who her *maman* is."

Bridgette understood her *petite* better than anyone, even her husband, and she walked out of the room, leaving Amalie alone with her child for the first time since she was a babe in arms. Her thought was to seek out the monsieur, but she had no need to look far since he was already approaching his wife's bedroom, with an angry scowl upon his face. She took his hand and led him away, deliberately leaving mother and daughter to become reacquainted.

Leopold asked, "What's going on, Bridgette? Where's my daughter?"

Bridgette said, "Follow me, and I'll take a glass of that fine cognac. She's with her mother, as is natural."

Some of Amalie's paintings had made their way to the London house, most particularly those of her parents and her as a little girl. Bridgette led him to the drawing room, which housed the portraits, as Leopold impatiently thought, *More revelations*. But he was happy to know that at least Cosette was with Amalie.

Bridgette stared up at the giant portraits, as did he as he waited for her to speak.

"A couple of years ago, your wife told you the story of her family life in Paris, or their life as she preferred to remember it. However, Georges Bouchard was not the saint she depicted. Oh, he was faithful to his wife, but perhaps that is the incorrect word to use. Georges Bouchard's family never approved of Amalie's mother, Mr. March's sister Marcia, and not too long after Amalie's birth, neither did he. He worshipped his small daughter and would deny her nothing. I think this was in part due to her uncanny likeness to him. Anyway, she was his pet and that of her grandparents, who never had the time of day for Marcia. Marcia loved her daughter too, and Amalie her mother, but Georges disapproved of every decision she made with regard to her, no matter how small and insignificant."

Leopold sat down beside Bridgette and was beginning to understand Amalie's strange behavior with regard to their beautiful child.

Bridgette continued, "It may have been different in the beginning. I wasn't there and can tell you no more than Amalie can remember, but in time, Marcia, who was very vivacious and charming, found love and admiration elsewhere. In essence she left Georges to their daughter, and Amalie's sweet innocence saw nothing amiss until the overheard argument shortly before the tragic accident."

Leopold said, "She told me much of this, Blanche and Cordelia too, but somehow she told it differently. I am not Georges Bouchard, and the love I have for my daughter is different and bears no resemblance to the love I have for my wife. I would die without Amalie; I hadn't known her a month when I understood that fully. Why can't she understand that? Am I not to show affection to our daughter? God knows how she dotes on her darling Leon."

Bridgette continued with her revelations, since she was not yet at the end of her narrative. "Exactly, sir, yet you employed a governess that she does not like or approve of, and Leon hates her. So how will he learn from her? It is not in Amalie's nature to look elsewhere for love and romance, especially since she has always loved—and continues to love—you more than you deserve. This much you know—I've no need to tell you—but push her away too far, and you may never get her back. Do you really wish to take that chance? I have heard you discuss commissioning a painting of your daughter, yet you never did so for your wife, in six years of marriage. That was sheer stupidity. Now I must go to my mistress."

Bridgette made to leave but then changed her mind and turned to him, having decided to divulge a secret she had thought she would never share with the monsieur, due to his past jealousy with regard to his wife—a jealousy that seemed no longer quite as pronounced.

"One final thing, monsieur: there was indeed a Russian prince—that was not idle gossip. It was Prince Vladimir Mikhailovich Ivanov. Oh, she never met him in person—perhaps saw a photograph—but he had seen her portraits, and as he stood in her father's study, watching her from the window as she played with her puppy, the prince impulsively asked Monsieur Bouchard for his daughter's hand in marriage. It seemed he had fallen instantly in love with her, as so many do, and Monsieur Bouchard was strongly considering an alliance, since he was titled and of high birth. However, he wanted to keep her with him a little while longer; therefore, his permission was not yet given, although it would have been eventually. I don't believe Amalie knew how far this almost went, but I have always made it a point to look out for ma petite, and she was so sheltered and innocent before she came to England and had to make her own way in the world. Anyway, he was a handsome man with riches and a palace, in his prime of life, but he would not have made her happy; I am convinced of that. There was so much in fate and destiny that brought you both together. I wonder how often Prince Vladimir Mikhailovich Ivanov regrets his patience with regard to a betrothal. I also wonder how many portraits he would have commissioned, had his life turned out differently. All turned out for the best, I would say. She has thus far been happy with you. I hope it will continue that way."

At this point, Bridgette finished her drink and finally walked away. She had never before spoken to Leopold Blakeley in such a manner, and he said no more as she walked out of the room without a backward glance.

He poured himself another drink and became lost in his thoughts. *There really was a Russian prince?* She had made it all sound like a big joke. *Some joke! Does she ever regret it?* Why would Bridgette decide to tell him this now? Was he not a good and attentive husband? Had he not lovingly cared for her these years? He knew his wife loved him, but why all this current drama? *Is this truly about our baby daughter? Or something else? Why haven't I ever commissioned a portrait?* He knew it was because he didn't want another man staring at her the day long as she posed for him. *Perhaps a woman? She knows enough educated ladies these days; surely, an artist or two might be among them.*

Amalie, at twenty-six, was in her prime of womanhood; she was his Venus, and that's how he wanted her painted. Never by a man, but perhaps by a woman? He also made a mental note to go through the box of numerous photographs at Blakefield Castle, knowing that if his wife had neglected to destroy the letter from Malcolm McFadden two years ago, she no doubt would have neglected to destroy such a photograph as mentioned by Bridgette, if indeed one truly did exist.

Leopold smiled to himself, in spite of all of these revelations about Amalie's youth that seemed to continually come at him. Her love for him was unmistakable, and he took much pride in knowing this as a certainty; her jealousy was almost worse than his. So he pushed all thoughts of Prince Vladimir aside. None of this solved the problem at hand. He already had known Miss Buchanan must go. He would not have his son broken—that was the easy part—but what to do about his beloved wife and daughter? Fancy words had never been his forte.

As he entered his wife's newly repainted lilac and sunshine-yellow bedroom, he witnessed a sight that he had been longing to see. Baby Cosette was fast asleep in her mother's arms, and Amalie whispered, "Cosette likes my lacy nightdress, so I promised her one the very same. She is my precious girl, and tomorrow we are going shopping in Harrods and then for ice cream and lunch.

Leon and you may come if you wish, but it's not necessary for you to do so, since we'll be shopping for girl things only."

Leopold's heart leapt in happiness, and he said, "What? And leave you two girls unsupervised to my account? We'll be coming too." He got into bed beside them and grew serious as he said, "Amalie, we are neither of us our parents; we are us. Perhaps we should remember that."

Amalie just looked at him and wondered what he meant— God forbid that they be like his parents. She was about to say this, but suddenly, she felt so tender toward him, remembering all that Bridgette had said to her that awful night before Cosette was born and how he had eavesdropped on most of it. It still made her ashamed to think of it, so instead she took his hand and kissed it, just as she used to do so often.

He thought of asking her about this Russian prince but decided it would keep. She seemed happy and content, so why risk further drama— or even worse, more revelations?

"By the way, I've been wondering if you know any lady artists," he said.

"Yes," she answered pleasantly, "indeed I do. A very fine one. Miss Imogen Armstrong. She doesn't usually paint children, but I can ask her."

Leopold thought that he might as well go for it. "Not for Cosette, for you."

Amalie laughed. "That's funny you should think of that now. She just the other day offered to paint me for free, but only under one condition, and you would be shocked."

Leopold said, "No, I wouldn't. What condition?"

Amalie quietly giggled and whispered, "In the nude."

She expected disapproval and was therefore quite surprised when he excitedly retorted, "Yes, if she's good, I'll pay her handsomely. Will she come to Blakefield?"

Amalie wasn't sure if he was serious. "Yes, I think so. But why? Where on Earth would you hang it?"

Leopold had already considered that question. "In my dressing room at Blakefield. No one but the maids go in there, and I can gaze at it every time you lock me out of our bedroom. You're not shy to do it?"

Amalie answered, "I find the whole idea quite thrilling. Can I have one in kind of you?"

Leopold's firm response of "No!" was accompanied by the appearance of his son, who was looking for his sister. When he saw his father, he began to whine about Miss Buchanan.

His father said, "We will discuss the matter tomorrow," with a wink and a tussle of the boy's curly locks as he jumped into bed beside them.

In the early hours of the morning, Bridgette found the family still asleep. Cosette was nestled with her mother, and Leon with his father.

Once again, Bridgette gave herself full credit for setting matters back in order, at least for the present time, as well she should have done.

CHAPTER 2
Lost and Found

Since they were leaving in just a couple of days, Amalie thought to seek out Imogen Armstrong to personally invite her to Blakefield Castle and discuss how her painting could be tastefully done. She knew she would find her in the British Museum, where she worked in the archives, and perhaps Imogen could show her some paintings that would be inspirational to her plan.

The previous day, she had gone shopping to Harrods with Leopold and the children, and it had been a lovely day. The sales staff had made much of the children, and this of course inspired Leo to spend extravagantly, especially on his daughter. Amalie was reminded of that day before Cosette was born, when they had gone there with Leon and her husband had spent so extravagantly on her, but she pushed that thought aside and enjoyed her day, even though this time they never quite made it up to ladies' couture.

Amalie had made a point of not mentioning to her husband when she was attending WSPU meetings in London, and often Bridgette would accompany her. On this occasion, however, she was merely meeting a friend and was more secretive than usual with regard to her outing, thinking she would surprise Bridgette and Leopold with her news later in the day.

Amalie set off alone, with McBride dropping her off at Harrods. She intended to purchase a sunbonnet for summer days in Blakefield's beautiful gardens, which she so happily anticipated. She would go there first and then off to the museum by hansom cab. She was happy and excited about the visitors as she left Harrods, having purchased three hats, one each for Cordelia, Blanche, and herself, which would be delivered to her home later that day. She had told McBride that she would be meeting the master so that Bridgette wouldn't worry about her. It also gave her a welcome sense of freedom, having the whole afternoon to herself, without questions and explanations.

The weather was fine, and Amalie decided to walk a little before hailing a cab. Unbeknownst to her husband, she had become quite adept at traversing the city. Of course, she would never tell this to him, in case he might forbid her to do so again, possibly even reducing the paltry amount of cash that he gave her, which already resulted in her frequently being indebted to Bridgette. After six years of marriage, it seemed she would never be given proper access to her money. She knew she could pursue it if she wanted, and he would have to acquiesce, but she was actually secretly amused by the whole thing. She had accounts everywhere anyway, and this was one thing she allowed him, since it seemed important to him, and perhaps he really was actually afraid of her taking off somewhere if she had the funds to do so.

Amalie was happily walking along Brompton Road, which was busy with shoppers and others just out enjoying the sunshine. A few gentlemen even tipped their hats to her, such was the mood of the day.

She was about to hail a hansom cab when her attention was drawn to a couple drinking coffee, seated at the window of an intimate café that she herself had visited a few times with her husband. They seemed to be engaged in serious conversation. When Amalie passed, the woman turned and looked out the window—and Amalie knew that she saw her. Lydia Sutton made no show of recognition, however, and turned her attention back to her male companion, Mr. Leopold Blakeley.

Amalie stood for a few seconds, stunned at what she beheld. She expected Leo to turn, but he did not, and she hurried past and hailed her cab. The sun had disappeared behind a cloud, as had Amalie's afternoon. She felt sick; her heart felt as if it would explode, and it took every bit of her inner strength, a strength she had thought she no longer possessed, to make her way into the museum in search of her friend—who, immediately upon seeing her anguished expression, grabbed her coat and hat and led Amalie along to her tiny flat, which was just a short distance away.

Imogen Armstrong boiled the kettle and handed Amalie a cup of tea. It wasn't until then that Amalie explained her original purpose for coming to see Imogen, with regard to her painting, and finally what she had seen as she made her way to the museum.

Imogen asked, "Are you sure she saw you? You say she is an old married acquaintance of your husband. Surely, this was something completely innocent. After all, he is commissioning a nude portrait of you—why would he want that if he is having an affair?"

The word "affair" stung at Amalie's very being. Never since meeting Leopold Blakeley had she doubted his fidelity, even when she'd accused him of it—when she had felt somehow neglected. If what she had seen was as it appeared, she felt she couldn't survive it. This was not her parents' marriage or any other where discreet marital infidelity might be tolerated. If this was true, her life with Leopold was over. It was beyond that even—her life was over.

Imogen Armstrong loved Amalie, as did so many others, and her love was such that it wrenched her heart to see her dearest friend so wretched. The tea was soon replaced with a bottle of wine, and eventually she allowed Amalie to fall asleep right there on her sofa—where she made her first sketches of her beautiful friend as she slept.

Lydia Sutton had appeared at Leopold Blakeley's office in a state of distress. It seemed that she and her husband were in the midst of a financial crisis that was heightened by a prolonged affair—which she had recently discovered—between her husband and a younger woman. Leopold was angry that she had chosen him to confide in and wondered at her reasoning, since his friendship with her husband these days extended no further than their club. He had distanced himself from these old acquaintances due to Amalie's concerns two years earlier and had most particularly avoided Lydia, who had set her cap at him many years before and had never quite given up her pursuit of him. Her appearance in his office had embarrassed him, and he had taken her to a café with the plan to send her on her way in a hansom cab once she had calmed down somewhat.

He felt quite successful in this endeavor when she appeared to cheer up considerably while he spoke to her, and soon he was making his way back to his office, completely unaware of the reason Lydia had suddenly brightened, for she had made no mention of seeing his wife.

When Leopold returned home much later than his usual time, due to their impending exodus to the country, he was met not by Amalie but by an agitated Bridgette, who asked him, "Where's Amalie? Didn't she meet with you?"

Leopold's head reeled as he discovered that she had not been seen or heard from since that morning, when she had set off to buy sunbonnets, telling McBride not to return for her since she was meeting Leopold.

"We made no such arrangement, Bridgette—you should have known that!"

"Why do you suppose I have been worried sick, monsieur? She told this to McBride but said nothing of it to me. Mon Dieu! What has happened to her? I checked with Mrs. March and Mrs. Allsop, even Lady Agatha. Beyond that, I was afraid to leave in case she returned with you safe and sound, having chosen for some reason not to tell me her plans."

Leopold exploded, worried beyond his wildest imaginings. He was reminded of the day he'd lost her momentarily in the sea at Cornwall, but this was much worse. "It has gone past nine o'clock—where could she possibly be? These damn friends of hers. I'm sure of it. I should have prevented it long ago. When I find her, she will never again be allowed to leave our home unaccompanied! Bridgette, I hold you responsible in the future."

"Yes, yes, monsieur, certainly, but first we must find her." As Bridgette spoke, she endeavored to sound calm. It was a calmness she didn't feel, but she could see the monsieur was terrified, such as she had never seen him, no doubt imagining that she had gotten lost in the wrong part of the city—or much, much worse.

Leopold rarely rode his horse in the city, but he did so immediately that night, accompanied by McBride, who knew various places where the suffragists held their meetings. It felt like they rode around for hours. McBride seemed to know all of Amalie's haunts, and Leopold was ashamed that he didn't know any and had taken so little interest in how she spent her days. Soon it was after ten o'clock, and the halls where deserted. McBride then mentioned that he thought he knew where her painter friend lived. She had told Bridgette that the friend had a flat near the museum where she was employed.

"Of course!" exclaimed Leopold. "The damn painting! But why wouldn't she come home?"

They set off toward the museum with no idea exactly where Imogen's flat was located, except that it was somewhere within walking distance. In his panic, Leo began shouting Amalie's name as they rode around the streets in the area. The neighborhoods were quiet at that time of night; just the voices of late-night revelers and rabble-rousers could be heard in the distance. He cursed himself for his neglect in not ascertaining where every one of these so-called friends of hers lived. He cursed himself for allowing her any freedom, absorbed as he was in his own moneymaking schemes. He was consumed with worry, since why would she do this to him unless something dire had occurred?

Eventually, Leopold just sat there upon his horse in the middle of the quiet street with his head bowed, feeling sick inside, for he had no idea what to do next. The hospitals? The constabulary? The river? McBride had no idea what further to suggest as he sat quietly beside him, uncertain of what he could say.

Several moments passed before suddenly, blessedly, he heard a beloved French accent shouting down from an upstairs window, above where he was seated dejectedly on Caesar.

"Stop shouting! I am in here, and I'm fine. Go away! I'm not going home with you!"

Immense relief washed over him, even as he wondered what in hell's name he had done to deserve such treatment. By then it was well after eleven, and he had begun to imagine the very worst.

In spite of her words, he ran up the tenement steps, two at a time, where the door was opened, presumably by her artist friend. Amalie clearly had been crying, and he said nothing at all as he grabbed her by her arm and carried her down the stairs, kicking and struggling. He forcibly threw her on his horse and took off for their home in Belgravia. His relief had given way to extreme anger, and he spoke not a word, not even when she eventually quieted down and stopped struggling and shouting abuse at him.

Bridgette was there, awash with relief, as he basically dragged his wife in the door, still having not said a word to her.

Amalie grabbed Bridgette's hand and ran upstairs with her. At the top, she shouted down to him, "I hate you! Go to hell!"

Leopold allowed her to go with Bridgette. Whatever terrible thing he had supposedly done, it really didn't matter. She was safe and unharmed, and he would deal with it after Bridgette had calmed her down. Meanwhile, his shipment of cognac had finally arrived from France, and a fresh bottle awaited him in his study. He felt in dire need of it because his mind was racing, and he was still imagining what might have been.

Upstairs, Amalie poured out her whole wretched story between sobs as Bridgette ran her bath. Bridgette had to undress her and cajole her into the warm rose-scented water, which eventually soothed and quieted her mistress somewhat, as did Bridgette's reassuring words. "Ma petite, why is it after all this time that you cannot understand how much that man loves you? Is he perfect? No, because no man is, but he comes close enough, and if he were to stray, which you should very well know he never would, why in God's name would he choose that old hag? Whatever they were discussing, it was not love, and she must have been overjoyed when she saw you. Why didn't you go inside, confront them, instead of causing such worry to us all? I have never seen such terror on your husband's face when he discovered you were not at home."

"I don't care about his face! Bridgette, they seemed so serious, and there is no reason or excuse for him to see her other than for …" Again, she started to cry. "He has broken my heart. I will never recover. I hate him, and I think I shall die! He has ruined my life!"

This said, Amalie chose to put on a white matronly nightgown, and as she began sobbing again, Bridgette was spared the need to share any further words of comfort by the appearance of her master, who was carrying his bottle of cognac and two glasses and told her that there was a bottle for her on the downstairs hall table.

He was greeted by his wife in the manner he expected, even as he handed her a glass of the amber liquid.

"Please get out of my room. You are loathsome and despicable, and I hate you. You can go to the devil, where you belong! You are the devil! You have broken my heart, and I am sure I will die, and then you will be happy, when I am in my grave! You want a divorce, you can have it, but I will ensure that my settlement will be so that you will be bankrupt and ruined, and no woman will want you then."

Amalie spoke while trying to push her husband out of the door, and Leopold was racking his brain for what his terrible transgression had been, but he could find nothing to cause what she had put him through that night. All he wanted to do, had wanted to ever do, was hold her close. A couple of hours earlier, he had been terrified by what could have happened to his most precious wife, and now she was telling him that he was loathsome and despicable and that she planned to ruin him?

Feeling it was finally time to talk sensibly, a skill he felt his wife often lacked, he calmly asked, "Amalie, beloved, what is this all about? You have terrorized me this night, and I can think of no reason for it. McBride and I were searching the streets of London for you, thinking you might have been attacked, anything, at that time of night. What am I supposed to have done to have deserved this?"

Amalie continued sobbing. She so wanted him to hold her, but she kept seeing that awful woman's face through the glass window. "I saw you!" she shouted finally through her sobs. When Leo still looked confused, she added, "And she saw me!" She threw herself on the bed and screamed, "Go to your mistress! She must be missing you! Please go away! Leave me to my heartbreak and misery!"

As the penny finally dropped, he started to laugh. "Are you serious? Lydia Sutton? At least allow me some taste if you are going to accuse me. What do you mean, she saw you? I took her for coffee to get her out of my office. They are in a financial mess, and her husband has cheated on her for years. I can't say I blame him. The woman disgusts me. She saw you? She said nothing. So that's why she cheered up so quickly. My God, Amalie, why didn't you come inside to confront me? It would have caused a lot less worry and stress."

At these final words and as her husband took a swig of his drink, Amalie stood up again. "Worry and stress? What I have gone through this very day! How can I believe you? How can I ever trust you again? You have torn my heart into tiny pieces! You are a beast! I promise I will ruin you!"

As Leopold turned to her, she looked so little and sweet standing there, calling him every name she could think of. He couldn't be angry with her, although he knew he should be. All was well again in his home, and even as she called him names and threatened to ruin him, he knew she was just looking for reassurance of his love, and not just by words alone.

"Amalie," he said calmly, "first off, you do believe me, and you do trust me, and you are not going to ruin me—well, not any more than you have already done. However, I'll agree with the beast accusation because I am taking you to Blakefield tomorrow, where I will not let you out of my sight. So it seems you will miss Lady Agatha's dinner party. I am also paying Bridgette back from your future allowance since I always know when you owe her money. Also, I can't take the chance of allowing you any money in the future with these threats of my ruination. As for your women's rights nonsense, and since you haven't yet achieved these rights, I'm exercising my rights as a husband. Now please take off your grandmother's nightgown and come here."

Amalie realized that Leo was telling her the truth. She also longed to return to Blakefield Castle, so tomorrow would suit her just fine. She didn't care about his threat to never let her out of his sight since that would require his full attention. As for money, she didn't need it at Blakefield anyway.

She felt a little sorry for what she had put him through, but not very, and said pettily, "If you want it off, you'll have to take it off me."

And that's exactly what he did, laughing in his profound relief at having her safely in his arms again.

CHAPTER 3
Secrets Revealed

Amalie awakened early the next morning to find Leopold still sleeping contentedly beside her. She had decided that she was not leaving for Hertfordshire that day after all, in spite of what her husband had *commanded* the previous night.

Her night had been restless in spite of her knowing deep inside that Lydia Sutton posed no threat to her. Leopold was always so much in control, or at least thought he was, but no matter what the reason, she was still irritated by the thought of him taking coffee with any poor "damsel" who chose to stop by his office. She thought, *What if someone had seen them together and thought the same thing as I did?* In addition, Lady Agatha had asked them to arrive early that very evening for her special dinner, and Imogen was most certainly owed an apology, especially if she was going to paint her, which was, of course, if Leo was still in that frame of mind.

She arose and stood looking down at him, still naked in their bed. After six years of marriage, she still thought him the most handsome man she had ever laid her eyes upon with his dark curls, muscular frame, and penetrating dark eyes. He took good care of himself too, and she thought it only natural that other women would find him attractive. She was glad that he was twelve years her senior. In four years she would be thirty, but he would be past forty, not that age seemed to matter as much in a man as it did in a woman.

As if he felt her staring at him, Leo squinted up at her. Checking the time, he said, "Amalie, it has just gone six o'clock. What are you standing there planning for me today, as if yesterday's escapades were not enough for the present time?" He reached out his arm to pull her back into bed beside him.

There it was, the "let's talk to Amalie like a child" voice. For as much as she never wanted to be easy prey to her husband, she inevitably always was—but not this morning, she decided.

"How many others?"

Exasperated, he asked, "Other what, beloved?"

"Damsels in distress?"

Leopold thought, *It seems she isn't done with my punishment yet*, and he responded, "It's hard to recall—ten, twenty, possibly more. I am such a sensitive and charming man after all."

Amalie knew he was making fun of her but decided to carry it on. "Actually, you are absolutely not sensitive or charming, well at least not to your wife, and any woman who would run to you for advice or sympathy must be either desperate or out of her mind!"

Leopold could tell that his Amalie was still very jealous, and he actually rejoiced in it. She looked so ravishing standing there, with her beautiful hair wild and wearing a negligée that did little to conceal her magnificent figure. She was looking at him with her eyes flashing. She was the most beautiful woman he had ever beheld, a woman he would kill for, and she was once again adorably trying to insult him. Her complete adoration of him still shone through so amazingly and unmistakably, but he was fully awake now and decided to tease her a little. "Amalie, you are being very hurtful, although if that is indeed the case, then you must have been very desperate to want to marry me in such haste. I didn't realize at the time that you were desperate—I wish I had known. Now I understand why you pursued me with such tireless determination."

Amalie, wide-eyed and playfully insulted, jumped on top of him on the bed. "You awful man! I was certainly never desperate in my life! I think you were the desperate one—desperate for some class and refinement—and I happen to know that I am very beautiful because lots of people say so, including you!"

With his wife seated upon his naked body on the bed, Leopold knew exactly where this was heading, but after the awful scare she had given him the previous night, he couldn't quite resist. "I said that? Really? I suppose that was because I wanted to get you into my bed." He held her close and whispered in her ear, "Forever and forsaking all others."

Of course, Amalie succumbed to him after that, but she was still irritated by the whole Lydia Sutton matter, and when she arose, she said, "I have decided not to let Lady Agatha down, so I will be attending her dinner this evening. Also, Miss Armstrong is owed an apology and explanation, more by you than me, but I must apologize on your behalf. Therefore, I am not leaving for Blakefield Castle until tomorrow. You, of course, must do as you choose. McBride can drive me both places."

Leopold was actually intending the same thing, but even after six years, he couldn't resist winding sweet Amalie up, and she certainly deserved it that morning, after what she had put him through the previous night, and even in spite of her sweet surrender to him. "I'm afraid that's impossible since I will be needing McBride today, so I suppose that means that you can stay here until tomorrow, if you prefer to do so, but Bridgette will be under orders to keep you at home."

Amalie was incensed, not by his words, because she knew

he didn't mean them, but by the fact that he felt he had the right to speak to her in that manner. "You, sir, are not my lord and master, but you are apparently McBride's. I will find my own way to both places, and I am quite sure there will be gossip when I attend tonight's dinner unaccompanied, but what do you care? You might have other plans in any case—more desperate damsels to console possibly."

Just then, Bridgette appeared with breakfast and said dryly, since she had caught the end of the conversation, "McBride asks if you are still taking that red car today."

When Leopold said that he intended to do so, she responded, "Good, I will let him know. Now I am off to see to the children and finish packing, although I may be forgiven for thinking I am currently in the nursery."

Leopold added, "You know, Bridgette, I am uncertain if I can afford your wages this month. You might want to alert the staff, most especially Monsieur Moreau. Your mistress has informed me of her intention of ruining me. Of course, she will need to find a lawyer to represent her pro bono, since I am stopping her allowance forthwith."

Amalie responded in French, knowing that although Leo's understanding of the language was somewhat improved, it was much less so when she spoke very quickly.

Bridgette just shook her head and went on her way.

Leopold meanwhile said, "I caught the word *cochon*—are you buying a pig, madam? Surely, you couldn't have been referring to your handsome husband. I may reconsider tonight's dinner if you bring me my coffee, and I'll have two of those croissants, with damson jam."

Amalie knew he was teasing her and said, "You are lucky I don't pour your coffee on your lovely head!"

Late morning, the Blakeleys set off for the museum in hopes of finding Imogen Armstrong available for lunch, which fortunately she was. She said she would work up her price for two paintings, with and without clothing, and showed them both the sketches she had brought with her in the hopes that they would stop by that day. Leopold was very impressed with Amalie's likeness, although a little embarrassed at the nude sketches. Imogen had clearly guessed at his wife's bare body, or at least he hoped she had. The woman seemed very solicitous toward Amalie, and he considered that she had made yet another conquest.

She went on to say, "I have ideas for a tasteful rendition of your beautiful wife, Mr. Blakeley, and I am assuming, of course, that there will be a private studio where Amalie can comfortably and discreetly pose for me. I expect to be with you at least two or three weeks, and as I understand you will have visitors there from America, I do not wish to be in the way, although it will be so lovely to get out of the city for a while."

Amalie cringed when Imogen mentioned the American visitors. Of course, she couldn't have known that Amalie had not shared this information yet with Leopold. Even as he cordially made arrangements and they bid Imogen farewell, Amalie fully expected an onslaught once they were alone.

Amalie would never admit that she preferred McBride's driving to her husband's, since the former was slow and steady, and Leo pushed the motorcar too hard in her opinion, and she regretted that it was Leo who was driving that day, since he yet again seemed angry at her, although he had said nothing so far. Amalie didn't venture to explain until he asked, which happened once they were seated in his car, which he had paid a young boy to watch for the couple of hours that they were away. She thought the red Daimler to be dreadfully ostentatious and always felt like hiding her face when he forced her to ride with him.

Before he started the engine, he said, "So Blanche and Cordelia are coming. Surely, that is good news. Any particular reason you neglected to tell me?"

Well, it was out now, and although she wished she was not currently seated in this red monstrosity that everyone who passed stared at, she said, "Well, you know Annabelle is married. She too is coming with her husband, Mr. Havemeyer. Also, another newly married couple …"

As she trailed off, Leopold exclaimed, "What are we now? A honeymoon hotel? When are they coming? And please don't say next week. Who are these other young lovers anyway?"

Amalie squeezed her eyes shut and responded very quickly, almost hoping he wouldn't hear her properly. "They are already on the ship. Um, Malcolm and Dolores. Lady Agatha says what fun—we can put on a play at Blakefield. I'm thinking Mr. Wilde's *An Ideal Husband*. It has two major couples and a femme fatale, and you can be Lord Arthur Goring, and I can be Miss Mabel. Lord Goring is a confirmed bachelor and—"

Finally, Leopold interrupted. "So McFadden will be back in town, with a bride no less. I hope she's pretty. Lady Agatha? Am I the only uninformed person as usual? What's all this nonsense about a damned play?"

Amalie responded, "Lady Agatha's idea. I haven't told her my idea yet. I'm sure Dolores is very pretty, although I don't know why you hope so, and Uncle March hasn't been told since he would have told you."

Amazingly, surprisingly, Leopold started to laugh. "A play in the midst of another summer pantomime. And a nude portrait of my wife being painted at the same time. Amalie, you are the most infuriating woman I have ever known. I suppose that's why I fell in love with you."

As Amalie stared at him wide-eyed, in shock at his reaction, Leopold kissed her nose and started up the engine. "Best get you home, Miss Mabel, so you can rest up and make yourself beautiful for your adoring public tonight. I wonder what Lady Agatha wants to talk to us about."

With that settled, off they drove too recklessly, narrowly missing running people over, or so it felt to Amalie, who for the most part had her eyes closed.

McBride took them to Lady Agatha's London home by carriage, much to Amalie's relief. She was wearing her new navy blue taffeta Lanvin gown to perfection with Lady Agatha's tiara, skillfully and lovingly placed by Bridgette in Amalie's lustrous honey-blonde hair. Leopold, as always, looked dashing in his formal dinner attire and gleaming white shirt, which contrasted so beautifully with his tanned skin. He was always the most handsome gentleman in the room, and she the most beautiful lady. This was often remarked upon by others in their acquaintance, as was how they seemed to have eyes only for one another.

They were shown into Lady Agatha's private parlor under a veil of mystery, until finally the reason for all the secrecy was revealed to them. Lady Agatha handed Leopold an envelope addressed personally to him on His Majesty's official stationery. He looked at her quizzically before opening it, even as she bade him to do so.

Upon reading it, stunned by the contents, he asked, "A knighthood? Lady Agatha, is this true? You are responsible for this? I hardly know what to say. The ceremony is September. Sir Leopold? I can't quite take this in."

Lady Agatha was very pleased with herself and his reaction as he solemnly kissed her hand. She had kept the secret beautifully, for she had been bursting to tell them her good news, and what was the use of being a duchess if one had no influence with the king?

Amalie remained seated in a state of shock, until Lady Agatha finally addressed her. "Lady Amalie, come and kiss my cheek. I don't believe I have ever seen you so quiet. Officially, you will be Lady Blakeley, but I much prefer Lady Amalie, so that's what it will be. To your servants you will be 'my lady,' and they will refer to you as such—all except Bridgette, who no doubt will do as she pleases."

Amalie said, "It's just too incredible. Lady Agatha, why? I mean, thank you, but oh, I don't know what I mean." Amalie's big aquamarine eyes filled with tears as she looked at Leopold, who appeared to be struck dumb.

Lady Agatha was very pleased with herself as they went in to greet the other dinner guests together. It was indeed an evening that had been worth postponing their return to Blakefield Castle, and Lady Agatha announced the good news to her guests, who congratulated Leopold, as expected, quite unenthusiastically.

Lady Agatha liked Amalie's choice for the play, and since Amalie had just finished reading her the book, the plot and various characters were much discussed by both ladies that evening, much to the chagrin of the other dinner guests, most especially Sir Leopold, who now knew that he was destined to be Lord Goring.

The next morning, the family and remaining staff set off for Hertfordshire. The household staff was most excited by the master's news, the likes of which never could have been kept secret for long, especially since the knighthood also elevated their status as servants.

Amalie sat dreamily looking out of the carriage window. She was happily anticipating sharing the news with the whole family, most especially Blanche and Cordelia. Blanche would be very proud of her brother. The Marches already knew, since Leopold had gone to see her uncle that morning, and all would be joining them at Blakefield Castle in a few days, even Freddie and Judith and their family. She hadn't yet mentioned to Leo that Freddie would be there, but there was plenty of room.

Lady Agatha was to join them for a week or so for the play's performance, after which they would accompany her to her country estate in Truro before heading off to their special cottage in St. Ives and seeing Marnie and Ned Tremayne once again. Amalie happily anticipated exploring the rugged coastline with her husband on horseback since this time she would not be under doctor's orders.

Finally, they arrived at Blakefield Castle, and after she had greeted the servants led by Mr. Carmichael, Amalie's first stop was her bedroom, recently painted lilac with pale yellow roses. The room was already dressed with the bedding and draperies she had shipped over from Paris. Her new area rug, in the same hues, also had arrived, and she was exceptionally pleased with the result. The room had been only half-finished when they left for London, and Maryia and her team of designers had done an excellent job bringing everything together. Amalie expected some pushback from Leo on the yellow roses, but what could he do about that now?

She then ran in to check on her other favorite rooms, for which she had given explicit instructions on freshening up for the visitors, since she wanted the new Mrs. McFadden, in particular, to be immensely impressed with her home. Amalie was so pleased with her designers that she decided to ask Leo to give them a special bonus, and she knew she must do it quickly before he perused the invoices that must surely be awaiting him in his study. She had had them sent to Blakefield as opposed to his London office in the hopes that once he saw how beautiful everything was, he would not be overly upset at the exorbitant price he had paid for such splendor.

Leon had dragged his father to the stables to see his pony Horsey, so Amalie fetched Cosette to show her the pretty flowers in the conservatory and garden. Her daughter's bedroom was a delight, with ballerinas and sugarplum fairies. Everything was pink with pale yellow and white accents. Cosette had inherited one dollhouse and two dolls from her mother, whose other toys had been put away until Cosette was a little older. Cosette was a gentle child who loved little animals, and Amalie had decided on a calico kitten, which Eloise was looking out for, and a puppy, perhaps a little pug, for Christmas.

She had decided that she and the children would not go to London that winter and that when the time came, she would make a very special Christmas for the children at Blakefield Castle— winter greenery in every room as well as an enormous tree in the great hall. She might even be able to persuade Blanche and Cordelia to extend their stay until the New Year, most especially if Leopold could be coerced into being "Father Christmas" for everyone's amusement, although Uncle March might be a better fit for the role.

Amalie felt at peace with the world as she and her baby girl picked flowers in the gardens where Leopold had kissed her for the very first time and finally proposed marriage. Her wedding day still remained the happiest day of her life.

Soon, these gentle reveries were interrupted by Bridgette. "He wants to see you in his study," Bridgette said. "I think he has discovered all the invoices. Mon Dieu, I knew this would happen. I will take Cosette upstairs with her flowers."

Amalie responded, "Yes, you may do so, but I will not be summoned to his study! Seriously, Bridgette? He has not been knighted yet. I will continue to explore the gardens, as I see fit."

Bridgette took Cosette's hand and walked away, saying, "I am only the messenger."

Shortly afterwards, Amalie was reminiscing about the time she got lost in the woods and was rescued by Leo, when she heard him calling out to her in the present.

She was hidden in the dense foliage and shouted back, "Go away! I am enjoying my walk and have no wish to discuss money!"

He didn't answer, and she carried on, only to suddenly see

him standing in front of her. He was smiling his devilish grin, and Amalie realized they were very close to the same spot where they had made love almost six years previously.

She said, "Oh no! I am a respectable mother of young children now." But she was laughing, much relieved that she was not about to be given another financial lecture.

Leopold was not to be put off. "I have already found the invoices and the yellow flowers in the bedroom. Don't expect mercy!" And indeed, no mercy was given.

When the Blakeleys were walking back to the house hand in hand, Amalie felt so very much in love, a feeling that didn't lessen when Leopold said, "I had decided to save the lecture for tomorrow, my beautiful wife, but then I remembered that I married a princess who deserves a hero, and it now seems I must also be her knight in shining armor."

CHAPTER 4
The American Invasion

Two days later, their London guests arrived, followed the next day by the arrival of the Americans.

As was their usual custom, the entire family and senior staff were lined up to greet the visitors. Bridgette stood with Eloise, Miss Buchanan, Cosette and Cousin Judith's girls, all the children were together except Leon, who insisted on standing with his parents. A little man now, although not quite five, he was assuming the role of future master of Blakefield Castle to the loving amusement of his mother and utter exasperation of his father, who had decided to keep Miss Buchanan on as governess to his little monster after all. Leopold loved his children, and even as he pondered how sweet and mild his baby daughter was, he was fully aware that Leon was dressed exactly like him, right down to his country squire suit and boots. The servants marveled at the boy's likeness to his father, and although loath to admit it to his doting mother, Leopold was immensely proud of his incredible young son.

Leopold looked down the line to where his daughter was

being held by Eloise, shyly hiding her face. Upon impulse, he strode down and walked back with her in his arms, just as the carriages were approaching. He would never allow her to hide in the background. One day she would be as great a beauty as her mother, who was standing beside him. Amalie had been allowed too much freedom after her father died, and although that had suited him greatly at the time, his baby princess would be well chaperoned by him and her mother, who would still be just as lovely as she was this very day.

Amalie found Leopold's gesture toward Cosette very sweet. She loved that he so loved the children she had given him. She had to stifle a laugh when Master Leon held out his arm for her to take as she approached the carriages, even as she observed her husband rolling his eyes as he watched his son's antics.

Amalie enthusiastically greeted Blanche, Cordelia, and Annabelle. She cordially welcomed Mr. Havemeyer to her home, and he insisted she call him Harvey. She instantly liked his warm and easy manner as well as his obvious adoration of Annabelle.

Finally, she dared to meet Malcolm McFadden's eyes, and what she saw there was the same affection as two years previous. They embraced, as would old friends, watched with curiosity by all, but most especially by Malcolm's bride, who shouted out incredulously, "You're the girl in the painting!"

By then Leopold had come over to welcome the newly married couple to his home. He and Malcolm shook hands, but the glint in both of their eyes was still apparent to Amalie, even as Leopold gallantly kissed Mrs. McFadden's hand.

Dolores McFadden was a fresh-faced pretty young girl of eighteen, and she appeared to be very much out of her depth with the sophisticated people around her. Her manner of dress was inappropriate as afternoon attire, and she had a mass of blonde ringlets, which by 1904 were woefully out of style.

Amalie wondered if Blanche had been cruel to Dolores on the

voyage over, as she had once been to Amalie, but then realized that Dolores posed no threat to Blanche, so she most likely had just ignored her. Amalie had hoped she would like Malcolm's bride, but she found she could not, most especially due to her opening remark but also due to the way she seemed to hold on to Malcolm. Why this secondary reason was the case, she daren't admit, any more than she would admit her pleasure at witnessing Malcolm's still apparent adoration, which inwardly pleased her, even as Blanche raised an eyebrow at her.

After everyone had been shown to their rooms and had freshened up, tea and refreshments were served in the conservatory. The conversation was fun and interesting as everyone caught up with one another. Soon Blanche was heard to exclaim, "My baby brother a knight!" and all excitedly congratulated Leopold. Several guests expressed their plans to attend the ceremony.

Henrietta March, of course, cried out, "But what does one wear when one is to see the king? Ladies, we must go shopping without delay—I am in need of your advice and opinion!"

Blanche consoled her with a wink to her brother, who proclaimed, "My dearest Henrietta, you will be the belle of the ball no matter what your attire!"

The general gaiety prevailed even as Malcolm said sardonically, "I wonder what you accomplished in order to be knighted, Sir Leopold. However, I very much congratulate you, most especially with regard to my lady Amalie, who is every inch the very finest of ladies."

Leopold responded, "No need to call me 'Sir' as yet, McFadden. 'Mister' will do just fine."

He then turned his attention toward Dolores. She seemed to be intimidated by the others, who were effectively ignoring her. He was reminded of years before, when his sister Blanche had been utterly awful to her now "dearest Amie." However, Amalie had been captivatingly beautiful, and Leopold had been completely besotted with her. Amalie also had possessed a certain poise and aloofness that this young girl lacked, so much so that he would feel like a cradle snatcher if he even considered flirting with her—as his wife was now doing quite openly with McFadden. He wondered why McFadden had brought her here. Why he'd married her was obvious enough, but he clearly had never fully recovered from the lovely Amalie. Leopold surprised himself by feeling no particular jealousy—he knew how much his wife loved him—but he resolved to speak to her afterwards, as she was currently displaying a side to her character that he had not often witnessed before.

Eventually, the McFaddens and Havemeyers went outside to explore the gardens, and the others retired to their rooms. All would assemble a while later for dinner. Amalie was about to make her way to Blanche and Cordelia's suite for their opinion of the new Mrs. McFadden when she was stopped in her tracks by her husband, who asked to speak with her.

"Well, my lady, I hope your behavior was not for my benefit. I felt very badly for the young bride. She is your guest and was completely out of her depth. The Amalie that I thought I knew would have made her feel just a little bit welcome." He spoke in a way that made Amalie feel quite silly and cruel, which of course was his intention. He then lay down on their bed and held out his hand to her to lie down beside him. She willingly complied as he let down her hair.

Amalie attempted to explain her bad behavior. "She accused me of being the girl in the painting. And what about that dress and those ringlets?"

Leopold responded while playing with Amalie's waist-length honey tresses. "My beautiful darling, you are indeed the girl in the painting, or you were. Do you remember the night I proposed to you? You wore a simple girlish gown, and your hair was tied with a blue ribbon. I thought you the sweetest, most perfect girl in the world, and I was overwhelmed with happiness, knowing that you would soon be mine. My sister made fun of you at dinner, and my heart ached at your humiliation. You were, and are, a goddess among women, and that idiot McFadden seems to still think so too. What do you have to say for yourself, my love? How would you feel if the situation were reversed?"

This was quite a speech for Leopold, and suddenly, Amalie felt quite ashamed. She had no further designs on Malcolm McFadden beyond his adoration. This she still possessed, and it occurred to her to wonder how she would feel if the situation were indeed reversed, if this man beside her whom she worshipped, body and soul, had feelings for another woman. Consumed with the drama of such an idea, she responded, "I would drown myself in your river, and you would be driven to madness until you also joined me in my watery grave!"

Leopold couldn't help but laugh. "That is not exactly what I was asking you, but perhaps I have made my point. By the way, I was reading through this play of yours. I don't really see you as Miss Mabel. I think that part should go to Dolores McFadden. You, my love, can be Mrs. Cheveley. I see you in that role, and I'm sure Lady Agatha will agree."

Amalie worriedly responded, "But if you're Lord Goring, you'll have to propose to Dolores McFadden!"

Leo pulled her to him and said, "But then again, didn't he and Mrs. Cheveley have a past together?"

Amalie finally made her way to Blanche and Cordelia's room. She had been bursting to tell them all her news and also to hear theirs, and there she found Henrietta, Annabelle, Judith, and even Bridgette all drinking tea and coffee and sharing their gossip.

Blanche moved over and patted the seat beside her. "What kept you, Amie? Is my brother up to his old tricks?"

Amalie rolled her eyes. "First, I received a lecture about Dolores and Malcolm, and then he wouldn't let me leave until—"

Blanche said, "Okay, we can stop you there. Bridgette has filled us in on the goings-on, including Lydia Sutton and my poor brother desperately searching for you at midnight! Amie, what would he want with that old sow when he has his beautiful French siren? We want to hear more about your suffragist friends, most especially the artist, Imogen Armstrong. When is she coming?"

Amalie responded casually, "In a couple days, after you've settled in. Leo has commissioned two paintings of me, one of them in the nude. Isn't that exciting?"

Everyone regarded her with shock, and Henrietta looked as if she needed smelling salts. Bridgette remarked, "I hadn't told them that part."

Amalie started laughing. "Lady Agatha is in full agreement, and the nude will be in Leo's private quarters." Then she changed the subject, even though her companions were sitting in shocked silence. "Annabelle, Harvey is so very charming, and he so obviously adores you. Oh, and Dolores with those ringlets? Leo *commanded* me to be nice to her. I swear, Blanche, sometimes your brother treats me like such a child!"

Blanche exclaimed, "Amie dearest, how Cordelia and I have missed you! You are the most endearing screwball that we have ever known on either side of the Atlantic. So are you going to be nice to the poor child? She must have been devastated to find you to be the girl in the painting. I do agree, however, that those ringlets have to go, and as for the dress? We will make Malcolm cough up some money and give her a makeover at Harrods."

All agreed, and Henrietta, Annabelle, and Judith left to change for dinner. Bridgette stayed behind along with Blanche and Cordelia, and Amalie asked her three best ladies in all seriousness, "Do you think Leo thinks she's pretty? He said before that he hoped she was pretty. I don't know why. Is that why he wants me to be nicer?"

Cordelia responded, "Amie honey, you know darn well you

are just fishing for compliments, and the flirting with Malcolm—maybe it is a little unkind? It seems he is still enamored with you."

Amalie couldn't deny this and was saved from responding by a knock at the door, followed by the entrance of Leopold, smiling happily and already dressed for dinner.

Blanche said, "I hope you haven't been eavesdropping on us girls!"

Her brother responded lightheartedly, "I know better than to do that, sister dear. Bridgette, what do you think? Ringlets for your petite this evening? She has a bit of younger competition. Maybe I can be of assistance picking out a suitable frock?"

Amalie gave him the meanest look in her repertoire of mean looks and chased him out the room and along the hallway.

Blanche then asked Bridgette, "Those two, they're doing okay? Cosette and everything? I swear, she's as jealous as him, maybe more so."

Bridgette responded, "I explained to the monsieur his mistakes. He was talking of having Cosette painted when he had never done so for his wife. But then that night she went missing, he was so afraid, and before they finally found her at Miss Armstrong's flat, McBride said that he had never seen him so terrified. They both thought she had been attacked or worse, although neither said it. When she suddenly shouted down for him to go away, he ran upstairs and carried her down screaming and shouting. She called him everything that night, but he didn't care. That's love such as I'll never know. That's why they sometimes act like children. And it's a beautiful thing. Never worry about them, unless one were to lose the other, for neither could survive that." Then Bridgette brightened. "But enough from me. Now I must see to ma petite's ensemble before the monsieur thinks of doing so again." She then followed her mistress to her bedroom.

After Bridgette left, Blanche said to Cordelia, "Wow, but then again, I don't believe I could survive losing you."

Cordelia responded, "Cocktails?" This made them both laugh as they made their way downstairs, hand in hand.

Amalie decided upon the navy blue taffeta that she had worn to Lady Agatha's dinner party. She did not don her tiara that night, but Bridgette paid special attention to her hair. She wore no jewelry other than her wedding rings, and as she gazed at herself in the mirror, she felt she presented a perfect picture of sophistication and poise.

Leopold was highly amused by his wife's apparent need to outshine her young guest and couldn't resist teasing her. "Bridgette, you have taken such special care of your mistress tonight. Is all this for me? I fear our guests must grow weary awaiting our esteemed company, and I also fear Mr. March is generously pouring out my best brandy."

Bridgette paid little attention to him as she declared, "Voilà! My lady is ready for her guests."

Everyone was gathered in the conservatory, as was often their practice on warm summer evenings, and Amalie's eyes were immediately drawn to a frothy pink nightmare in ringlets. She stood alone as Malcolm chatted with Harvey Havemeyer and Amalie's uncle March, and Amalie suddenly felt dreadfully sorry for the young girl. She clearly had no idea of style, and her husband did not appear to be very caring.

Malcolm immediately approached Amalie and, kissing her gloved hand, told her how very well she looked, as he gazed longingly at her. Amalie smiled warmly at him, but her attention was more drawn to the awkward young girl who looked like she would rather be anywhere other than where she was, neglected by her husband and ignored by the other guests.

Amalie made a decision. Her special attentions usually were paid to those less fortunate than she, women like Maryia or Eloise who just needed a little financial help and encouragement, since they already possessed the personality and style that caused her to notice them in the first place. However, Dolores was already rich, or at least her husband was. Her clothes were expensive—just completely lacking in style. Malcolm, for whatever reason, had married a shrinking violet, and Amalie intended to help her to bloom.

She made her way over to the young woman and asked her if she liked to ride, which Amalie assumed she did, coming from Texas.

Dolores smiled gratefully as she responded, "I surely do ma'am, but I didn't bring the right clothes. I think I got everything all wrong, and I'm sorry that I blurted out about the painting, but we all thought that she was a princess, and Malcolm never said she was you."

Amalie noticed that the young girl was quite pretty—she clearly simply had no feminine guidance, and this assessment was confirmed when Amalie learned she had four brothers, and her mother had died when the children were little.

"My father is not rich, not like Malcolm's family anyway, and Mrs. McFadden, his mother, doesn't like me much. I'm beginning to think neither does Malcolm, and he so admires you."

Amalie was aware of the others watching them. She took Dolores's hand and led her aside, behind some of the lush, giant leafy plants, and said, "First of all, it's Amalie, not 'ma'am.'" Then she stretched the truth a little, just to make the poor girl feel better. "Malcolm is like a brother to me. I am twenty-six, yet I am still the youngest woman in my acquaintance, or at least I was until now. If you will allow me to be your older and wiser sister, I will help you with your style, and with style comes confidence. I am very good at that sort of thing, and then we shall see how much Malcolm loves you."

The poor girl looked so happy that Amalie regretted her meanness to her when they'd first met. Amalie added, "Don't worry about Blanche—she used to hate me too!" and Dolores cheered enormously.

As they all walked arm in arm into dinner, Leo said to Amalie, "Yet another reason that I adore you." And she perfectly understood what he meant.

The next morning, Leopold went to his river, where he found Malcolm already there, as expected. He remembered how Malcolm used to like to criticize his treatment of Amalie—since he completely misread him and his love for his wife—and as they were saddling up after their swim, he decided to turn the tables. "Dolores is very pretty. Amalie has decided to provide her with some fashion sense, and knowing my wife, that won't come cheap. I hope you've got the cash to fork out for it."

Malcolm's response quite shocked Leopold, who expected anything other than what he said. "She's nothing like Amalie, maybe a watered-down version. No, not even that. I made a terrible mistake marrying her, and what a total embarrassment at dinner. I could tell what everyone was thinking, but maybe she'll improve a little if Amalie teaches her how to dress and fix her hair. Possibly she will learn a little from Amalie's poise and charm—if that's even possible with Dolores, which I somehow doubt."

For a moment Leopold wanted to punch him. Even married, McFadden still had designs on his wife, a woman he would never have. And that poor girl—she knew it. He decided to talk to Blanche. Amalie had agreed to take Dolores McFadden under her wing, but she was also the object of this misguided man's desire. He said, "McFadden, I would have thought better of you. Why'd you marry? No, forget that. None of my business. Just keep away from my wife, and remember, like it or not, you have a wife of your own now."

When he got home, Leopold ran upstairs to see Amalie. He had a change of plans and needed to talk to Blanche too. He was surprised to find Bridgette and Dolores with Amalie in her room, sorting through Amalie's clothes. Bridgette immediately noticed his expression and made to leave with Dolores, who was holding several of Amalie's dresses.

It was Amalie's and Bridgette's turn to be shocked when he took the dresses from Dolores and threw them on the bed. He ushered both Bridgette and Dolores out of the room, closing the door behind them.

Amalie shouted, "What in God's name was that about? I thought you wanted me to help her. The poor girl! You're crazy."

Leopold made to move the dresses and lie down on the bed, but Amalie, now in a temper caused by her embarrassment at his behavior, shouted while pulling his arm, "Don't you dare! You stink of the river! Go take a bath! You are a crazy man, and that's my new coverlet all the way from Paris!" She ran and turned on the water in their newly installed bath, in their beautifully appointed en suite. She ordered him into the bathroom as she took off to Blanche and Cordelia's room, shouting, "You're a crazy man!"

Blanche and Cordelia were about to make their way down to breakfast when they were stopped in their tracks by the noisy commotion down the hallway. They waited, and as expected, Amalie appeared at their door.

"Blanche, your brother's a crazy man. First, I have to help Dolores, and then I'm not to help her, and he threw my dresses on the bed and—"

Before she could finish, Leopold appeared. "Blanche, I need you to sort out Dolores. She's not getting dressed up as my wife!" That said, he turned to leave. "Now I'm going to lie down on Amalie's new coverlet that I paid a fortune for."

For once in her life, Blanche was at a loss for words as her brother took off again, presumably still dirty, with his wife running after him, yelling, "Stay off my coverlet, you crazy man! You stink!"

By now Annabelle had appeared with her husband, as had the Marches, to the sight of Amalie chasing her husband into the bedroom, still screaming at him to stay off the bed. Since this behavior wasn't terribly unusual, Annabelle just explained, "They're really very fond of one another."

Henrietta said in all sincerity to Blanche, "Blanche, my niece's beautiful new coverlet! Please see to your brother!"

All suddenly went quiet, and those assembled were about to go down to breakfast when they were stopped in their tracks by the sound of Amalie crying and Leopold laughing.

Blanche had had enough and opened the door to find them both fully clothed and soaking wet. She then simply turned around and said, "They're fine." And she made her way downstairs with the others.

Harvey Havemeyer was very amused by the Blakeleys' antics and found himself very glad that he had agreed to this holiday, as the English called it. It seemed the upper classes, at the very least, were just as batty as he had been led to believe.

Meanwhile, Amalie was still glaring at Leopold as she got undressed and returned to the bathroom for a proper wash, her hair soaking wet. He followed her and laughingly begged her forgiveness, which she eventually granted, especially since, at the very least, she had kept him off the new coverlet.

CHAPTER 5
What Next?

The following day, when Amalie went upstairs to rest before changing for dinner, she decided to do so in her newly appointed turret room.

Leopold had been busy working as usual with her uncle March in his Colquhoun tartan study—the project that she eventually had gotten around to completing the previous summer. She had chosen the tartan simply because she liked it. It wasn't too dark or too bright. She had kept Leo's worn leather chair, which held such sweet memories for her, but replaced the other chairs as well as one wall with the beautiful colorful tartan. She'd had the remaining walls and carpeting matched to the exact shade of green in the multicolored tartan, with accents of blue and black to pull it all together. When he was working there, she chose red and orange flowers with leafy green filler in a beautiful brass vase that she had unearthed from the attics for his desk, which she had had French-polished to a lustrous sheen—bringing it back to life after many years of neglect. Her final addition had been a vintage French globe drinks cabinet, upon which she had spent far too much money but which she could not resist. The result was amazing, and sometimes when he was not at home, she would sit in there by herself behind his desk with a small glass of his best cognac and imitate him for her own amusement.

Most importantly, Leo loved the room, and she felt it was the first time he had truly appreciated her God-given talent in interior design.

Amalie had decided it best not to inform her husband of the east turret room project due to his past comments on the stairs being dangerous. However, Maryia had seen to it that at least some repairs had been made to the stairs, and a proper handrail had been installed. This was one of Amalie's favorite rooms, and she was looking forward to showing it to her lady guests, who would be under strict orders never to mention it to the men. While Amalie worked on Leopold's study, Maryia and her team had utilized the carpets and furnishings from Amalie's bedroom that had been redone. Window seats in blue and yellow velvet fabric with multiple pillows added such a level of luxury and comfort to the turret room, and Amalie's remaining dollhouse, her favorite, was displayed along with the dolls that had been left behind by Cordelia and Judith's girls. She intended to use this room for her sitting with Imogen Armstrong. It was private, and the light was perfect for it.

Eventually, she would share her special room with Cosette, but not until she was older. She had thought of showing the room to her and to Leon, but Bridgette correctly cautioned that they might try to find their own way there if they knew it existed, Leon especially, and the stairs were indeed still quite dangerous, especially for children.

When she ran upstairs, she was thinking she would bring Blanche and the others up the next afternoon for a private tea party, and she was humming happily to herself as she opened the door. But she was stopped in her tracks by the sight of her husband sitting cross-legged on the floor, going through her boxes of childhood papers and photographs.

Amalie was livid. "What are you doing here? You are not allowed in here! Who told you about it? Whoever it was is in big trouble! And get out of my things! They do not belong to you!"

Leopold laughed at her, which only served to make her angrier.

"What is so funny, you awful man? Please leave immediately—and get out of those boxes!" Amalie spoke while attempting to grab the boxes away from him, though to no avail, and for all her anger, he seemed to find the whole situation very amusing.

"I thought I told you that you weren't allowed up here," he said, "and now I find it so nicely appointed with all your toys and private possessions. Very disappointing, Amalie."

There it was again, the "let's talk to Amalie like a child" voice.

"So what? You are not my lord and master—I live here too, and this is my special room, so get out! Now!"

To Amalie's relief, although she would never admit it, he still seemed to find the whole situation highly amusing. "First of all, I am actually master of this house, and some might even say your lord and master. Did you think me too feeble-minded to figure out what the invoices for this little confection were for, so well mixed-up among the others? There was no need to keep it a secret. When have I ever denied you anything? You were with child when I forbade you to come up here, remember? And now, even though I know you have been sitting at my desk tippling on my brandy, I just want one thing."

Amalie answered quite peevishly, "What? And why do you always know everything? Oh, this is really quite vexing!"

Leopold responded with a wide grin, "Remember, I'm better than you and faster than you, and now I want the photograph."

Amalie recalled the first time he'd said those words to her

and had to laugh herself. "As I recall, sir, that was on a horse! I suppose you mean Prince Vladimir Mikhailovich Ivanov. I have no idea why Bridgette told you that. I didn't like his photograph one bit. He had a big belly and lascivious lips. He was just plain awful. He probably has eleven children by now, and if Papa had pursued it, I would have run away!"

Leo persisted. "So where is the photo?"

Amalie said, "Don't make me. You will laugh!" But she was laughing too by this time.

Leopold stood his ground. "I'm not leaving until I see this lascivious man."

Amalie dug through her boxes and found it. She threw the photograph at her husband and stood with the petted lip he adored.

"Well, my darling, you really did do very well when you captured me. I'll need to get Bridgette on this. She said he was handsome—no doubt to make me jealous."

"Okay, now leave!" Amalie felt embarrassed because indeed, the photo she had shared was of no handsome prince, and she opened the door for her husband's exit. But she couldn't resist remarking, "I don't think much of your past admirers either!"

Leopold said, "But, my dear, you only saw two of them." Upon saying this, he stood up and closed the door.

As he locked the door, Amalie said with her special little smile and her best cockney accent, which was really very bad, "Is it payment you demand for the room now, Sir Leopold, sir?"

He responded as he started removing her dress. "Just the first installment."

The first installment also turned into the second and third, and no one knew where to find the Blakeleys that afternoon. Leopold lay naked, lovingly watching as Amalie pulled out a colorful satin caftan from an ancient oak chest, yet another item she had rescued from Blakefield's enormous attics. She and her designers had gone exploring up there many times for inspiration and had actually used several of the pieces they had unearthed in their designs.

He asked quizzically, "My darling, what is that you are wearing? And I'm not letting you out of here dressed like that, half-naked."

Amalie responded, "I found this and others like it in that chest. I don't believe they have ever been worn. There are several white ones too. Bridgette had them cleaned, but really, they weren't soiled." She threw a much larger caftan at her husband and said, "Try it on."

Amazingly, he did, and as they stood together and looked at themselves in the full-length mirror, Leopold commented, "I wonder who they belonged to."

Amalie responded, "I was hoping you would know. It seems as if at least one of your ancestors led an interesting life. Look, there are also strange leather shoes, the likes of which I've never seen. I'm actually glad you came up here today. I've decided it will be our secret room. Well, Bridgette knows about it, but she knows everything."

Leopold was intrigued. "I haven't been up in the attics for years. God alone knows what secrets are buried there. The family goes back at least three hundred years. I used to hide up there as a boy until one day my father discovered me, and I was forbidden to ever go up there again. I was too afraid to disobey him and afterwards just lost interest. Amalie, I don't know if I've ever said it, but you saved me. I would have grown old counting my money otherwise, holed up in this mausoleum. You actually brought us both back to life."

Amalie kissed her husband's hands, as was her habit when she felt especially tender toward him. She considered that this was a mood she had not quite seen before, and she liked it very much.

They were still standing in front of the mirror when Leopold suddenly said, "Here, put on the shoes. Let's go up there now!"

Amalie was shocked and laughingly said, "Leo, we can't! Look what we are wearing. What if someone sees us?"

"I know another way up there," he said, "and I'll go first. No one is allowed in that part of the house. I keep it locked. No one will see us."

Leopold led Amalie to the back of the house, the section that had always been locked and for which none of the house keys fit. Amalie, being Amalie, had on several occasions tried to unlock the door and had always been curious about what was kept in there but had hesitated to ever ask him about it. She had tried to do so once, when they were newly married, but he had been completely closed up on the subject. Now it seemed, after six years of marriage, he was showing it to her without her asking him to do so.

The massive oak door groaned when he unlocked and opened it, and Amalie was suddenly hit with the musty smell of neglect. Clearly, no one ever came into this part of the house, not even Leopold, and as he led her by the hand, she quietly followed him. Amalie wanted to ask about the closed-up rooms they passed but didn't dare. Up they went instead to the attics, where Leopold opened and closed ancient oak chests and wardrobes, examining their contents, which consisted mostly of old moth-eaten clothes, and Amalie found herself feeling sorry for the poor souls who'd had to carry all the heavy pieces of furniture up there.

Meanwhile, Amalie studied the huge paintings in the dinginess, most particularly the ones of Leopold's father and mother. She found it strange that his father, as a young man, had had a kind face, whereas his mother, although quite beautiful, had displayed cruelty in the curl of her lips and in her eyes. She wondered anew what the true story of their marriage really was.

She was soon aroused from her reverie by Leopold taking her hand and saying, "Let's go back downstairs."

She wondered anew why he had suggested such an expedition since he didn't really seem to enjoy it. Perhaps it just made him feel easier to have her there as he explored it—the little boy inside of him.

They were again quietly making their way along the musty unused hallway when he suddenly stopped and said, "I want to show you something." He slowly unlocked a door, and as they entered the room, Amalie somehow knew. Her darling hadn't been conceived in the room she now occupied, the room where she and Leopold shared their love. It had happened in here, with several items of furniture thrown asunder, and no one had ever set the room back in order.

Leo spoke quietly but not bitterly as he said, "I understand he dragged her along this corridor, screaming and fighting him all the way. The story goes that she bit him so fiercely that she drew blood. She tried gin and other old wives' remedies to get rid of me, but it seemed I was destined to live, because thirty-two years later, I was to be given an angel who would make up for everything."

Amalie's tears flowed freely, and her heart was so full of compassion that she felt it might burst in her love for this man standing before her, this man who was her life. She realized he was smiling at her, his demons gone.

He kissed her tenderly before saying kindly, "Lady Amalie, I give you full permission to bring these rooms back to life, as only you can, and please use all the roses you find appropriate." He gave her the key to the room.

"Blanche?" she asked.

"Really, I don't know. You can tell her and Cordelia, I suppose, but please no others. Edward knows but will never speak of it, not even to his wife."

Somehow Amalie felt unworldly, dressed as they both were, and deliriously happy. They left the dark hallway behind, and Leopold turned and locked the door, giving Amalie the other key.

They turned around, and just as had happened on their wedding day, there was Bridgette. "Mon Dieu, monsieur! We have been searching everywhere! Where have you been, and what are you wearing? I found your clothes in the turret. Ma petite, you are half-naked! Monsieur!"

As Bridgette ushered them into the bedroom, they were quite dirty from their day's adventures but were laughing. Although Bridgette was much relieved, she told them she must inform Blanche. Dinner had been held back, and a search party was being considered. Although she was berating her master, Bridgette could see the sheer joy on her petite's face, and she began to laugh, a sight quite unusual for Bridgette.

Blanche and Cordelia soon appeared, and Blanche was uncharacteristically speechless.

Amalie then told them that Leo was allowing her to get to work on the rooms in the previously locked backstairs hallway. Blanche, of course, knew about the room and that her brother had taken a giant step forward in exorcising his demons.

"What in the name of Jesus are you wearing?" Cordelia asked.

Amalie, looking down at the curled-up toes of their shoes, said, "I have no idea, but I found these in the attic, and there are other similar pairs. They are all clean—well, these once were too. You ladies can both take one pair a piece and a caftan too. They are really most unusual."

Blanche was by now laughing. "That's our Amie, always willing to share."

"Well," she replied, "perhaps everything but my husband!"

It was decided to allow the guests to commence dinner with the excuse that their host and hostess were both indisposed, and Bridgette would bring them up a tray after they'd each had a bath.

Leopold and Amalie were pleased with the turn of events as they bathed together and stayed in their room the entire evening, basking in intimate conversation and in their love for one another.

At dinner Malcolm McFadden asked if there was anything he could do.

Blanche responded, "No, Malcolm, my brother has everything under control."

All resumed their meal, each person with the idea to find out what actually had transpired the following morning.

Amalie, meanwhile, had no intention of telling them, the whole truth at any rate.

CHAPTER 6
One Big Happy Family

Blakefield Castle had never seen so much activity going on at the same time. And Amalie was in her element!

Imogen Armstrong had arrived by first-class train ticket, paid for by Leopold, who also had cheerfully paid for two giant stretched canvases, new oil paints, and sable brushes. Amalie had not ever seen him so congenial, and sometimes she had the feeling she was holding her breath, in case suddenly that should change.

Ever since their day of exploring the attics and the back hallway that had been locked up for so many years, he seemed to be agreeing with every suggestion she made, and his agreement to some things truly shocked her, due to the price involved.

Amalie spent her mornings posing in the east-wing turret with Imogen. Sometimes Leopold joined them, although Imogen would never allow him to see her work, so he was forced to patiently wait for the final products to be unveiled. He surprised Amalie by actually speaking intelligently with much interest regarding Imogen's passion for the women's rights movement and her role in the WSPU. Of course, he also explained why he preferred his wife to temper her involvement, most especially with the knighthood and her new position in society. Imogen and Amalie didn't really set much store by this, knowing full well that upon her return to London, Amalie would—as was usual— make her escape to meetings as often as she could. At any rate, they just agreed with him, thereby keeping the peace and tranquility that seemed to permeate the whole household.

Leopold Blakeley appeared to be a contented man in the early part of that summer. The rooms in the back of his castle had been cleaned out, and Amalie, Maryia Smith, and Maryia's team, as well as all of Blakefield's visitors, were making suggestions or, in the case of Blanche, demands on how the section would be utilized.

Blanche and Cordelia would be moving to a larger suite in that part of the house, so that eventually, their current suite could be repurposed for Cosette. This was, of course, not to occur until Leon was sent off to school, an inevitable future for him that Amalie planned to put off as long as she possibly could. Leon and Miss Buchanan were finally getting used to one another, with Miss Buchanan's temperament much improved—an anomaly that Blanche put down to the country air.

The bills were arriving fast and furiously, and still nothing phased Leopold.

The ladies, including a more stylish Dolores McFadden, took afternoon tea together on these idyllic days, and on one such occasion, Blanche asked what they all were wondering. "Amie dearest, I have to ask because I just can't seem to get my head around my brother's new and improved behavior. What have you been putting in his cognac?"

Everyone laughed, and Amalie responded, "I promise, not a thing! I have wondered just how long this will last a great deal myself!"

Annabelle said, "Well, he has always loved you most ardently, but somehow now even more so, and I cannot remember the last time he snubbed you at the dinner table."

Henrietta was about to reprimand her daughter for such a remark, but Amalie was laughing. "That is truly the case, Annabelle! It has been quite an age!"

Dolores McFadden, who had been sitting quietly, smiling, then quite shocked the others when she said, "Amalie, your husband is so handsome. How did you make him fall in love with you?"

Amalie was at a loss for what to say. She had never completely warmed up to Dolores, although she had tried. Dolores understandably was jealous of Amalie's friendship with Malcolm. However, Amalie felt there was more to Malcolm's apparent disdain for his wife than his feelings for Amalie. During the past weeks since their arrival, she had noticed the distance he kept from Dolores. At times Amalie had thought of asking Malcolm about it but had decided it was really none of her business. Blanche and Cordelia had taken Dolores to Harrods for new, more appropriate apparel, and Bridgette had shown her how to style her hair, but all this had had little effect on Malcolm, or really none at all. The others, even Leopold, felt quite sorry for Dolores, but Amalie couldn't find it in her heart to do so. She kept these feelings to herself, for fear of censure, even from Blanche and Cordelia, but they could see it, as could Bridgette. Leopold couldn't, however, and also seemed not to notice the attention that Malcolm was still paying to Amalie.

Amalie eventually responded quite lightly, "I didn't make him do anything. He did so by his own free will. I will agree, however, that he is really rather handsome, as is your husband, Dolores."

And that was the end of the discussion.

During those summer evenings, rehearsals had begun for Lady Agatha's play. Fortunately, the duchess had insisted on Amalie playing Miss Mabel, so she was no longer assigned the role of

Mrs. Cheveley; to everyone's delight, this role was snapped up by Blanche. The remaining cast was rounded out by Annabelle, Harvey, and Malcolm. Dolores had declined to act in the play, with the excuse that she couldn't possibly remember her lines, and the others just left it at that.

Imogen was the obvious choice for stage manager, and Cordelia kept the Marches and indeed everyone quite inebriated by the end of the evenings. Freddie and Judith had returned to the city with their three children because it seemed that Judith was once again with child and was plagued by morning sickness, besides which Freddie was finding his host's new affability quite vexing; it seemed to Freddie to be combined with an even greater conceit than usual, no doubt due to his impending knighthood.

One afternoon before the Allsops left for London, Freddie took Amalie aside. "You know I often feel responsible for bringing you both together. I just want you to know that Judith and I are just an hour away should you ever need us."

Amalie thanked him, of course, but was later bothered by the statement. Malcolm had once said almost the same thing to her. Did they see something in her husband that she didn't? She resolved to speak to Blanche and Cordelia. She knew she should be happy, and indeed she was, but somehow something had changed after their magical day in the turret and the attics. Leopold was kind to her, but she missed his sarcasm, his moods, and if she was honest with herself, his passion. Perhaps he regretted his honesty in telling her such sad and dreadful details about the night he was conceived and about the gin and all of those wretched things. Her heart broke for him, as such was the depth of her love. She had been especially amiable and compliant since then. Perhaps that had been a mistake. She was beginning to realize that the new and improved Leopold Blakeley was not the person she had fallen in love with, and perhaps it was time to goad him out of this new complacency.

While Cordelia and Blanche were dressing for dinner one evening soon after the Allsops' departure, Cordelia said, "Do you feel that little Amie is happy—I mean, with the new affable Leo? I've seen her watching him with a confused look, and yet she hasn't sought our counsel as she always has before. That day they were running around the hallway, they were so happy. That's just a few weeks ago. Something is different."

Blanche looked thoughtful. "Yes, I sense something too. At first she seemed to enjoy my new, kinder brother. I'm not sure if that is still the case. Let's see how dinner goes tonight, and then maybe we should talk to her—find out what's going on in her new lilac and yellow-rose bedroom."

However, it was not necessary for them to wait until dinner. A knock at their door soon produced a sad-faced sister, whom they loved so dearly, and they sat her down with a glass of sherry and bade her to speak to them.

"At first it was fine—I mean, really nice. But I feel like he is slipping away from me. It could be boredom, but why wasn't he bored just a few short weeks ago? I was the happiest I have ever been, and so, it seemed, was he. He told me things that day in that awful room. Perhaps he regrets it? He didn't seem to at first, but …" Amalie blushed and took a sip of her drink before continuing. "He hasn't made love to me in over a week. I don't think he will do so ever again."

At this point Amalie began to cry. "I don't know why he is continuing with the nude portrait either. It makes no sense. I wish I knew how to make him mean again."

Blanche and Cordelia exchanged glances. They understood perfectly. Little Amie loved Leo's moods and unpredictability. But what to do? Of course, he was still in love with her. Perhaps, upon reflection, he did regret his honesty. Perhaps he felt somehow exposed. Perhaps he felt the telling of the final part of his wretched start to life had made him less of a man in his adoring wife's eyes.

When the ladies expressed these thoughts to Amalie, she responded, "But he is more a man than any man on earth. And I've been so sweet and kind to him. How could he think that?"

Blanche responded, "Exactly, possibly too sweet and kind. Where is he anyway?"

Amalie responded, "He went downstairs, saying he would leave me to get dressed." Amalie looked expectantly at Blanche, the big sister who would make everything right again.

Blanche responded, "He possibly might regret that soon. Where's Bridgette?"

Blanche went looking for Bridgette and soon returned with her. Mumbling to herself, Bridgette sought and found the now famous Parisienne black confection, worn only once six years ago, although an attempt had been made in the summer of 1902, when Amalie first discovered that she was with child.

Amalie giggled, shocked at Blanche's plan. "But isn't it too old-fashioned? Will it even fit me?"

It seemed that not only did the dress fit, but it looked sensational—Amalie looked sensational.

Cordelia responded, "Well, dearest Amie, it seems that it does fit, and holy cow, if this doesn't put him in some sort of passion, good or bad, I can't imagine what will. Also, no one downstairs has the faintest notion of fashion."

Blanche instructed Bridgette, "Her hair—she can wear it down. Do we have any black velvet ribbon?"

The ladies were immensely enjoying themselves as they anticipated Leopold's reaction to this siren who just happened to be his wife.

Satisfied with their handiwork, the ladies made their way downstairs with instructions to Amalie to follow ten minutes later. She was to hide in Bridgette's room until then, just in case Leo came looking for her. As Bridgette led her by the hand to the west wing, she said, "Mon Dieu, I'm not taking the blame for this!"

When the ladies entered the conservatory where all were gathered, Leopold asked, not unpleasantly, "Where's Amalie?"

His sister answered sweetly, "Doesn't she usually come down with you, Leo? She'll be down in a few minutes. Some last-minute adjustments."

Leopold had been presenting a pleasant facade to his guests. Furthermore, he had been presenting it to his wife. He felt her confusion. They had been so especially close to one another since he took her to the accursed room, a room she was already working her magic on as she chased away the shadows of the past. She had been so tender and loving to him after that day that in his self-pity, he was worried that she now pitied him. However, he had been finding it difficult to keep up this pretense of composure, even as he watched McFadden flirting and fawning over Amalie while all but ignoring his own pretty wife. Leopold hadn't made love to Amalie in days, although he desperately wanted to. He missed her drama and laughed inwardly about how her wifely devotion and deference were beginning to irritate him.

Now, as the others were partaking in Cordelia's cocktail hour, he stood there with Edward and their customary glasses of cognac with his back to the door, until McFadden's sharp intake of breath and the others' looks of amazement, accompanied by his sister's smirk, caused him to turn around.

Although she felt exceedingly self-conscious, Amalie Blakeley floated into the conservatory—to the shocked silence of all assembled—looking beyond sensational and apologized sweetly for being late. Her guests' facial expressions soothed her damaged ego, and Malcolm jumped over to kiss her hand.

But Malcolm was stopped in his tracks by his angry host, whose charming veneer had suddenly cracked, although he did manage to say, "Please excuse my wife and me for a moment."

Diane Coia-Ramsay

He took Amalie's arm and led her from the room, but not before noticing his sister smiling at him. *My God*, he thought, *this completely inappropriately dressed goddess is my wife.*

However, he was not in the mood for paying compliments. He led her out into the rose garden, where he had first kissed her so passionately, and as he scowled forbiddingly at her, Amalie's heart soared with happiness.

"Take it off," he said. "I thought I forbade you to wear that dress!"

Amalie responded, "What? Here? I don't think so. I think I look rather nice, and I'm sorry you don't think so. Nevertheless, it's staying on. Anyway, I didn't think you would notice or even remember it."

Amalie made to walk away, smiling at herself, but Leopold grabbed her arm and pulled her further into the garden.

"What are you intending, my dear husband? To strip me of it yourself, right here in the gardens? Very well, but you'll have to help me with the fasteners."

Amalie turned her back to him and lifted her hair. She could feel the intoxicating nearness of him and yet his hesitation. She waited, thinking of the humiliation if he just walked away.

But he didn't do that, not this time. He wrapped her hair around his fist and with his other hand pulled her to him, still with her back to him, and began passionately kissing her neck and shoulders. He then pushed his free hand down her bodice until, wide-eyed, she exclaimed, "Leo, not here! What are you doing?"

"I think this might have been what you had in mind, coming down half-naked for dinner," he said. "I am assuming that I was to be the lucky man—after all, it's my castle and my gardens, and you're my wife."

He turned her to him, and Amalie, overjoyed, exclaimed, "What if someone comes looking for us? My aunt? Blanche and

Cordelia? Oh, Leo, no!" But she was laughing. He was back, and Amalie was still so utterly besotted with him.

He briefly drew back and said, "I don't want your pity. The things I told you—you kept them to yourself?"

He looked so vulnerable for a split second, but Amalie knew the correct course of action. "Pity? For a smug, conceited, crazy man about to be knighted?"

It was indeed exactly the correct response. He again took her by the hand and led her to the stables, where he grabbed a blanket and his horse, which he quickly saddled up.

"Where are we going? Are you kidnapping me? I think this knighthood has gone to your head, Sir Leopold!" Amalie was immensely enjoying her husband's antics, and by now he was immensely enjoying himself too.

"I'm taking you somewhere where no one will find you. No mercy, my lady, after tonight's little performance. I assume it was for my benefit, so I fully intend to enjoy it."

They rode off toward the river, and Amalie hoped he did not intend to throw her in. She happily held on to him as he led her further down than she had been before, to his childhood hiding place.

As he lifted her down from his horse, he grew serious. "This is where I used to come as a boy. No one could ever find me here, not even Blanche, who, by the way, I assume was behind tonight's little performance."

It was a beautiful summer's evening, and Amalie took the blanket and laid it down on the lush grass. "Did you ever bring a girl here?" she asked.

"Amalie, beloved, as if I would tell you if I did. But truthfully, no. I only came to nurse my wounded pride. I even did so the day Freddie put a pellet in my face."

He took his flask of brandy from his saddle and passed it to her as they both sat down on the blanket. "McBride's a good chap—always keeps it replenished." Returning to her question, he added, "I used to think about it, though."

Amalie responded, "Anyone in particular?" She felt a pang of jealousy and wondered, not for the first time, about his years as a young man. She was twenty-six and had been married to him for almost six years. When he was her current age, he had still been free, with six more years of freedom still ahead of him before they would even meet.

He didn't answer her but just smiled.

She pursued her line of questioning, her jealous curiosity getting the better of her. "Were there lots of girls? Did you ever, you know, with anyone I've met?"

Leopold started to laugh as he took a swig from his flask. He then screwed on the lid and tossed it aside. "My darling, I didn't bring you here to tell you secrets, but no one you've ever met, and I never said I was a saint. For God's sake, Amalie, I was thirty-two when we met. I wish I'd met you ten years sooner, but I don't think your father would have permitted me to take you away."

"Leo, I would have been ten! Anyone special?"

"Amalie, this is all I will say on the subject. No, I was never in love before I met you. I thought I was incapable of it. I never seduced a young maiden, most especially since, given my family background, I had no intention of being trapped in a loveless marriage. Most importantly, you completely took my breath away. I was so grateful for your little uppity ways, since I was sure that if you were nicer, you would have been snapped up already. Even when you were attempting to snub and insult me, I could tell that you'd never been kissed, and I was determined to be the only man who ever would do so."

Amalie was enjoying the conversation and asked, "How could you tell? I don't know if I believe you."

Leopold just said laughingly, "My beautiful darling, it couldn't have been any more obvious if you'd worn a sign around your neck. You mentioned my castle twice upon our first meeting, when I had never mentioned it to you. A sophisticated woman wouldn't have made such a blunder."

Amalie grew thoughtful. "Hmm, I knew that was a mistake. I worried that you thought me a gold digger."

"No, I didn't think that. You trembled when I kissed your hand. I may not have wanted to know it just at that moment, but wanting you was like a fever, and I knew that marrying you was my only option."

Amalie asked coquettishly, "So are you glad you married me?"

Leopold lifted her chin and kissed her gently as he looked deep into her eyes. "Amalie, you are my life. Come on, I'm taking you home."

Puzzled, she said, "But I thought …?"

Leopold helped her to her feet. "I think rain is coming, and I won't have you catching a chill. You've caused me enough worry in the past. Besides, there's a big comfortable bed waiting for us. We'll just go straight upstairs. I'm not in the mood for McFadden."

Amalie happily obeyed since her dress was far from comfortable; however, it had played its part so well that she would have it cleaned and packed lovingly away. She then noticed that Leopold's suit was quite dirty and hoped no one would see them before they went upstairs.

They rode back in blissful anticipation of a night of romance and passion. Leopold stabled his horse while Amalie watched him, and they returned to the house just as their guests were leaving the dining room.

Amalie, aware of their bedraggled appearance, was reminded of that night six years earlier when she'd gotten lost in the woods and Leopold found her.

It seemed he was reminded of it too as he said to one and all, "Mrs. Blakeley got lost in the woods. I merely rescued her."

But this time he walked upstairs with her, as she called back laughingly, "I did get lost!"

Blanche turned to Cordelia. "I remember that night. God, how I wanted to get her away from him."

Cordelia laughingly responded, "And tonight you just handed him to her on a plate."

Blanche laughed out loud as she took her lady love's hand on their way into the conservatory for after-dinner drinks.

CHAPTER 7
An Unexpected Visitor

The next morning, Amalie was happily humming a tune as she went to fetch the children to take them to the kitchen garden and teach them the names of herbs. She enjoyed doing this when she was in an especially sunny mood. Leon was very solicitous toward his little sister, and he and his mama laughed at the faces Cosette made as she smelled the herbs and attempted to pronounce the names of each one in French as well as English in her sweet baby voice.

Leopold joined them for a little while. He had been out riding the estate with Blanche and Cordelia, who had not returned with him, and Amalie laughed happily when he caught sight of his daughter's calico kitten, which she was carrying in a little basket. Eloise had finally tracked down the perfect one, and Cosette had cried with delight when she was presented with her new kitten, which—after much consideration and suggestions from her brother—had been named Kitty. Amalie might have chosen something more original; however, the important thing was that they all, including Cosette, had been sworn to secrecy, since Papa would say that cats belonged in the barn.

As expected, Leopold said to Amalie, "Cats belong in the barn and not in the nursery." But they both knew full well that this particular kitten would be remaining in the nursery, lest he break his daughter's heart, which he had little intention of doing.

Amalie responded, "Oh, Papa, she found it in the garden one day. What else could I do but allow her to keep it?"

As she spoke, Cosette was pulling at her father's arm, saying, "Papa, Maman got me a kitty."

Leopold asked lightheartedly, "So which one of you ladies am I to believe?"

Leon was the one to answer. "Maman!" By this time his baby sister was nodding her head vigorously in agreement as she clung to her kitten.

Leopold turned to his wife and said, "Yet another Lady Amalie conspiracy." And to his children he said, "I suppose I cannot now say no. Just make sure you look after it." However, he was more amused than angry, and Amalie winked at her children as he walked into the house.

"Well, *mes enfants*, at least we have no need to hide Kitty in the future, but we shall keep her away from Papa, nevertheless."

Amalie watched her husband walk away and smiled to herself as she remembered the previous evening, when they had eaten supper in their room, and he had made love to her so passionately that she had cried with happiness.

First thing this morning, she had thanked Blanche and Cordelia for their usual guidance, and Blanche had laughed and said, "Who would have thought, once upon a time, that I would become your spiritual advisor?"

Cordelia had laughed too, remembering how different things used to be.

Cordelia understood Blanche better than anyone. She had loved her for many years, and their partnership was one of mutual respect and happiness.

No one could have rejoiced more than Cordelia at the coming together of Blanche and her brother, a situation that never would have come about but for the intervention of a beautiful French girl in the summer of 1898.

Since then, she and Blanche had become very close to, and protective of, their little sister Amie, as they had come to think of her. They had both helped her through the delivery of her two children, through pneumonia, and through many other dramatic events that, in all truth, she mostly had caused herself in her besotted adoration of Leopold.

Cordelia had met Leopold Blakeley only one time prior to that summer. She and Blanche had voyaged to London and Paris in 1895 and met him once for dinner in the Savoy. She had thought him to be a singularly unpleasant man and had been glad when he finally took his leave of them. He did not invite them to Blakefield Castle—the setting of Blanche's unhappy childhood— nor did Blanche show any interest in going there, and the two siblings who had shared their unhappy childhood together neither kissed nor embraced upon parting.

Cordelia had been most unenthusiastic about their planned visit to Blakefield Castle three years later and had not approved of Blanche's scheme in going there. She'd never had any intention of going along with it, even when her inheritance was uncertain, but upon reflection, she was overjoyed that she had agreed to the trip in the end. Had she not, then none of what had occurred afterwards could have possibly come to pass.

Cordelia had been able to tell that very first time she saw them together, coming in from the gardens—the day Amalie Bouchard arrived at Blakefield Castle—that they were in love, possibly before they knew it themselves, and she had marveled at the change in Leopold, a completely different man. She had thought it sweet and quite amazing, the transformation in him, and the young woman who was responsible for it was clearly as besotted with him as he was with her. She was glad of it, although she didn't say this to Blanche at the time.

Just a few short months later, Blanche would be matron of honor at their wedding, and since then, she and Blanche had seemed to spend as much time in England as they did in the US. Who ever would have thought such a thing during that dinner in the Savoy in 1895?

⁂

It was getting close to the children's lunchtime, and the sun was high in the sky when Amalie told them it was time to go inside. As she stood and waited for Leon to gather up his toy soldiers, carrying the kitten in the basket in one hand and holding Cosette's hand with the other, she spotted a man seated upon a black stallion approaching her from the distance.

Amalie stood rooted to the spot—for a moment and from a distance, he almost could have been her husband. His black curly hair and dark skin and even his stature were familiar, but as he came closer, it was easy to see the differences. This man was not as handsome, and his face was not as kind. He was a bit older than Leopold but not by too many years, and as she sent Leon inside to fetch his father, she knew it, straightaway: he had come from Spain and was here to somehow cause turbulence in her idyllic summer and in her happy home.

She looked up at him as he dismounted and waited for him to speak, all the while hoping that Leon was not tarrying in his mission to fetch his father.

He smiled at her with little warmth and said, "What a charming scene, a graceful little mother and her beloved children.

But I forget myself. I am Xavier Cortez, cousin of Leopold Blakeley—or should I say Sir Leopold, although not quite yet. He is a very fortunate man, if my assumption is correct and you are his beautiful bride."

Amalie bristled. His English was perfect although his accent was unmistakably Spanish. She looked toward the house and still saw no sign of her husband. Instinctively, she lifted Cosette, who had been hiding her face in her skirt, and the kitten jumped out of the basket.

The stranger retrieved the kitten and handed it to Amalie, who still hadn't spoken a word. He said, "I understand you are French. You are very lovely, but I think you already know that."

Still, she did not speak, and finally, Leopold appeared at the doorway. When he at first beheld his visitor, he looked surprised, shocked even, but not unpleasantly so.

As the cousins approached one another, Amalie said, "Excuse me," and simply walked away, still carrying her baby daughter and her kitten. She passed her husband, whose attention was not upon her but upon the stranger, as she walked back into the house.

Bridgette was running down the stairs to greet her. Clearly, Leon had run up to fetch her. "Here," Bridgette said, "let me take Cosette to the nursery, and I will come to your room. I only know that according to Leon, 'the man who looks like Papa is talking to Maman.'"

Amalie quickly obeyed and was anxiously looking out her window for Blanche and Cordelia when Bridgette re-entered her room.

She turned and spoke quite nervously. "He's his cousin. Here from Spain. I don't like him. I don't think he means well, and he seems to know an awful lot about us, or should I say me? He even knows I am French, and I've never heard of him! I didn't even know Leo had a cousin. I'm looking out for Blanche. After all, he's her cousin too."

Bridgette responded with a tone of conspiracy. "I imagine he read about the knighthood in the *London Times*. Possibly there was a short description of those about to be honored by the king? I wonder what he wants because I'm sure he wants something. I saw them walk into the house and toward the monsieur's study. They look alike, but the monsieur is more refined, and his bearing more noble. He is also younger. What did he say to you?"

Just then, Amalie spotted the ladies walking over from the stables. They were accompanied by Malcolm and Dolores, whom they must have met during their ride. Bridgette said it would be better if they all met in Blanche's suite, just in case the monsieur came upstairs.

"No!" Amalie declared dramatically. "The turret. We must fetch my aunt too. She is resting in her room. Uncle March went to London with Harvey and Annabelle today."

Ten minutes later, all including the McFaddens and Imogen Armstrong had gathered in Amalie's secret room that previously none, except Imogen and Bridgette, had known existed. Amalie had intended this to be her and Leopold's special room, but that no longer mattered to her.

The paintings were covered over, and Malcolm, who had overheard that one of them was a nude, was intensely interested in seeing them. He knew Blakeley would never allow it, but he thought, *Maybe I could come up here when no one else is around.* Looking over at the lovely Amalie, wide-eyed with drama, he regretted his marriage. Nothing could alter his contempt for a girl who had lied to him, a girl whose youth and pretty face hid a wanton nature. No matter how Blanche and Cordelia dressed her up, she would never be anything but tarnished in his eyes. He wanted to spend time alone with Amalie, just walking and talking as they had done that first summer, since he knew that was all their relationship could ever be, and he needed to find a way to shake off Dolores.

"I never knew we had a cousin," said Blanche, "but come to think of it, it seems quite natural that we should, possibly many more—they are Roman Catholic after all."

Amalie and Bridgette were at first indignant since they shared that faith. However, the others laughed at the remark, and soon, so did they, even as Henrietta exclaimed, "Sakes, Blanche! What a thing to say!" The remark was typically Blanche.

"Tell us what he said to you, Amie. You seem upset by the encounter," Blanche continued, growing serious.

Amalie spoke with great drama, as was her endearing way. "He is a horrible, nasty man. He called me little, French, and beautiful, in a way that seemed insulting, and he knew about the knighthood. Then Leo came out and walked right past me, as if he was a long-lost cousin. Well, of course, he is a long-lost cousin, I suppose, but nevertheless …"

Cordelia asked, "Does he have a name, this nasty villain?"

Amalie declared with great aplomb, "Señor Xavier Cortez! Leo better not ask him to stay for dinner!"

Blanche looked thoughtful. "It seems he has been doing some research. I wonder what he is after. Money, I expect. Can't imagine my brother parting with any of that. I wonder what they are talking about."

Cordelia said, "You have every right to go and find out—and for that matter, so do you, Amie."

Blanche was in the course of responding that she had no interest in so doing when Leopold suddenly appeared. Amalie strained her neck to look behind him and see if he was accompanied, and he was not. She looked at him expectantly, as did the others, all waiting for him to speak.

"To quote Cordelia, I see the gang's all here, even McFadden and Dolores. My love, did you also alert the village of our visitor? Bridgette, please see to Lady Agatha's suite. Amalie and Blanche can stay. Will the rest of you please excuse us? McFadden, I hope you weren't peeking at my wife's portraits."

Malcolm patted Amalie's shoulder as he walked out, a protective act that didn't go unnoticed by Leopold.

Blanche said as the others were leaving, "Cordelia is staying."

Amalie, indignant, said, "So is Bridgette. And that man is not staying in Lady Agatha's suite. I don't want him touching her things, and it is too close to the family's bedrooms! He can stay at the Black Raven. He can dine there also!" But even upon saying this, she knew that Leopold would do as he saw fit.

He responded, "No, my love, I'm afraid not. It seems he is my only surviving cousin, who I had no idea existed until today. I would be grateful if you would at least attempt to make him welcome. He has traveled all the way from Cadiz. He will not be staying at the village inn. Blanche, aren't you at least interested to meet him?"

Blanche responded sarcastically, "No, little brother, not particularly so. What is he after anyway? Money?"

As he turned to walk away, her brother said only, "Don't call me that at dinner, Blanche. Amalie, wear something nice."

After they heard his footsteps descend down the winding staircase, the remaining four women stared at one another.

Amalie exclaimed, attempting to imitate her husband's voice, "Amalie, wear something nice! He will be most vexed when he discovers that I will be taking dinner in my room—permanently!"

Bridgette said with much drama, "Why don't all you ladies wear something very special for dinner? Who says that you must be nice to this ignorant man who insulted ma petite? I will ensure that there is nothing valuable left in that suite. I am certain Lady Agatha will not be amused if she hears about this. Ladies, hide your jewelry and make sure to lock your doors. I fear nothing good will come of this unexpected visit."

The ladies acquiesced and arranged to meet in the Marches'

suite for afternoon tea—none of them wished to encounter Señor Cortez until the evening. By that time the others would be back from London, so they would be eleven at dinner.

Amalie remarked, "Really, there will be so many of us this evening, there will be no need to speak to him at all. Perhaps he will be offended and leave in the morning! Blanche, will you please take my place at the dinner table? I don't wish to sit beside him, and you are much more condescending than I."

Blanche laughed out loud and said, "Amie dearest, we all know you can be very uppity when you choose to be; however, I will be happy to oblige."

Later that day, when it was time to rest before dinner, Amalie found her husband already doing so as she entered their bedroom.

When she walked in, he opened his eyes and sat up. "So, my dear, a private meeting in what I thought to be our special place. It seems you have taken an immediate dislike to a man—my cousin indeed—that you just met fleetingly in the garden this morning. Perhaps you will find him more amiable upon further acquaintance."

Amalie was incensed. "I desire no further acquaintance with such a nasty, horrible man. I want him to go away, and for all your reputed genius, you certainly seem to lack judgment of character. He wants something, dear husband, and if you cannot see through him, I certainly can. He has come here to cause havoc and discord in our happy home, and you, it seems, similar to my uncle March, cannot see further than the end of your nose! I do not believe that I will dine with my family and guests this evening. I feel a headache coming on."

Amalie did not join her husband on their bed, as was her usual custom, but instead walked over to her chaise.

Leopold, exasperated, stood up and walked over to sit with her in an attempt to smooth things over, in order that he might enjoy his dinner that first night. But as usual, he got it all wrong. "What did he say to you, my darling, that was so upsetting? He was very generous in his compliments toward you and the children. You know that on occasion, you are inclined to be oversensitive."

Amalie was outraged. "Oversensitive indeed! He introduced himself very arrogantly and told me in a belittling fashion that I was little, French, and lovely. Oh, but I already knew that. He also knows about the knighthood! I don't wish him to remain here, and until he leaves, you best keep your safe locked. Bridgette has advised us ladies to hide our jewelry."

Leopold laughed. "Well, dear heart, all of what he said is true, and indeed you do know that you are lovely—everyone tells you often enough. My safe is always locked, lest you decide to rob me, and I am quite certain your jewelry is safe, even Blanche's considerable collection. I would prefer, however, that you indeed play the role of my charming wife and hostess this evening and take your proper place at dinner, with Xavier on your right-hand side. Blanche can be seated on his other side, and I will leave the rest of the seating up to you."

As Leopold stood up, he concluded, "Amalie, with regard to what he wants, please remember that I'm not a total fool. He gave me a bunch of my mother's letters, written to her mother and her brother, his father, Alejandro Cortez. I threw them in my desk drawer, and perhaps Blanche will want to read them since I'm not sure that I will want to do so. He has seven surviving children and—as he put it—a very plump wife." He then repeated, "Wear something nice," and as he left the room, he stated his intention of speaking to Blanche.

Amalie then pondered, *Well, if I am to be seated thus, Malcolm will be seated on my left side. Cordelia can be next to him, and Blanche can sit across from Cordelia so she can stare him down as only she can. Dolores and Aunt March can sit on either side of my husband, so he can enjoy their conversation, and everyone else will sit in between. Perhaps he will leave tomorrow.*

When Bridgette came in to dress her mistress, she told her that the seating arrangement would be taken care of and that Chef Moreau was creating several culinary masterpieces. Mr. Carmichael and his footmen had meticulously set the table, which was complemented by beautiful flower arrangements that Imogen had generously taken on as a welcome break from painting. Her nude was coming along nicely; she had chosen an Eastern theme, using silks and satins of exotic shades draped on her beautiful friend, in such a way that the painting was even more alluring than had it just been done as a completely naked woman reclining on a sofa. She considered it her finest work thus far, and this was no doubt due to her special love for her exceptionally beautiful friend. Although the nude would be in Mr. Blakeley's private collection, she knew she would use the likeness as inspiration for other nudes she intended to paint in the future. She had included Amalie's husband in the second painting since he so often sat with them—when Amalie was clothed—and she hoped he would be pleased and not upset that she had chosen to do so. Amalie was in on her plan, and they were such a striking couple in their prime of life that it just seemed the correct thing for her to do.

Bridgette, of course, took very special care of Amalie's hair and toilette that evening. She had bathed in rose water and donned her stunning new Jeanne Paquin aquamarine silk. However, and most especially, after Blanche stopped by and told her that she too had been given her orders for dinner that evening, it was decided that "gloves were off." Blanche mused, "My brother giving lectures on etiquette—never thought to see the day!"

Amalie at the last moment chose to wear her diamond tiara in her immaculately coiffed hair.

It seemed that Leopold was determined to make his guest comfortable, since he had gone down a little earlier to offer him a glass of cognac. Amalie had not yet donned her new gown at that time, and he had left her to walk down with Blanche and Cordelia.

She knew she looked stunning. She also knew that her husband was well aware that his guest made her very uncomfortable. As she was about to take the ladies' arms, she spotted Malcolm at the top of the grand staircase. It seemed that Dolores had already gone down, and he had come back up to fetch her reticule.

As Blanche and Cordelia exchanged glances, Amalie walked over and took the arm of a very grateful and dashing Malcolm McFadden. He had dressed that evening, as he had once before, in his full Scottish clan regalia. It had been a last-minute decision of his to bring it along with him, and on that particular evening, he was very pleased that he had chosen to do so.

Malcolm enthusiastically complimented his beautiful hostess, and indeed his heart quickened when he saw her approach him. As they walked down the grand staircase together, he allowed himself to imagine that they were indeed a couple and what happiness he would know if that were truly the case.

The conservatory went silent when Malcolm and Amalie walked in, and Amalie was conjuring up thoughts of her autocratic father and his friend Count Victor Le Clair as she proudly glided past her husband and his male companions—with her nose in the air—and issued the briefest of greetings. "Good evening, Señor Cortez. I hope your room is comfortable. Harvey, Uncle March, Leopold."

She did not wait for their return greeting as she made her way over to be seated with Annabelle and her aunt, but she couldn't help but witness the look of naked hatred that passed between Malcolm and Leo. It appeared that Señor Cortez most certainly noticed it too. The remainder of the assembled guests were already quite familiar with the looks that passed between these two men, who it seemed were still rivals, and consequently, they set no store by it.

Leopold and his cousin soon walked over to Amalie, who by now was chatting animatedly with her aunt and Annabelle, with Malcolm standing close by. Leopold said, in a determined effort to sound pleasant and unconcerned about the manner of his wife's entrance into the conservatory, "My dear, please allow me to properly introduce you to my cousin, Xavier Cortez, whom you met briefly earlier this morning. Xavier, my wife Amalie."

Amalie stood up as Xavier gallantly kissed her hand, and she simply smiled sweetly and said, "Señor Cortez."

He responded, "Please, we are cousins after all. Please call me cousin Xavier, as I have asked my cousin Blanche to do also."

This was met with a smile but no further conversation as Amalie simply excused herself for the second time that day and walked away. She could tell that Leo was angry with her. It was in his eyes if not his smile, but she didn't care. He should have waited to walk her downstairs. He should have respected and understood the fact that this long-lost cousin had been very rude to her—in front of her children—earlier in the day.

Amalie felt that her husband had completely disregarded her feelings, and she was as angry with him as he might have been with her. She could tell that Blanche felt similarly by her stance and demeanor.

Meanwhile, Leopold was furious with both his wife and his sister, who he felt were behaving very badly to his cousin and special guest.

After Amalie walked away, Xavier said, "I may have appeared rude to your wife this morning, but it was certainly not my intention. I was simply overawed and charmed by her sheer loveliness and motherly attention to her children. Perhaps I will be given a second chance."

Leopold was about to respond that he expected that he would be so given when his cousin continued speaking. As he watched Amalie laughing at something Malcolm was saying to her, his forlorn wife looking on and unsuccessfully attempting to join the conversation, Xavier remarked, "Your American guest is quite neglectful to his wife, and yet she is quite pretty. Of course, she is not on the level of your Amalie."

When dinner was called, Leopold approached Dolores and said, "I understand you will be seated with me this evening, Dolores. Let me escort you to your chair."

Such gallantry, Amalie thought, as seething inside, she begrudgingly took Xavier's proffered arm.

Dinner was served, and Monsieur Moreau exceeded all expectations with each course that was served to the family and guests that evening at Blakefield Castle.

Amalie was certainly gracious to her Spanish guest but by no means friendly, and there was an occasion when his leg accidentally brushed hers—at least she hoped that it was accidental. She jumped, and he apologized profusely.

For the most part, she chatted easily with Malcolm, and she was so glad he too was seated beside her. Blanche was being Blanche, sitting across from Xavier and majestically looking down her nose at him. Cordelia, who was seated beside him, was left to provide at least some congenial intercourse for their Spanish guest, since the others around him were making little or no attempt to do so.

Xavier Cortez was not unaware of what was going on with those he was seated beside. He knew he was being snubbed by the French woman and her American guests. Even his cousin Blanche was very American with her colloquialisms, spoken in a most English upper-class manner. He found the whole charade quite amusing. Of course, he himself would never tolerate such behavior from the women in his home, and it seemed to him that although his cousin was watching the women with a less-than-pleased countenance, he was very possibly quite used to such behavior from his wife and from his sister.

There was one point when Blanche said, "I wonder, Cousin Xavier, that your wife did not travel with you to England."

He responded, "Indeed, Cousin Blanche, she, unlike you ladies, has little time for dressing up and travel. She has seven children to care for and a husband with very exacting expectations."

Dear God, poor woman, thought Amalie.

Blanche calmly responded, "My my, how different we are in the rest of the world since most gentlemen in our acquaintance must pander to their wives."

Such was the conversation at one end of the table, while at the same time, Leopold sat at the other end between two women who prattled away all through dinner, even as he tried to shut them out and ascertain what was going on at the other end.

He could tell that Amalie and Blanche, in particular, were completely shunning his cousin. He could also see that McFadden was lapping up the attention being paid to him. He saw his wife jump at one point and Xavier apologize; for what he couldn't tell, but he was determined to find out. Amalie, looking magnificent, was ignoring him too. No smiles for him, as was her usual habit when they were seated thusly at dinner. He could almost imagine that she did not belong to him, seated as she was, like a stranger. However, she did belong to him, for all her airs and outrageous flirting with McFadden. He knew it was all for his benefit, and she would be made to pay later. Two years earlier, he had been almost driven mad with jealousy, but now he knew her every little idiosyncrasy, and he loved her just as much as he knew that she was in love with him. Therefore, Leopold was not upset by his wife's and sister's bad behavior, but more amused by it, since he too was well aware that his cousin's visit was not some spontaneous urge to connect with his English family. He knew there was a reason for it and would be patient enough to let that reason unfold.

Eventually, the ladies withdrew and left the gentlemen to their port and cigars.

Harvey Haversham was an even-tempered successful businessman who had been raised, like Cordelia, in a prosperous and loving home in Upstate New York. He found the drama that was usually on display in this beautiful family country home, or rather castle, to be most entertaining. When his wife had told him the story of her family and home, he had assumed there were some exaggerations; however, it seemed his sweetest Annabelle had not been exaggerating in the slightest.

Annabelle had told him her wonderful news that morning, and he knew she was making her happy announcement to the ladies at this very moment. At forty-seven and with two grown sons, he was delighted to again be a father, and since the conversation in the dining room seemed fraught with undertones, he very soon made the suggestion that they join the ladies. His host had suggested billiards, but he had declined, as had Malcolm, and the idea of playing billiards was abandoned, much to the chagrin of Harvey's father-in-law.

From his observations, Harvey could tell that Edward March and Leopold Blakeley were as thick as thieves. Malcolm McFadden was cast as the rival for the lovely Amalie's affections—thus the abandonment of billiards—and now entered Xavier Cortez, the Spanish villain.

Harvey wondered at the necessity of putting on a play for the benefit of, of all people, a real duchess, since theatrics were clearly ongoing every day at Blakefield Castle. The cast was rounded out by his eccentric mother-in-law; a French servant who ruled the household; his host's completely outrageous sister and her companion, a millionairess and part-time bartender; and finally, a militant lady artist who was—or so he had been told—in the process of painting a nude painting of the wife of his host, a man soon to be knighted by the king. Harvey Havemeyer was having the time of his life and wasn't ashamed to say it!

When the gentlemen entered the conservatory, the room was abuzz with Annabelle's news. The ladies were enraptured and completely surprised, and Annabelle, who had had her condition confirmed by Bridgette and Dr. Matthews, was absolutely over the moon. Leopold and his cousin had held back a while in the dining room before joining the others. Edward March had left them to it as it seemed this stranger had something of a private matter to discuss with his nephew.

By the time Leopold and Xavier joined the others, the champagne was already flowing in celebration, and all thoughts of Señor Cortez and his real intentions took a back seat to everyone's elation.

Xavier, of course, was forced to join in the congratulations and felicitations to the happy couple. His true objective, the real reason for his coming to England, must yet wait a while, and besides, he found himself enjoying the engaging interactions between his cousin Leopold and his wife and guests, an atmosphere that was at once as incomprehensible as it was entertaining.

Blanche and Cordelia had shipped over the latest Victor Victrola from New York that spring and had brought along several popular records from the United States. Soon the company had moved into the great hall, where the Victrola proudly stood. Amalie loved to play her new contraption, and in the gaiety of the evening, some began dancing to the very latest recordings, including Amalie's favorite, "Meet Me in St. Louis."

Amalie was happily singing along, and although still not

immensely pleased with her husband, she danced over to where he was standing with her uncle and his cousin. "I just love this song!" she said. And then she laughingly asked him to dance with her.

But Leopold refused, citing the fact that he was not overly fond of modern music and most particularly that song.

Amalie covered up her intense humiliation by saying lightly, "Very well, old man. I will dance with myself." She turned to walk away but was stopped in her tracks by Xavier Cortez stepping forward and asking her to dance. As a gracious hostess, she had no option but to accept, even as she looked helplessly at the ungracious host, who just basically left her to it.

Xavier Cortez was an accomplished dancer, unlike Leopold, who usually had to be coerced into dancing, unless he had partaken in several glasses of his preferred beverage. Xavier's manner was pleasant enough, and again Amalie marveled at the striking similarity between the two cousins. However, there was something quite wrong with this man's features, a callousness that was real and not the act that her husband put on for the world— inside, she knew Leopold to be kind and caring. However, as she turned toward him to rescue her from this man, who was by now holding her too closely, so that she longed for escape, she saw, incredulously, that her husband was dancing with Dolores McFadden. Xavier was smiling at her in a way that made her feel increasingly uncomfortable, until she was unexpectedly and thankfully tapped on her shoulder by Malcolm McFadden, who asked if he could step in, smiling pleasantly.

Once they had danced away, Amalie thanked him for rescuing her. He responded, "I could see you weren't having fun. There is something sinister about that man. I think your husband should keep a sharp eye on him. Remember, Amalie, my offer still stands. It will always stand. I made no wonderful declarations of love when I married Dolores. She had a pretty miserable life with her father and brothers. I merely rescued her, knowing my heart's desire would never be fulfilled, at least not while Leopold Blakeley walked the earth. She has a better life now, traveling Europe and dancing with your handsome husband. Look at her smiling adoringly up at him. What a foursome we make, for sure."

Amalie looked over at Leopold and Dolores and wondered what cruel game her husband was playing. If his intention was to upset Malcolm, he had missed his mark, and if the show was for her sake, she couldn't really understand why. She responded thoughtfully, "Malcolm, you are the nicest man I have ever known. You make me feel comfortable and safe, and I'm sorry for the words I last spoke to you when you were in England. You mean a great deal to me, but—"

Malcolm interrupted, "No need to continue. I know the 'but.' Do you think I should go rescue my wife? Not that she appears to want rescuing, although she's had too much champagne, I think."

Amalie smiled and agreed that it might be time to wind down this most peculiar evening. Her evening had started with Malcolm and ended so, with little or no discourse with her husband in between.

Blanche said to Cordelia, "It might soon be time for me to intervene. I'm not sure what game Sir Leopold thinks he is playing. Poor Dolores. And he might just be a little too sure of himself with our Amie."

CHAPTER 8
Do You Really Want to Risk It?

Amalie was exhausted when she finally made her way upstairs. Bridgette had come down to fetch her. It always seemed that Bridgette knew when something was wrong, and she too disliked this cousin of the monsieur and mistrusted his motives.

Blanche and Cordelia came to her once she was safely in her room. She locked both doors before confessing, "I am so confused. I don't understand what has happened to my Leo. He was so horrible to me today and especially this evening. This man is sleeping in our hallway, and he was most inappropriate, the way he danced with me. Thank God that Malcolm rescued me—because I could see my husband had no intention of doing so. I am afraid of this stranger and afraid to be alone in case I come upon him. I don't believe that Leo will protect me either. It's like all of the sudden he hates me. I don't understand why."

It had been such a strange and unusual day, and they were all tired, but Blanche could see the fear in little Amie's eyes as she started to cry in her confusion. "Okay," said Blanche, "the rest of you get to bed. Amie, do you want to go with Cordelia or Bridgette? Whatever this is about, it needs to stop. I will wait here for my brother since this stranger is apparently my cousin too. I won't have him causing havoc in this family!"

Amalie seemed afraid to stay in the east wing, so it was decided that she should go with Bridgette. Bridgette put her to bed and soothingly stroked her hair, so that she was soon fast asleep. Bridgette had been witness to the monsieur's many moods, many times, but this was somehow different. Her sweetest petite was afraid, and it was as if he didn't care or even was glad of it. Bridgette recalled that the previous morning this had been a happy home and he a loving husband. Could this one man really have changed all of that?

Soon she crept in beside her mistress, just as she had done many times before Leopold Blakeley and his castle, before England, and before her young mistress's world was turned upside down.

It was the wee hours before Leopold crept silently into his bedroom. He undressed quickly and then opened the door to peek into his wife's room. He was quite shocked not only to find his wife's bed empty but also to find his sister asleep on the chaise. His heart skipped a beat as he went and shook Blanche gently awake.

Blanche took a moment to realize where she was and to remember what had occurred the previous evening. "What time is it?"

Leopold quickly answered, "I don't know, possibly 2:00 a.m.? Where's Amalie?"

Blanche stretched, stood up, poured herself a glass of water from the carafe by the bed, and took a drink as he stood there, impatiently waiting. Finally, she answered, "She's gone, Leo. She is leaving tomorrow morning. She is spending the night with Bridgette, and they are both leaving with your children first thing in the morning. She is afraid for their welfare. She is afraid of your cousin, for I won't call him mine. I can't say I blame her. We will all soon be behind her, since no one wishes to remain here any longer. You saw to that tonight."

Leopold scratched his head in disbelief. He had heard such things that night. He had even read some of the letters, or as much as he could stomach, and now this? He felt befuddled since he had drunk too much and fallen asleep in his study.

He was about to speak when Blanche said, "Anyway, I said I would let you know since she does not want to see you again. I didn't mean to fall asleep. But there you have it. I'm off to bed."

Her brother finally seemed to come to his senses. "What do you mean, leaving? You have no idea what transpired today— what I have been told!" He then took his sister's hand, and they sat down on the bed. Looking down at the floor, he said, "I suppose it is for the best."

Blanche couldn't believe her ears and couldn't hide her disbelief. She had expected protestations, anger, demands to see little Amie. Whatever had happened, whatever this wicked man had said to him, she needed to find the letters.

It seemed he had nothing further to say. Blanche stood up and stared at him for a moment before saying, "Well, I suppose that's that then. I'm off to bed. Sweet dreams, Sir Leopold." She then slowly walked out and closed the door.

This was worse than she had imagined. But what to do? It was the middle of the night, but she was wide awake. *I need to fetch Amie*, she thought, *and have her go to him.*

Blanche crept along to Bridgette's room, feeling like a thief in the night. She regretted telling her brother that Amie was leaving. Usually, that sort of talk shook him out of his black moods. She knew she had gotten it wrong. Whatever he was afraid of, he needed to share it with those who loved him. *To every problem, there is a solution*, she thought as she lightly tapped on Bridgette's door.

Amazingly, she found both women awake and drinking tea.

Bridgette explained, "She had a nightmare. This is a terrible state of affairs. Can I pour you a cup?"

Blanche gratefully accepted the tea. She knew she would never sleep that night till she fixed things. "Amie, I got it all wrong. Whatever that man said to him, he is feeling hopeless. I've never seen him like this. I think you should go to him. I know it's money, because it always is, but I think it might be blackmail—humiliation for all the world to see, when he is about to be honored by the king. You both know enough about our parents. Perhaps there's more. We need to find those letters. Bridgette, do you think Lady Agatha will help us? She knows all the renowned barristers and judges in London. She is very fond of my brother and little Amie."

Bridgette said there was no harm in trying, since it would all come out anyway. "I'll have McBride take me to the station—the early train—unless your brother is going into London, and then I will take the next one. We won't tell him I'm going. I will speak to Her Ladyship plainly."

That decided, Amalie finally spoke. "Poor Leo. I am so stupid. I should have understood. I will go to him now."

Blanche walked Amalie to her room. At first she panicked when she realized the bed had not been slept in, but when she opened the door to Leopold's dressing room, there he was.

She quietly crept in bed beside him and wrapped her arms around his warm body. He awoke and said, "I thought you were leaving me."

Amalie immediately understood that this had come from something Blanche had said to him, and she held him tighter, her whole body caressing his. "What made you think that? Leo, I will never leave you. You are my world."

Leopold turned around and sleepily stroked her hair. "He intends to reveal my wonderful family secrets right before the ceremony—abject humiliation. How can I put you through that, my love? It will be the gossip of London Town, the dysfunctional Blakeleys, all completely mad. And our children—what of them? He wants money, of course. I know better than to give it to him. I won't be controlled like that."

Amalie took his hand and kissed it. "What do I care what the English have to say about anything? They all have skeletons in their closets. That's blackmail, Leo, and blackmail is a crime. It won't come to that, but even if it does, it would never change us or my love for you. At least now I understand. You were pushing me away last night. Please never do that again, or you'll break my heart."

These words seemed to lift his spirits somewhat, and he said, "I need to go to London this morning for a few hours, and then I'll see him gone. Now that I know I have you, I will figure something out. Please stay with Blanche and Bridgette this morning. Stay away from my cousin. I'll fix this or turn down the knighthood—as long as I know you are with me in this."

Amalie considered telling him of the plan of Bridgette going to see Lady Agatha to ask for help, but she thought he might prevent it, so all she said was, "Did you really think I took my marriage vows so lightly? After two weddings?"

Leopold smiled sleepily, and just before again nodding off, he whispered, "And stay away from McFadden too."

Amalie was soon asleep as well, back in her husband's arms where she belonged.

Leopold awoke early. He thought of going to Scotland Yard; perhaps Cecil Pickering could advise him. He and Cecil had been at Cambridge together, and Leopold recalled the fracas that had ensued when his friend disregarded his family's wish that he enter the church and instead joined the London Metropolitan Police. He had risen in the ranks since then, and Leopold hadn't seen him in several years. It was an outside chance, but possibly Cecil could advise him. He was being blackmailed for actions and deeds that were not his, but the shame and humiliation that he and indeed his family would suffer if these letters were somehow made public was too terrible to even contemplate. He had lived a solitary life before Amalie. He had friends, but he kept them at a distance. She had opened up the world for him, made it full of life, and he had been so very happy since then.

He thought of his business, of Edward March, who would be labeled along with him. Leopold Blakeley was a proud yet private man who was being forced to confide somehow in someone who could help him, for the sake of his family. Cecil seemed the best choice, given his chosen career and expertise.

However, even as he boarded the nine o'clock train, he couldn't see how his family's shameful past could be hidden. It seemed his mother had been a prolific letter writer who'd shared her great misery in the finest detail with her Spanish relatives. No wonder his father had been driven mad. And from what Leopold had read, it seemed to him that his mother had not been what she should have been even when they first married. He had known his father was a cruel and unhappy man. He had known his mother was desperate and depressed. What Leopold Blakeley had not known, however, was the scandal surrounding his mother that had necessitated her leaving Cadiz, nor had he known of his father's debauched behavior and gambling debts, which had brought about their unhappy union. Leopold thought of Amalie's and Cosette's sweet, innocent faces and of his son's adoration, and he felt ashamed of actions that were not his but that seemed bound to follow him through life.

Sweet Amalie, he thought, *sweet and pure when I found her. Yet it seems she is bound, along with our children, to bear the shame that should be mine alone.* He thought of Blanche too. Amalie had brought him and his sister together. Proud Blanche—she had been through enough already without this.

Leopold had hurried but missed the eight o'clock train. This was just as well since Bridgette had boarded it with plenty of time to spare.

Bridgette had risen at the crack of dawn. McBride had taken her to the train station early enough so that he could be back in time to take his master. He had cited trouble with the Daimler as the excuse to delay them enough to miss the earlier train. His master seemed too distracted to notice that there was treachery afoot, and thus their plan was successful.

Bridgette rang the front doorbell of Lady Agatha Pengallon's London home. She had drunk tea often enough with the grand dame not to be intimidated by her. Her Ladyship was a formidable force, that much was true; however, if she liked you, she was actually very kind and had a keen sense of humor. Fortunately, she liked Bridgette.

The butler who answered the door told Bridgette to go around to the back entrance, and when she refused, he closed the front door upon her. She waited no more than a few moments before Lady Agatha's butler returned and begrudgingly showed her into the front parlor, where she was greeted with urgency and great concern.

Tea was ordered, and Bridgette began explaining her sudden visit in the manner she had been rehearsing since McBride left her at the station. When she finally concluded, she sat silently awaiting Her Ladyship's support or derision. Bridgette wasn't sure what to expect since the duchess had not spoken a word during her long and passionate dialogue.

Eventually, she said, "Leopold should have come to me, but no matter. I am very well aware of the scandal and stories surrounding his parents. I met them, you know, though obviously many years ago. He wasn't well liked, but she was really quite an appalling woman. She was very beautiful, but there was a cruelty to her, and it was evident in the way she treated her husband. When she died, I followed the news of the whole sordid affair, and my heart broke for the young boy left with the monster his father had become. I grieved for his sister too, but Leopold was special."

The old lady became tearful. "I had just recently lost my son, my only child, around that same time, and watching from afar as Leopold grew into a fine young man was a favorite occupation of mine. I had little else to concern me, a widow with no children to care for, only the same tedious people surrounding me—hoping, no doubt, to be remembered in my last will and testament. I do have a great-niece, and for a while I entertained the notion that perhaps she and Leopold could marry. He was handsome and becoming very successful in his business affairs. I went to see him in his office, ostensibly about my investments. I was very impressed with him, and soon he was handling all of my finances. I brought him and my niece together several times; however, she had nothing in particular to recommend herself, and he had no interest in her, even for a dukedom. Then one day I found out he had married some little French heiress. I knew he didn't need the money, so I assumed—correctly, it seemed—that it was a love match. He could afford to marry for love, and so, it appeared, could she. I resolved not to like her, and when I finally met her several years later, I could understand why he'd fallen so hard. Well, you know the rest, Bridgette. Now she is my dearest Amalie, the sweetest girl, and so much in love with him."

At this final remark, Lady Agatha arose and rang for her butler. "My guest and I will partake in a light luncheon, and then I will need my carriage."

Bridgette looked at the great lady, who majestically, with a look of determination, said, "My dear, we are going to see my good friend Sir Charles Webley. He will see to it that this Cortez fellow is thrown out of our great country and sent on his way from whence he came."

This was much better than Bridgette ever could have hoped for, and soon she and the duchess were being driven in Her Ladyship's crested carriage, followed by a carriage containing two senior officers from the Metropolitan Police. *Of course,* thought Bridgette, *we forget how powerful Her Ladyship truly is.* They picked up Edward March at his London office before leaving town, and Bridgette sat very proudly across from the duchess as both carriages made their winding way to Blakefield Castle.

Leopold Blakeley had boarded the train to Hertford earlier that day. He was returning home as he had done so many times. However, on this occasion he was not happily anticipating his wife's latest antics. This time there was murder and hatred in his heart.

He had stood across the street from Scotland Yard's imposing building and realized that he could not seek help from his former friend. He could not lay himself open to gossip and speculation. After all, he hadn't seen this man for several years. What could possibly be his motivation to help Leopold?

He had decided instead that he alone must face this challenge, and he had walked the streets of London deep in thought, until finally ending up in St. James's Park, close to Buckingham Palace, where he walked among the American tourists and the nannies walking and chatting to one another, with their charges safely tucked away in elaborate perambulators. The summer day was warm and sunny, and he passed half an hour playing football with some London lads as they laughingly kicked a leather ball, possibly found in a dustbin, since it had most certainly seen better days.

It felt like everyone around him was happily going about

their business. He had thought of going into his office but found that he couldn't face his staff or even Edward, who no doubt was wondering what had happened to him. The faces of his wife and children took turns spinning around in his head. He knew how much Amalie loved him, her hero. He didn't feel like much of a hero but had resolved finally to turn down the knighthood. He would return home and throw this long-lost cousin out of his house. He would give him one hundred pounds to see him on his way, certainly not the thousands he was demanding. There would be a scandal, but it would be short-lived, and he thought as he walked past the guards at the palace that at least he wouldn't have to face King Edward VII with all the unpleasantness that enveloped his family name.

Meanwhile, at Blakefield Castle, Amalie watched Xavier Cortez from her bedroom window as he rode off on his magnificent black stallion. She wondered briefly how he had come upon such a fine creature; however, there was no time to waste on such thoughts. The previous night had somehow emboldened her. How dare this man threaten her dearest Leo? She ran along to Lady Agatha's suite, where he had spent the night, to search for something, anything, that she could use against this evil man, but the room was devoid of anything other than a few items of clothing. She then rang for the housekeeper, Mrs. Mowbray and asked her to have the maids pack up the guest's belongings and place his leather bag in the great hall. She instructed her housekeeper to have the room thoroughly cleaned and aired with fresh linen and to ensure the door was locked when they were done.

She then quickly made her way down to Leopold's study. She needed to find those letters to discover just what was so terrible and what could possibly be worse than what she already knew about his dysfunctional family.

Amalie had waited most of the day for the opportunity to search in Leopold's study. Xavier had arisen very late, and she had spent the morning out riding with Blanche and Cordelia. Malcolm and Dolores had accompanied them for a while, but it seemed they must have been arguing, probably about the previous evening, when Dolores had developed an apparent crush on Leopold, due to his inappropriate behavior. *Still*, thought Amalie, *it is no more than Malcolm and I deserve.* Nevertheless, she resolved to put an end to it. Amalie knew their interaction had meant nothing to Leopold, or at least she hoped that it hadn't, and she was well aware that even as Malcolm was most caring and solicitous toward her that morning, Dolores couldn't seem to look her in the eye.

After her ride, she had sat for a while with Imogen in the turret, who after some persuasion had showed her the portrait of her and Leopold, since she had just applied the finishing touches to it and was now putting most of her efforts into the nude. Amalie loved it and exclaimed her praise of it and how Imogen had captured his handsome features and penetrating eyes. It was the first portrait she had ever seen of her husband and the first of herself as a woman. Blanche and Cordelia, who upon orders were staying close to Amalie, declared that they must have an official reveal of the portrait for all to see, once they had gotten rid of the Spaniard, of course, as Blanche called him, refusing to admit to any family connection.

Amalie first checked Leopold's desk drawers—but only after she opened the windows to air out the room, which still smelled of brandy and cigars. Leo let the maids into clean only when he was home. He was very private about that room, and Amalie smiled to herself, remembering how he had told her that he was well aware that she would sometimes sit at his desk when he was in London. She really did so because she liked to feel his essence around her, when he was gone most days to his London office. She liked to imitate him for the amusement of Blanche and Cordelia, as well as for Leon, who also would insist upon playing the ham.

Having allowed her thoughts to wander to happier times, she hurriedly resumed her search, but to no avail. As she wondered whether Leo might have taken the letters with him, she was suddenly startled by the appearance of Xavier Cortez, who stood in the doorway, holding the letters in his hand.

"Are these what you are searching for, cousin Amalie?" He sneered at her as he spoke, and he was blocking the doorway.

Amalie wondered how she ever had thought that he resembled her husband. He had the same black curls, but there the similarity ended. In the darkened room, he looked somehow debauched. His mouth was salacious; his dark eyes held no warmth. Amalie's pulse was racing with fear and discomfort as she said, "Kindly get out of my way."

He didn't move but smiled and said, "But don't you want these?" He waved the letters in front of her as he took a step toward her. "Very entertaining, or at least your husband thought so."

Amalie felt trapped and afraid. She tried to look beyond him toward the great hall, in the hope that someone would appear. She was scared to attempt to move past him but gathered her courage enough to try.

Then everything happened so quickly. Blanche was suddenly there, screaming at him. He grabbed Amalie's arm and twisted it behind her back, and she was struggling to get away when quite suddenly, seemingly from out of nowhere, Leopold appeared.

McBride had picked him up from the station, and he had walked in the front door exactly in time to see his sweet Amalie struggling against this monster. Every bit of rage and hatred he had been feeling toward this man, and indeed toward his whole dysfunctional family, exploded as he ran toward this interloper, grabbed him by his hair, and dragged him into the front courtyard, where he lunged at him, grabbing and punching him until both men were rolling around in the dirt.

This was no gentlemen's boxing match, but a street brawl, and Leopold was definitely getting the better of his cousin, who soon was trying to get away from him. However, Leo wouldn't let him go. He had his hands around Xavier's neck, and there was murder in his eyes.

By now, all the household had started to appear, but Amalie didn't notice that. The letters had fallen to the floor when Leo grabbed his cousin, and she had quickly picked them up and secured them in her pocket. Now she leapt forward in an effort to stop this since it seemed that Leopold wouldn't let up.

Finally, Malcolm and McBride came along, and as Malcolm pushed Amalie aside, it took both men to pull Leopold off his cousin.

Everyone else was standing in shock, and Henrietta March looked as if she once again required her smelling salts. McBride had taken a hold of Xavier, and Malcolm was still holding on to Leopold. Cordelia and Annabelle were helping Amalie to her feet as she insisted, even with her disheveled appearance, that she was fine. Suddenly, everyone's attention turned from the two men, torn and bloody and still being held back from one another, to a crested carriage followed by a black Metropolitan Police wagon driven by two constables.

As the household, including many of the servants, continued to stand there in shock, Lady Agatha majestically stepped down from her carriage, assisted by Edward March and Bridgette, who rushed over to see to her mistress. Amalie was standing in a torn, dirty dress and by now was being held back by Blanche and Cordelia from running to her husband.

The two constables took hold of Xavier Cortez and proudly announced, "We got 'im, Your Ladyship. We'll see he's on the next boat to Spain."

Leopold had relaxed somewhat, and Amalie broke loose and ran to him in time for Lady Agatha to raise her bejeweled spectacles, which were hanging amid the multitude of pearls around her neck, and look them both up and down. She declared, quite calmly, "Well, I can see you're both fine. Henrietta, is there any tea to be had? I am quite parched—such a dusty road."

Blanche had run inside for her cousin's leather bag, and as the police led him away, Leopold handed him the one hundred pounds, as he had intended to do earlier in the day. "Your passage home," Leopold said. "Now get off my land."

Edward March at this point calmly mentioned, "We missed you in the office today, son."

As everyone trailed back inside the house, including Lady Agatha, escorted by the bloodied and dirty future Sir Leopold and Lady Amalie Blakeley, Harvey Havemeyer was heard to exclaim to his wife, "Annabelle honey, your family is beyond entertaining. I may never want to return to New York."

Annabelle responded, "Oh, Harvey, I told you that you would like them."

CHAPTER 9
They Shoot Horse Thieves, Don't They?

That night, Leopold was still shaken and sore. It had been many years, after all, since he had gotten involved in a brawl—and even then, it had been a drunken one. He worried about whether he would have stopped if it hadn't been for McBride and McFadden. *McFadden saves me again*, he thought, *this time from myself*. It seemed that the women in his home had handled the whole situation better than he, and he was incredulous that while he was walking the streets of London, Bridgette and Lady Agatha had been summoning the troops, so to speak.

Lady Agatha had left before dinner. However, she had taken Amalie aside first and said, "You did the right thing, sending Bridgette to fetch me. I can see Leopold is still shaken. I will leave you to settle him down, and I'll be back to check on you soon, my dear."

Amalie had never seen her Leo so angry, and she worried about when he would have stopped if Malcolm and McBride hadn't appeared. She was glad when she was finally alone with him in their room. He didn't seem to be too badly hurt, other than a bruised jaw and knuckles, and Amalie insisted on seeing to him by herself. He was quiet and thoughtful, as was she, uncertain what to say as she ran his bath. She remembered that just a few days before, they had been so happy; she hoped they would soon be happy again.

As Leopold gratefully sank into the warm bath, he seemed to cheer slightly as he watched his Amalie being a good wife, gathering his clothes and examining the damage. "What have you put in my bath, beloved? It smells of flowers," he said lightly. He could tell that Amalie was nervous from the way she was bustling around the room, and indeed she was—she had witnessed a side to him that she had never seen before, and it scared her a little.

"Lavender," she responded. "It has a peaceful, relaxing aroma that soothes the soul."

Leopold laughed and called her to him. "Do you think my soul needs soothing, Amalie?"

"Possibly," she answered, still standing out of his reach.

"Do you think I'm mad then? As you asked me all those years ago?"

"No, "she replied. "At least I don't think so."

"Good," he said, smiling. "Will you wash my hair?"

Amalie was surprised by his request but willingly complied. She could sense him relaxing as she massaged his scalp ever so gently.

"We've no need to endlessly discuss the last couple days," he said, "but thank you, my love."

These words again surprised Amalie. "For what? What did I do?"

"At first, I worried tonight, *Would I have stopped?* When I saw you struggling with him, I thought I would kill him. But I now know that I wouldn't have done so. It wasn't McFadden who prevented it—I just now realized that, watching you nervously being a good wife. When I saw you standing there all torn and dirty, after trying to join in the fight, I had a fleeting thought of what life would be without you, without ever making love to you again. I saw your love for me so apparent to all, and the desire to see that man dead finally left me. I just wanted him gone." He then made to stand up. "Will you help me get dried off? I'm a bit sore, I'm afraid."

Again, Amalie happily obliged. She felt him coming back to her and the sheer awfulness of the past couple of days melting away.

He then lifted her chin and gazed adoringly into her wide aquamarine eyes with his dark penetrating ones. Amalie felt herself melt as he said, "You are the most beautiful woman that I have ever beheld, inside and out—the sweetest, most adorable wife that a man could ever ask for. I love you, Amalie, my love. *Je t'adore.*"

All this was almost too much for Amalie to take in, and all she could manage, still staring into his eyes, was "My dress is wet."

"So take it off," he said, still staring into her eyes.

She didn't move, and he gave a soft chuckle and turned her around as he began to unfasten her damp gown, still standing completely naked. Amalie thought, *This is quite a different mood, and I think I like this one very much.*

He led her to the bed, where he made love to her so gently, as if he feared she would break. Amalie sensed that he needed her gentle touch after the day's violent encounter, and she gently touched and caressed him until he fell asleep in her arms.

It was a while before Amalie fell asleep. It was still quite early, after all. However, Leo looked so peaceful and content, and she just stroked his head gently until eventually she drifted off too. However, that night she had nightmares about the violence she had witnessed that day. Leo had said he would have stopped, but he'd had both hands around his cousin's neck, and it had taken two men to pull him off him. Amalie decided that she must, of course, believe what her husband had told her, and when he had reassured her, she had believed him. Still, she hoped the memory of it would soon fade away. She was anxious to make everything normal once again in the morning. This worry was just the darkness playing tricks on her mind.

Leopold awoke early, and anxious to put things back to normal, he rode off to the river for his morning swim. He laughed to himself upon his return to Blakefield Castle. *Normalcy again. Last night sweet Amalie bathed me in lavender and caressed me until I fell asleep. This morning I will be getting told to stay off her French coverlet, just as I should be.*

Leopold didn't want her to feel nervous around him, watching his moods. However, it seemed she often did, unless, of course, she was angry at him. He wondered how she put up with him but was pleased that she did.

It wasn't until he returned Caesar that he remembered about the horse. The black stallion on which Xavier had arrived most assuredly had been stolen. He wondered why he hadn't questioned this before—horse thievery was a very serious crime, and this particularly fine specimen must surely be missed by its owner. He needed to set about finding the owner, or he would be the man arrested for the crime, and he might need to turn down the coveted knighthood yet. He spoke to McBride, who would keep the horse fed and watered and well-hidden until Leopold could send out feelers with regard to the owner. Another mess his cousin had left behind. He wondered where Xavier was that morning. He hadn't thought of it the previous night, relieved that he was gone, but now he thought, *He must surely still be in England.* He had thanked Amalie but no one else, not even Lady Agatha, and he realized that the whole sorry business wasn't over yet.

When he returned to the house, it seemed the whole household was hungrily tucking into breakfast. He had hoped to catch Amalie alone, but here she was smiling cheerfully at him, dressed up in riding apparel, as if nothing particularly unusual had occurred the previous day.

"Good morning, Leo. Did you enjoy your swim? I'm thinking of taking Louis-Alphonse out for a ride—that's what I plan to name him, the black stallion, since we don't know his name. Oh, and please stay off the coverlet until you have bathed. Bridgette just had it washed and pressed, an enormous endeavor."

Blanche and Cordelia were especially amused at little Amie's comments, and trying not to smile, they awaited his response.

Leopold filled his plate with his usual bacon, sausages, and scrambled eggs and sat down before responding. This morning, with a house full of visitors, with his wife's ridiculous comments, and now, it seemed, with Dolores making cow eyes at him too, was exactly what he needed to restore him.

"Amalie, my love, I had no idea. Did the horse's owner give you permission to keep his fine steed? How very generous of him, especially since he easily could have you up in front of a magistrate for horse thievery. And with regard to your fine French linens, perhaps I should look for some of our old dowdy English ones and carry a blanket around with me, in case I feel suddenly inclined to have a lie down on our bed."

Before Amalie could answer, the others erupted in laughter. Henrietta March exclaimed, in a disapproving tone, "Sakes, Leopold, talking of thievery and beds at the breakfast table."

Even Leopold had to laugh at this, and as he apologized, tongue in cheek, for such inappropriate conversation, Amalie stared at him wide-eyed.

"I thought you would let me keep him," she said. "You

can find the owner and pay him, or perhaps he doesn't have an owner—perhaps he's all alone in the world. Also, you promised me a horse. I have to be so gentle with Belle. I love her dearly, but there are times I feel like a good gallop. Louis-Alphonse will suit me perfectly. I'm going to keep him, I think."

Leopold laughed. "No, my darling. I must find the owner; a horse of that caliber is very valuable, and I doubt that he came here all the way from Spain. I'm sorry, my dear, but you can't keep him. Furthermore, you are too small for a stallion. I will find you the perfect filly, and I will help you train her. You have never ridden a stallion, and I fear that you never will."

This response was as she'd expected, but still she thought, *Here we go with the old "let's talk to Amalie like a child" voice, after being so sweet last night.* Now looking peevish, she insisted, "What if you can't find the owner? What will you do then? Why am I too small? I've ridden lots of stallions in France."

Leopold laughed out loud as he took his wife's hand and kissed it. "Lots of stallions, really? I'm sure your father allowed that, most especially in the middle of Paris. There will be an owner, and I must take care of this quickly, before I'm the one who is arrested."

A moment later, Amalie was aghast, as indeed was everyone else, including Leopold, when Dolores said, "Leo, I've ridden stallions before on the ranch. Can I ride him till you find the owner?"

Leopold just looked at her incredulously. This comment was not going to go down very well with his wife. He quickly finished his breakfast, stood up, and announced, "McBride is under strict orders—no one will be riding that horse!"

Amalie followed him upstairs, her indignation consummate. "I can't believe she asked you that! After I was told no? Sitting, making eyes at you all through breakfast. You will need to nip this in the bud!" She spoke while guarding the bed, as Leopold pretended to try to get around her.

"Oh, I see, my love—only you are allowed ardent admirers."

Amalie knew he was making fun of her as she followed him into the bathroom. "That's different! She's eighteen! Mon Dieu! You, sir, are old enough to be her father!"

Leopold was having fun. Amalie was jealous—about nothing, as usual—but he thought that he may as well enjoy it. "Ouch, that hurt! However, I seem to recall that I was once mistaken for your father."

Amalie said, "That's different. That was Blanche. She's not sitting with you at dinner either."

Leopold couldn't help himself. "But my darling, it was you who placed her there. Now am I clean enough for the French coverlet?"

Amalie pouted. "I hate you!"

Leopold responded glibly, "That's a shame. I suppose that means I shouldn't buy you the pure white filly I've been negotiating with Sir Archibald Beaton about. I should let him know my wife's not interested."

Amalie's eyes lit up, just as her husband knew they would. "Oh, Leo, seriously? I do love you so! Who on earth is Sir Archibald Beaton? I swear, you keep such secrets!"

"Amalie," Leopold said as she threw herself upon him in delight, "isn't that the pot calling the kettle black?"

CHAPTER 10
It's Not Over Yet

More than a week had passed, and still the stallion's owner had not been located. This concerned Leopold, and he and Edward wondered why neither of them had thought to ask Xavier Cortez about it. Clearly, he hadn't brought the animal from Spain.

There were no markings or initials on the horse's leather saddle, which was old and well worn, as was the blanket beneath it. None of this made sense with such a beautiful animal, still in its prime of life. Leopold had taken to exercising the horse himself; he wouldn't have McBride get in trouble should he be seen with it, nor McFadden neither—although he'd offered—and thus the beautiful stallion began to grow on him. He had placed advertisements in various newspapers. He had inquired at several constabularies in London and beyond and had spoken with certain magistrates who he thought could help him, but still nothing. He at the very least reassured himself that should the owner eventually turn up, he would be able to prove he had made the greatest attempt to locate him.

It seemed to him that by now his cousin must be gone. He was saddened by the way things had turned out. That first morning, he had hoped for something different. Leopold believed that under other circumstances, he might have loaned him the money or even invested in his vineyards in Cadiz. It seemed his cousin was afraid of hard work, but he had seven children, four of whom were sons, and they were his blood. These were thoughts he spoke to only Edward about, since he didn't want to upset Amalie, and Blanche refused to talk about it.

He realized he had his own children to worry about, although both were so very young. Xavier must have been desperate to plan such an ill-fated course of action. These thoughts brought his mind back to the letters. Were they still in his desk drawer? How could he have forgotten about them?

Leopold searched his office and worried that his cousin might have taken them back, in which case, whose hands were they in now? The whole sorry business might yet still not be over.

That night was to be the big reveal of Amalie's painting, the one with her fully clothed, and once again the house was full. Even Lady Agatha had come for the grand event, and Leopold, still unaware that he was in the painting, had resolved to stop worrying about something that might never happen. He did, however, decide to tell Amalie about the missing letters.

When he mentioned the letters to her, Amalie stared at him wide-eyed. He had never before brought up the subject, and she had therefore been afraid to do so. Even Blanche had not mentioned the letters. Amalie had told Bridgette that she fully intended to burn them, and Bridgette had raised her eyebrows as to why she hadn't yet done so—if that was indeed her intention.

"What is the matter, Amalie?" asked Leopold. "Well, I suppose I understand. You are afraid that they may have fallen into the wrong hands, as am I."

"Not exactly," she said hesitantly. "I thought you knew I had them! Honestly. And I was going to burn them. I promise I never read them."

Amalie stood nervously, and again Leopold wondered, after six years of marriage, how he could still make her feel so. Was he really so terrible? He gave her a great beaming smile. "My wonderful girl! Was that what the struggle was about? Why didn't you tell me?"

"Yes," she said, "but he dropped them when you grabbed him. I picked them up and put them in my pocket. I was afraid you would be angry with me, and I really didn't read them. I've no need to know their terrible contents. I think you should burn them."

"Amalie," he said, lifting her face to his, "you must know never to fear me. I'd sooner cut off my right arm than hurt you. I nearly killed a man for hurting you. Don't you remember?"

Amalie remembered it only too well and responded, "Of course, I know that, Leo. It's just that I prefer your many kind moods to your sometimes unkind ones."

She was so serious when she said this that he had to smile. "Well, at least the kind outnumber the unkind. Am I really so moody?"

"Yes," she said matter-of-factly.

Leopold simply shook his head as she rummaged in her giant wardrobe and eventually produced the letters and handed them to him.

He counted them. "They are all here, you wonderful, beautiful girl! It seems you saved me a second time within the past week." He casually perused the letters and said, "Strange really, they appear all to have been written in English. I would have expected Spanish."

Leopold was about to leave with the letters when Bridgette entered the room to assist her mistress in dressing for dinner. She saw them in his hand. Before he could exit, she said, "Please, monsieur, remember that Lady Agatha is dining tonight. Please be on your best behavior and stop encouraging that silly Dolores."

Amalie smiled a little nervously as her husband responded, "I see you are no longer knocking, Bridgette. I am well aware you saved my skin, but even my gratitude has limits."

Bridgette threw a towel she had been carrying at him as he walked away into his dressing room, and Amalie felt somewhat relieved to have gotten the matter of the letters over with, at least for the present time. However, she knew that she should tell Blanche that Leo now had the letters, so she ran along to Blanche's room before getting dressed for dinner.

"I'm so sorry, Blanche. I wasn't sure what to do or say. I didn't read them, I promise, and I thought if neither of you ever mentioned them again, I would burn them, and that would be the end of the matter. I don't know what Leo intends to do. He was so pleased that I had them but then just took them away. He didn't say any more, and I hope he doesn't ruin dinner, especially with Lady Agatha and the painting. I hope he doesn't mind about the painting—I mean, that he's in it. Oh, it's all so worrying, and I really don't feel very well."

Blanche took Amalie's hands in hers. "Amie, this is not a problem of your creation. Stop making it into yours. You're tying yourself in knots. Stop worrying about him. He will do what he will do, as he always does, and I, for one, don't care to read them anyway or know the contents. Come here, honey." Blanche embraced Amalie, hoping her brother would just set the letters aside, at least for that night.

Amalie, somewhat mollified by Blanche's comforting words, was about to return to her room when Bridgette appeared. "Lady Agatha sent for the monsieur to come to her room and escort her to dinner. She asked that you go down with Blanche and Cordelia this evening."

"Oh dear," said Amalie worriedly, and Bridgette led her back to her room to get dressed.

They soon heard Leopold exit his room to the hallway, presumably on his way to Lady Agatha's suite, and they just looked at one another, surprised that he didn't tell Amalie what he was doing.

Bridgette seemed exasperated. "Petite, stop worrying about him. There are many sides to that man, most of them good, some not so good. I saw the same thing as you that day with his cousin. But he did stop, and I believe it was because of you."

Amalie turned to Bridgette. "Do you think he looked a bit crazy? I mean … I hope … oh, I don't know what I mean. I find I can't keep up."

Bridgette sat her down on the bed and spoke quietly. "The monsieur is as sane as you and I, if that's what you are worried about. However, perhaps his mother was not—perhaps that's what he saw. He read some of the letters at least but did not reveal the contents to anyone, unless to your uncle March. He talks to him. I wish I had burned them myself since nothing good can come of them. In the meantime, petite, try to forget they even exist. Now, do you wish to wear your tiara? Let's fix your hair."

Amalie quietly complied. However, she was reminded of how he had said sardonically, all those years ago, "No known madness in the family, as yet diagnosed anyway."

Those words and why he had said them to her when she hardly knew him were coming back to haunt her. She had really quite forgotten them until she'd read the letters, although his words had concerned her at the time. But she had been falling so much in love with him, so she had never dared to ask him why he'd said such a thing, when she was only asking about the history of his family—a history she still knew so little about, though everything she did know was appalling. How she wished she had burned the letters and told him she had done so. But what would have been his reaction to that? How she wished she hadn't read through them and seen their terrible contents. She hadn't read them at first, but her curiosity had gotten the better of her. Then she had seen such things. She so wished she had just left them in her wardrobe, and now she had lied to everyone. She felt truly unwell and hoped she wasn't coming down with a cold.

She put on a brave face and kissed Bridgette before making her way to fetch Blanche and Cordelia. She wasn't sure why, but the excitement of unveiling the painting had quite forsaken her. Was it guilt about lying or fear about what she had read in the letters? She could feel quite a headache coming on.

Amalie thought she understood Isabella Blakeley so much better now and the fear she had lived with each day. She was no longer just "Leopold's awful mother"; she had become a person, a woman in her own right, with thoughts and feelings, who had been abused and desperate—the last Mrs. Blakeley.

c✢✦✦✤✤✦✦✢

She was met, as usual, by Malcolm in the conservatory. The butler, Mr. Carmichael, was fixing drinks, and although Amalie already had been a little late coming down, there was still no sign of Leopold and Lady Agatha, and therefore dinner was delayed. Amalie felt self-conscious when her aunt remarked, "I wonder what's keeping them?"

She wasn't sure what to do and was considering whether to go upstairs to fetch them when they finally appeared. Lady Agatha was as gracious as ever, and Leopold was smiling, but not at her, as they all made their way into dinner. Lady Agatha was on Leopold's arm, and she on Malcolm's, with Dolores walking behind them on her own.

Amalie just wanted dinner to be over. There was a certain polite awkwardness to the general conversation, and she decided not to mention the painting, hoping everyone else had forgotten about it. Imogen had it set up in the parlor for the footmen to bring through at the appropriate time. Amalie couldn't seem to rid herself of her headache or the knot in her stomach, and she couldn't seem to enter into the conversation going on around her.

Eventually, just before dessert was served, Lady Agatha loudly said, "Amalie dearest, you are so quiet tonight. When is this unveiling to be?"

At this point, Imogen nodded to the footmen, who went out to bring in the giant canvas. Amalie had imagined this so differently. At this particular moment, the painting was the last thing she wanted to see, and as they lifted off the covering, there was a short silence until Amalie heard Leo laugh and say, "I'm in it too?"

Everyone began exclaiming about the painting's beauty, about the fine brushwork and how Imogen had captured their likenesses. Amalie said not a word and felt otherworldly. Leopold was laughing as he closely inspected it with the others who had gone over to examine it more closely too. Only Malcolm and Amalie remained seated at the table, and Malcolm was looking at her with some concern. Dolores trilled about Leo's likeness and how dashing he was, and she then turned and shouted over, "Amalie, there are so many paintings of you, but you are much younger in my husband's painting."

Amalie could have stated the obvious, that she was just sixteen when it was painted but she discovered that she couldn't find her voice. Only Malcolm saw something change within her, even if the others did not, and he felt so very sorry for her and very concerned. It was meant to be her portrait, but no one seemed to care that she was in it. He asked her if she was okay as he handed her a glass of water, but Amalie wasn't okay. She felt dizzy and unwell, and her headache had gotten worse. There was a sickness among Leopold's tenant farmers, especially with the children, and she had been worried about that. She had taken a few of the young families some clothes that her children had outgrown and had been warned about the illness during her brief visit to them.

She quietly excused herself, but only to Malcolm, since all the others were still talking at the same time as they examined the painting, and no one was paying attention to her. She easily managed to slip out unseen by all. Malcolm wanted so much to go after her but knew full well that he could not.

Amalie felt the need to get away from everyone and from that house—the secrets and mysteries, moods and forgiveness, passion and hate, joy and despair. For the first time since coming to England, she felt like a stranger, an outcast. She felt French and wanted to be in France. She wanted her father, but she couldn't have him. She needed to escape. She would take Bridgette and the children, Eloise too. As she made her way toward the derelict folly, her secret place, her mind was going in every direction.

She had given her life up to a stranger, a man she knew nothing about. She would have Bridgette write to Freddie, who had offered to help, and then she would make her way to France—to Victor Le Clair. He would help her, she was sure. She had money and now needed access to it. Victor would deal with her husband on that matter. *Husband*, she thought. *What sort of husband is this?*

She had references; she could find work as a designer too. *I am done with it. I am finished. I've put up with so much, always forgiving, yielding. I need to get away, someplace I can think, among people like me.*

It seemed no one had missed her. They might have thought her to be in her room. Only Bridgette knew she ever came to this place. No one else did, and she prayed that Bridgette would come now.

She finally heard voices shouting, including Leo's, and he sounded angry. She felt too paralyzed to move. Thankfully, Bridgette appeared.

Everyone was used to Amalie's tears. She shed them often enough—when she was sad, when she was happy, and when she was afraid—but this was so much worse than Bridgette had ever beheld. Amalie said between sobs, "Bridgette, help me get away. Let us take the children. Please help me get to France. The count will help us. I know he will."

Bridgette was confused, so much so that she spoke her given name. "Amalie, what is wrong? What has happened? What has he done?"

Amalie just repeated herself again and again, until Bridgette said, "Okay, I don't know what this is about, but okay. You will need to return home now, however. They are looking for you."

Amalie complied, but when they arrived, she said, "Please take me up the servants' staircase. This is not my home."

Bridgette was almost crying too. What was suddenly so wrong? Amalie was shaking, eyes wide with fear. Surely, this was not all about a painting. Bridgette had warned the monsieur often enough, as had his sister. Had he finally pushed her petite too far? She felt Amalie's brow and found she was burning up. "God no!" she shouted finally to herself. "Not again!"

They stepped stealthily around by the kitchens and were about to go in when suddenly Leopold confronted them. Amalie tightly squeezed Bridgette's hand. He looked more angry than concerned. Even Bridgette was surprised by his demeanor, especially when he said, "You will need to explain this behavior to your guests. Lady Agatha is wondering where you are. This childish behavior is unacceptable—"

Bridgette interrupted him there. "Kindly say no more, sir. That's enough!"

Leopold, angry about being spoken to this way, made to grab Amalie's arm to lead her back to their guests, but he finally noticed that Amalie was sweating, and a red rash was appearing on her face and chest. He had had it as a boy, but how could his wife have gotten it? He knew it had appeared among a few of the children on the estate, but she was never near any.

"Bridgette, there is an outbreak of measles among my tenants. Has Amalie been among them?"

Bridgette was livid. "Yes!" she said. "She took some of your children's outgrown clothing over to a few young families. Any particular reason you didn't tell her about this?"

Bridgette made to move on past him, supporting Amalie, but he intervened, and she allowed him to carry his wife as the most sensible course of action. But once they were upstairs, she shouted at him to get Dr. Matthews and stay away from her petite. As she shouted orders down to the servants, the whole household appeared from downstairs, and Bridgette informed them, "You all must leave in the morning. My mistress has contracted measles and is still contagious."

Both Lady Agatha and Henrietta tried to refuse, but they knew it was for the best. Lady Agatha regretted not having included Amalie in her conversation with Leopold that evening, but really that wouldn't have changed anything. Nevertheless, she felt ashamed.

Blanche, Cordelia, Imogen, and Malcolm were the only ones other than Leopold and Bridgette who refused to leave. Eloise was sent to the Marches' home in Belgravia with the children, and Dolores accompanied them there, as did Annabelle and her husband. Lady Agatha returned to her London house, after much persuasion. She felt so guilty about that last evening. How could she not have noticed that Amalie was unwell?

When Leopold returned with the good doctor, measles was confirmed. Both he and Blanche had had it as children, but that didn't matter. In her delirium, Amalie screamed as Leopold entered the room. Dr. Matthews regarded him suspiciously as he requested that he stay outside the sick room since she seemed to be afraid of him.

Suddenly, they were back in 1902, but that had been pneumonia, and this was different. She seemed terrified somehow and wouldn't allow Bridgette to leave her. She was speaking primarily in French and was calling for her papa, crying for him and begging to go home.

Leopold was confused. He tried several times to go to her as she cried to go home, but she seemed terrified of him. He felt so much regret. He thought that she would die hating him, and he too was sick, sick inside, as he said to Blanche, "I see it now, probably too late. I could tell she was nervous around me, afraid somehow that I would turn on her. I have never hurt her. She is my body and soul. I can't go on without her, and if she beats this, I know she will leave."

Blanche wasn't quite sure what to say to him, but she tried. "Leo, I know deep inside she has not stopped loving you. I don't understand this fear, however. What did you do?"

He shouted back, "Nothing! Everything was fine! I don't understand either! I was at first angry when she left the dining room without a word and without saying anything to me, but—"

Cordelia then interrupted, "I believe she told Malcolm, as the only person who had noticed that something was badly wrong with her. Why did Lady Agatha want you, by the way? And why the secrecy?"

"No secrecy. She knew about our parents and said she had been paying special attention to me since I was a boy. I never knew that. I was very surprised, and I'm grateful to her. She helped me get started in my business as my first major investor, but I didn't know that was her reason. I had no idea about any of this—really something."

Cordelia responded, "Yes, I'm sure it was. Any reason you didn't take Amalie with you to her room, the one she designed? Any reason you ignored her at dinner? Maybe that sweet girl read some of those letters after all and found out you are all crazy. Or should I say mad? I'm going to go relieve Bridgette."

Cordelia left the room, and Blanche and Leopold just looked at one another.

"Perhaps we never deserved such happiness after all," Blanche said as she too left the room.

$$\mathcal{C}\!\mathcal{F}\!\mathfrak{O}\!\mathfrak{G}\!\mathcal{T}\!\mathfrak{O}$$

Cordelia found Bridgette asleep in a chair next to Amalie's bed in the darkened room. She nudged her gently and sent her off to rest and then sat down and took her place at the bedside.

Amalie slept peacefully for a while. She looked so little and sweet, even with her red face and arms, although thankfully, the red seemed less angry than a day or two previously. Cordelia found herself wondering what was indeed contained in those letters. However, even if this accursed and feared madness had been somehow evident in their parents, she was fully aware that no such thing was evident in their offspring. "Nonsense," she said aloud, thinking she just needed to convince both siblings of it, and she regretted speaking to them the way she had just done. But what about little Amie? What did she believe? They needed to bring her back from whatever dark place she was in.

Cordelia considered that of all the women in England, Blanche's brother had had to choose this fragile little French girl, so sweet and somehow so innocent, in spite of everything. The last thing she had needed was the ordeal caused by the appearance of Xavier Cortez.

Blanche appeared at the door, and Cordelia motioned for her to come sit with her. "I'm sorry," Cordelia simply said, and Blanche took her hand and kissed it.

"Where's your brother?" Cordelia asked.

"Afraid to come in, poor man. I feel so badly for him. He doesn't deserve this," Blanche said sadly.

Amalie seemed to awaken, but it was clear this awful malady had not yet left her, and soon she began thrashing around in her bed, coughing and mumbling in French, but not very clearly. Neither woman could understand much of it; they just knew that she was extremely agitated and was crying out for something or someone. Not yet wanting to awaken Bridgette, who would be able to understand, they simply attempted to speak to her soothingly, and she finally settled down.

❧❧❧

By this time Leopold was fearful that he had truly lost his Amalie, without knowing why. Measles was a childhood disease, and many had it as children. He should have known that Georges Bouchard would have prevented anything contagious from coming anywhere near his daughter. She clearly had been better cared for by her father than by her husband. He sat dejectedly in his study that his wife had decorated so lovingly and wished he knew how to bring her back. *She loves me,* he thought. *She's just forgotten somehow, and I need to make her remember.*

There was a knock, and Bridgette appeared, having been unable to rest much more than an hour. "Monsieur, Count Le Clair is on his way here. It seems Mr. Allsop sent for him. McBride wants to know if he should go fetch him at the station."

Leopold simply responded, "She's still too weak to travel, if that's why he's here." He arose to refill his glass. Events were unfolding all around him, and he felt he had lost control of them.

Bridgette watched him sadly and said, "If you don't mind me saying, monsieur, that will not help you. Why not go have a swim and a good gallop out on Caesar and come back refreshed so we can work together to bring her back to you? I swear, she is not going anywhere or leaving with that man."

Leopold smiled sadly and quipped, "Is that an order, Dr. Bridgette?"

"Yes," she said.

And amazingly, he put down his glass and obeyed.

CRORO

When Leopold returned to the house, he found the count seated in the great hall, drinking coffee and reading a London newspaper. He seemed relaxed and looked up when he heard Leopold's flat greeting to him.

"Freddie Allsop sent for me, but I fear it might have been quite unnecessary. I have been upstairs to see Amalie. I reassured her that I was here. She seemed to understand, but she is still quite ill. Dr. Matthews is with her. Most have measles as children, but Georges Bouchard was very protective of his daughter. What has happened? I'm afraid I don't comprehend this sudden need to return to Paris or her fear. Can you enlighten me, Leopold?"

Leo led him into his study and said, "She is too ill to travel, at least at the present time. At any rate, as her husband I can prevent her from doing so, even when she has recovered." He was angry at Freddie and wondered what he had written to the count, to bring him to England with such urgency. "So what tales have you been told?"

"That she wishes to leave England and wants me to demand you return her inheritance. Of course, this is all nonsense. I fear the child has gotten lost in one of her novels. I don't see that she could ever live without you. Still, something must have occurred to so suddenly threaten her adoration of her husband. I understand that Blakefield Castle received a visitor from Spain."

Leopold felt his heartbeat quicken. Whatever was wrong

with his wife, whatever she believed, would surely be explained and sorted out. Victor Le Clair had little intention of rescuing her from him, and clearly, he did not believe, as did others, that Leopold had done something terrible.

"I don't understand any of this, and I am relieved that you have not come here to judge me, as it seems others have done."

Leopold went on to explain about his cousin and the events that had led up to Amalie's illness and apparent phobia. "I may have been insensitive but certainly not threatening, and before this, she was very happy, spending money and enjoying all her visitors. I was completely blindsided by this turn of events. Perhaps I should allow her to leave—perhaps call her bluff. For once I am not the villain in this."

The count could sense his friend's anger, and he felt it was justified. "Leo, you do not mean that. If you don't mind me asking, what was in the letters?"

Leopold had little intention of revealing that and said, "It doesn't matter. She didn't read them. She was adamant about that, although no one had accused her of it ..." His voice trailed off. "Of course," he said. "She must have done so."

Victor laughed. "Amalie? Leo, my dear friend, how could you have thought otherwise?"

"I suppose I didn't quite realize that my loving wife could lie so convincingly."

"Well, I will not inquire further if you do not wish to share the details with me. However, rest assured, it would not go any further than this room, and perhaps I could be of assistance to you. I have one young woman living under my roof. I have no need of another arriving with her nannies and her children."

Leopold smiled thoughtfully. This man was already so intertwined in his life—his connection with Amalie's father, his affair with her mother. It was embarrassing, to say the least, but the count was a very astute man, and Leo knew he could rely on his integrity.

It was early evening by now, and he poured them both a large cognac as he began to tell the abbreviated history of his wretched family, including his mother's love affair with a peasant boy that had necessitated her family marrying her off to his father, their miserable life together, his own pitiable childhood, and finally the worry his mother had expressed in her letters, the ones written just before her death, about her husband's plans or threats to have her committed.

"So," Leopold continued, "is that it? How in hell's name could she believe such a thing of me? She knows how much I love her. She has never had cause to doubt it. It seems I'm not the one who's crazy after all!"

The count spoke up at last. "My friend, I wouldn't say that within her hearing. What is Malcolm McFadden doing here, by the way? Possibly filling her head with this nonsense?"

Leopold explained, "He's on honeymoon with a bride he doesn't appear to like very much. She's eighteen and in London right now. Most everyone in the house went there when Amalie was contagious, but he refused to leave. He's standing guard over her, I believe, in case I get out of hand."

"Ah, younger competition. I hope you are not flirting with the young American?"

Leopold didn't answer this, so the count drew the conclusion himself. "I see. That's two reasons I know of already to account for such insanity. Actually, four—there is also her illness, of course, and her own guilt about lying. Family meeting? Bridgette also?"

And so it was agreed. The two men gathered along with Dr. Matthews in Blanche and Cordelia's suite, leaving Imogen to sit with Amalie.

"Why do you think she did this? My petite does not lie!"

Bridgette was indignant before she became pensive, as the others in the room already were.

It seemed that Blanche had overheard many of her parents' heated discussions and was not surprised by the letters' content in the least. "I should have known it. That's why she was so adamant about not reading them. Well, first let's get her well, and then I'm quite certain she will blurt it out to at least one of us. It will eat her up otherwise. Maybe you should try to go in to see her, Leo. Don't mention the letters, though, at least not while she's still in this state. We will get her well first."

Victor Le Clair mused, "Amalie is fortunate to be part of such a family. You are all so understanding."

Blanche simply said, "Well, we love her, Victor. She's very special."

Leopold said, "That is why, no matter what, I'm always the one in the wrong."

Dr. Matthews sensed a certain self-pity in Leopold's response and said, "Leo, she is not out of the woods yet. Go to her kindly or not at all."

❧

Imogen left Leopold to sit with Amalie. It was the first time since her illness began that he had been alone with his wife, but she was sleeping, and he was aware that Bridgette was probably standing guard outside the door.

His heart was heavy, and he was hurt, saddened that she could think him capable of such cruelty when all he had ever done was love her. He felt tears in his eyes as he watched her, her rash still very visible, her breathing labored; she was still coughing occasionally, although it sounded less harsh. He felt ashamed of his earlier anger. How could he be angry with her? For whatever reason, to her the fear was real, and his heart melted.

"Monsieur, why are you sad?"

Leopold looked up. Amalie was awake, or was she? He was suddenly afraid. He had been so busy worrying about himself, and he was ashamed. He rolled up his sleeves, took off his boots, and decided that it would be he who stayed with her through this. "She must get well," he whispered to himself, "even if she forever hates me. I can't walk the earth without her."

Amalie apparently had heard him, and she smiled before drifting off again. "You must love her very much. I am sure she will come back to you. You are nice."

Just then Bridgette reappeared. "Shall I stay with her now? She has been that way. I worry."

Leopold attempted to reassure her, although he too was worried. "Well, at least she called me nice, Bridgette. I would rather stay with her now."

That night Amalie's fever reached a pitch, as did her coughing, which seemed to be racking her poor little body. Leopold refused to leave this time, and neither Blanche nor Bridgette argued with him. They could see the fear in his eyes.

She was thrashing about and coughing and rambling in French. Her words were garbled, and only Bridgette could make any sense of them as she responded and spoke soothing words to her in their native language.

At first Leopold held back, scared she would be afraid of him, as she had been the first few days, but then it occurred to him that she didn't even know who he was. He asked Bridgette what she was saying, and when Bridgette didn't really answer him, he berated himself for not having become fluent in her native tongue and mentally promised her that he would become so, if given another chance.

They were applying salve to ease her inflamed skin and trying to make her drink tepid fluids and an elixir to ease her sore throat and quieten her cough.

Early morning, her fever broke, and she suddenly sat up and shouted, "Leo!"

He pushed in and took her in his arms, and as she clung to him, she fell fast asleep. She said nothing further, but it was enough.

CHAPTER 11
All Better Now

Amalie finally awoke the next day. Her fever was gone, although her throat was still sore. The cough had lessened, and she felt very hungry.

She wasn't quite sure what had happened, but she knew somehow that she had lost several days. Leopold was beside her, sleeping, but he was fully clothed and lying on top of the bed. The summer sun was shining bright, and she arose to greet the day.

As was her normal habit, she looked into her full-length mirror. She was at once shocked at what she saw—the rash, her hair unwashed, her eyes gaunt—and it all came back to her. She remembered the letters, the painting, Leo's anger. Was the count really here? Or had she dreamed that? She had lied—had they discovered that? She thought about Leo's anger, his mother's fear. What had happened to her? Where was Bridgette?

She slowly backed away, staring at her husband. What had happened to her? She wanted to scream for Bridgette but was afraid to awaken him.

Suddenly, he opened his eyes. He was smiling at her, and then he wasn't. What had happened, and why couldn't she remember? She felt faint. She felt weak and afraid, and as he arose from the bed, she fell to the floor.

Leopold quickly ran over to her. He took her in his arms, and at first she struggled, but he wouldn't let her go. He told her over and over again how much he loved her. Crying, he asked her to come back to him.

She remembered. "Oh, Leo," she sobbed, "what have I done?"

Leopold was relieved. It seemed she was back. "Nothing," he said. "You've been very ill. Measles. You're over the worst. We will get you well."

Amalie braced herself; she was ashamed but couldn't hold it inside of her. "Leo! I lied. I lied to you—to everyone!"

Leopold once again saw her fear and felt his heart would break for her. *People lie all the time*, he thought. *My sweetest Amalie feels she has done something unforgivable.*

"Amalie, my dearest one, I already know that. We figured that much out. It's not so terrible. How can you even think that? I was the one who was wrong. I should have understood. You were frightened by my cousin, the fight, and the letters. But all is well now, my darling. Remember, you're mine, and I'm keeping you."

Amalie smiled weakly. "Please don't tell me the count is here. Did I dream that?"

Leopold gently said, "I'm afraid you didn't, but he was great. He understood."

"Leo, can I have a bath?"

Leopold laughed, much relieved. "It will be my pleasure."

Bridgette knocked and came into the bedroom, but they didn't hear her from the bathroom. She could hear the monsieur singing to her petite, who was laughing. He was giving her a bath. Bridgette had never heard him sing before, and it lifted her spirits enormously.

She decided on a good, hearty breakfast. Surely, they both

were hungry. But first she must tell Blanche and Cordelia. It was early, but she knocked on their door.

Blanche came to the door, and Bridgette said, "He is giving her a bath and singing to her—a fine voice too. I have never before heard him sing. He is singing 'Meet Me in St. Louis,' her favorite, with all the wrong words."

Blanche laughed, as relieved to hear it as Bridgette was to tell it.

"Now I must go see to their breakfast." And off Bridgette went as Blanche told Cordelia the good news.

Leopold's heart was overjoyed, and he found he didn't care much about anything other than his darling girl as he gently washed her hair and soaped up her body, singing to her all the while as she laughed happily at him.

Amalie was relieved and happy and couldn't quite understand the blackness that had overwhelmed her. As her husband gently dried her with a big, fluffy white towel, she said thoughtfully, "Leo, what if I stay red?"

He turned her around to her full-length mirror and answered, "See, it's already fading, but either way, I'm keeping you." He then found her nightdress and dressed her in it and sat her down to brush her hair.

Bridgette returned with two maids and a pile of linens. "Monsieur, please excuse us as we freshen the bed."

Amalie and Leopold sat on the chaise, and when the maids had finished, Bridgette said, "Now both of you, back into bed. A full breakfast is on its way."

When Bridgette and the maids left the room, they both did as they had been told, as Leopold said in jest, "You see, my love, how that woman speaks to me?"

Amalie smiled, but the smile faded as memories came flooding back. "Oh my God, Leo, how can I ever face anyone again? I could die of embarrassment. And what I put you through is unforgivable, but it was all so real. I don't think I want to ever leave my room again. I'm too ashamed."

A short while later, Blanche and Cordelia appeared, and Amalie started to apologize and tell them how ashamed she was. They could all see that she was still afraid, only now it was because she thought she deserved to lose all the love they had so freely given to her.

"I lied to everyone. I looked in the letters, and what was in them became so real. Perhaps because I was getting sick? Blanche, please don't hate me! Please forgive me!" Amalie was crying again, feeling that she had let them all down. She felt she just wanted to hide away forever.

Blanche then took control. She held her and let her cry it out, saying, "It's over, Amie. We love you, and all the rest is over. The count is leaving today. We will tell him you are still unable to see anyone. No one else knows anything except that you had measles. It's none of their business anyway. I'm your sister. Cordelia's your sister. Leo's your husband. Now let's just get you better, honey."

Bridgette appeared again with the maids, this time bearing trays full of breakfast meats, eggs, fresh coffee, and brioche. Bridgette remained after the maids left, and Amalie cheered at the sight of her dearest people all gathering around her, sharing a makeshift breakfast buffet, right there in her bedroom.

They were all talking happily, relieved that the worst was behind them, when Cordelia exclaimed, "Ladies, it seems our princess has fallen asleep. We should leave you now, Leo."

Amalie had drifted off with both hands still tightly holding on to Leopold's arm, and although he was growing uncomfortable, he allowed the others to leave, knowing he would remain for as long as she needed him to do so. He did attempt to remove his arm from her grasp, but she held on to him even tighter. He knew that she was on her way back from wherever she had been the past days but was not quite there yet, and he spoke reassurances to her, uncertain but hoping that his words were reaching into her heart.

The count refused to leave without first speaking with Amalie, and she understood. Quite frankly, she knew it was only right that she allow him to do so. By early afternoon, Bridgette had helped her get dressed, and she settled down on her chaise, awaiting an embarrassing lecture from the man who, it seemed, had taken over the role of her father.

He came to her kindly and addressed her in French. They both looked at Leopold in a manner that prompted him to excuse himself, although they asked for Bridgette to remain. Leo felt a little irritated to be excluded from whatever they were planning to discuss but thought it best not to show it, in the hope that Amalie would tell him about it later.

He found the others seated in Amalie's rose garden, drinking coffee. As Blanche poured him a cup, he explained, "It was strongly hinted that I should leave them to it. Bridgette stayed, and when I left, they were all conversing in French. I have decided to retain a French tutor to come to my office a few times a week. It is about time I learn to speak the language and to understand it beyond a few words spoken slowly. Please don't mention this to Amalie as I intend my education to be a surprise—or a secret if I turn out to be a miserable failure at it."

Malcolm expressed some surprise that Leopold had never considered this before, and for once Leopold didn't bristle but said, "Prior to this summer, it never seemed to matter, but these past days I have felt very much at a disadvantage, at the mercy of whatever Amalie or Bridgette, or even the count, has chosen to share with me, and now they are upstairs and in my home, and I am excluded from a discourse that I would barely understand had even I been allowed to remain."

Malcolm arose to get ready to join the count on the train to London, since he had volunteered to update the family on

Amalie's recovery and to bring back the children and remaining guests. Leopold had thanked him, almost begrudgingly, aware that McFadden had somehow become a part of his extended family, a circumstance that Leopold never could have imagined that first year he'd come to Blakefield Castle.

After Malcolm left them, Cordelia said, "I wonder, Leo, and please don't be offended, but why do you always refer to 'my home' and not 'our home,' even when speaking with Amalie? I suppose that's how you still see it. It's just something that always strikes me—not important really."

Leopold had decided it was time to leave them to the garden and go about his business when Amalie suddenly appeared, smiling, still displaying the remnants of her rash. She obviously had heard at least some of their conversation and said happily, "That's all right, Cordelia. I really don't mind. I haven't had my own home in seven years after all." Then turning to her husband, she said, "Leo, will you take me out on Caesar for a little while? I feel too shaky to ride on my own. I'd really like that. I hope you weren't offended earlier, by the way. The count just wanted to talk to me privately—well, with Bridgette too—mostly about my parents, private matters that really don't concern you."

Before Leopold, who was somewhat bothered by this comment, could answer, she was off to ring for fresh coffee. Blanche said quietly, "Something still is not right. Leo, I think you should ask Bridgette what was said."

Leopold was thinking the same thing and said as much. When Amalie returned, he said to her, "Darling, I think it's a little soon. In fact, I'm surprised to see you downstairs already. Please sit down at least. I'll take you riding soon—another day, I promise."

Amalie surprised them all by saying, "No matter. That's all right. I don't mind." Then she turned and went back inside the house, all thoughts of fresh coffee apparently forgotten.

Blanche said, "Let's ring for Bridgette. I want to know what he said to her. This is strange behavior."

Bridgette soon appeared, and Leopold asked her straight out to tell him, since something was clearly not right with his wife. He intended to go and find her, but first he needed to know what was going on, since she was not acting her normal sweet self.

At first Bridgette seemed reluctant to speak, saying it wasn't her place, but she saw the pain and confusion in her master and relented. "First, I must ask you a simple question, monsieur. Did you say something about your wife being crazy?"

Leopold didn't answer at first and then remembered. "When I was angry and hurt. It was just a turn of phrase. For God's sake, Bridgette, are we back at the letters again? What is this about?" He was becoming frustrated and angry.

Bridgette answered, "I know, I know, monsieur, and I'm glad that man has left us, and I'm angry with Mr. Allsop for bringing him here under such a terrible pretense. He went on and on, lecturing her and cautioning her to keep a check on her behavior. He told her that she was fortunate in her loving and understanding husband and family but that she shouldn't tempt fate—his words—and that he sees her father in her, most particularly this year. He said this as if this was not a good thing, and he told her that her mother had not had a happy life with him, due to these traits of his character, which Amalie apparently shares. He fell short of mentioning his affair with her mother and said all this in a kind enough way, but it is all nonsense. I am sorry to say this, monsieur, but if anyone has flaws in their character, it is he! I have told ma petite this. I don't think she paid me mind, however, possibly because of the letters, which I wish she had not read. Now we need to somehow get this nonsense out of her head. I want my spirited mistress back, no matter what it takes!"

Leopold looked shocked and angry, but it was Blanche who was first to speak. "Leo, I am listening to this with disbelief. She now seems to believe that she must behave, or she will be sent away or even put away! You will have to somehow convince her otherwise. If you can't, I'm taking her to the States for some normalcy. This has become ridiculous!"

Cordelia interrupted what sounded like Blanche working herself into a temper. She placed her hand on Blanche's and said, "Listen, we all know little Amie has quite a temper. It was just a few weeks ago that she was chasing Leo along the hallway, calling *him* crazy. Leo, if anyone can work her into a rage, you can. Make her angry. Tell her you're getting your study redone because you don't like it or that the bedroom roses have to go, or you've changed your mind about her new white filly. Be outrageous! If you can make her really angry with you, we will soon have her back. I'm sure of it. What do you all think?"

Bridgette was in such agreement that she kissed both ladies. She stopped short of her master, but he took her hand and kissed it in pretend gallantry. He was smiling broadly as he said, "Okay, ladies, watch me!" Then he turned to go back into the house.

Leopold found Amalie in the bedroom. It seemed one of the maids, or perhaps Eloise, had brought in a profusion of yellow roses. She was sitting in that childish way she had, looking out upon the gardens in a chair she had pulled over to the window. He had to admit that his wife's taste was indeed exquisite. He was so fortunate to sleep amid a sea of yellow roses beside a rose-scented angel. It was so difficult for him to be mean with her. He really just wanted to take her in his arms and caress her so tenderly after her ordeal. However, more than that, he wanted his spirited wife back, so he set about his plan to make her angry with him, in spite of the fact that she once again appeared nervous, perhaps even to be alone with him.

His task turned out to be much easier than he possibly could have imagined. She turned and smiled and told him his gardens were beautiful at this time of year, and this was his opening.

"Too many damn roses!" he said. "Too much tartan and too many damn roses. You will need to get rid of the tartan in my study and the yellow rose wallpaper in here." He could feel himself cringing as he spoke, but he carried on. "You have completely taken over my home so that I hardly recognize it."

At first she looked quite shocked. Amalie had been pondering the count's advice and had already been thinking that he possibly had given it in an effort to keep her in England and away from his château—though she no longer had any intention of going there anyway. She was totally astounded at her husband's words; he was making no sense at all. What was he even talking about? Return his castle to the gloomy old-fashioned way she had found it? Still, she attempted to be nice, as indeed the count had counseled her. "Leo, excuse me, but I don't understand. I thought you liked your tartan study. You asked me to do it, after all. And the rest of the house, my bedroom, the drawing room? What about the back of the house? You actually just asked me to reconfigure and design that whole wing. I'm afraid I'm a little confused. Do I understand you correctly?"

Leopold was still inwardly cringing, but he knew he was hitting his mark, since although she was smiling sweetly at him, there was a definite glint in her eye. So he continued. "Your bedroom? You mean my bedroom, madam, and yellow roses are not to my taste. If you don't want to change it, I can always bring in an English designer. You can take your yellow roses over to the west wing if you like. In fact, I believe I will have my bedroom completely redone—burgundy, I think. Yes, burgundy walls and carpeting and English bed linens."

Amalie was staring at him wide-eyed, and by now he was finding it difficult to keep a straight face. "Too much French stuff in this house. No more silk coverlets from Paris either, and I want everyone to speak English at all times. Did you not know that an Englishman's home is his castle? That applies to an Englishman's castle too! Time for some major changes, which have been a long time coming."

Amalie stood absolutely aghast. Had he lost his mind? And the count had her worried about her behavior? In spite of what the count had advised, this was really too much and completely unacceptable. "To hell with your Englishman's castle, and to hell with you! My taste is exquisite! Ask Lady Agatha! Your English taste is ugly and stodgy as was the taste of *all* of your nasty ancestors! Nothing to be proud of, I am sure! I will be happy to remove some of the 'French stuff' you suddenly find so abhorrent, you crazy man, in the form of me! Your French wife! And you can enjoy all the burgundy you want because I will no longer be sleeping in this house or with you!"

Leopold allowed her to storm out of her beautiful yellow-rose bedroom. It was her room, and that was why he loved it, just as he loved her every coverlet and lacy thing that she had shipped over from Paris for some ridiculous price. She was back! He was smiling happily to himself, indeed laughing, as he allowed her sufficient time to unload on the ladies, who surely had been waiting in hopeful anticipation that he would hit his mark and that she would do exactly that.

Amalie was surprised to find Bridgette with Blanche and Cordelia as she stormed into their suite but was too incensed to wonder why. "Blanche, that man has gone crazy! How dare he criticize my taste when he has absolutely no style at all! He wants everything to be burgundy again and dares to tell me that my bedroom is actually *his*! He can have his ugly old castle back again, even uglier than I found it, and bring in his horrible English designers to bring back all the burgundy and bring down all his ugly ancestors' portraits from the attics. I am far too good for him, and my paintings are far too good for his horrible castle! Bridgette, we are moving to my house in London, purchased for me as a joint birthday and wedding present, and I am changing the locks before he can get his hands on it with his ugly, nasty, beastly English taste! And just dare he try to take that house back! I will have him in front of a magistrate!"

At this point, Amalie was running out of breath, and she suddenly realized that the ladies and even Bridgette seemed to be laughing at her. At first she was confused, indignant even, and then she heard a familiar voice behind her.

"Ouch, that hurt! I thought I had good taste, in women at the very least. I suppose I will see you in court then? Shame, really, since I've decided to keep the tartan and yellow roses after all."

Amalie turned around, and there he was, laughing too, and she felt suddenly deliriously happy. He hadn't meant a word of what he'd said. He didn't want her to be nice and compliant. It seemed he loved her just as she was, with her temper and idiosyncrasies. Still, she said, by now laughingly, "You horrible man! I was doing my best to be nice to you, and you set me up! You didn't mean one word of that, did you?"

Leopold responded, "Beloved, if I wanted nice, I would have run out of your aunt's house one night long ago and missed my exquisite five-course dinner!" Turning to the others, he said, "This summer alone, I have been threatened with ruination, with the magistrate, and oh, with my wife throwing herself into my river so she can drive me mad from her watery grave. Have I missed anything, beloved? But I've decided to keep her, since she is really quite pretty."

Amalie playfully slapped his arm and then hugged him so happily that the others, who still hadn't said a word, felt tears in their eyes. Leopold joyfully lifted her into his arms and carried her lovingly back into her exquisitely appointed lilac and yellow-rose bedroom, where he passionately made love to his still red-spotted, slightly crazy wife, whom he wouldn't want any other way.

Once the couple was gone, Blanche said, "I'm a bit disappointed that she didn't need to chase him down the hallway."

To this Bridgette responded, as she left Blanche and Cordelia, "Just give them a few days. Well, that's me off-duty. No need to assist her with her bath this evening. I will have Monsieur Moreau send up something special for dinner—a bit later on, of course."

CHAPTER 12
The Actress, the Prince, and an Abandoned Dinner

Several of the rooms in the back of the house were nearing completion, and Amalie had forgone the riding party to show Annabelle and Imogen the recently completed rooms. She also was seeking ideas for her newly imagined "summer room." Her aunt March had accompanied them that afternoon as well, and the only remaining men, Leopold and Edward March, were again ensconced in the billiards room—or as Henrietta now referred to it, their counting house.

The play was set to be performed that Saturday, and Lady Agatha was expected to arrive Friday and remain for a week. She was forestalling her return to Pengallon House in Truro until the Blakeleys could accompany her there, and Blakefield Castle was far too busy with visitors that summer for them to possibly consider such an undertaking until September, after the knighthood accolade.

Maryia Smith was showing the ladies around the rooms and

asking Amalie's advice on which pieces of furniture could be tastefully employed and which should be stored or otherwise disposed of.

"Nasty, heavy old pieces," declared Amalie with a sneer. "I can't imagine the Blakeleys were ever renowned for good taste. I'm almost tempted to say, 'Get rid of the lot!'"

Annabelle was laughing as Amalie fought to open a door in an old oak armoire. "So you found nothing of interest in anything? I wonder why this piece is locked. Perhaps it contains priceless artifacts!"

The ladies sent for McBride to break open the armoire, and once he had arrived, they watched excitedly as he performed the task. He wasn't completely happy about it, but he considered that there was unlikely to be anything of value contained therein. After all, many choice pieces had been sold by the old master to help finance his debauched lifestyle, and McBride's current master had shown little interest in all the goings-on in the back of the house.

Finally, the lock gave way, and the doors sprang open to reveal several drawers within. McBride quickly left the ladies to it, and as Amalie began to rake through the contents, her feminine companions stood in amazement.

Therein were ladies' undergarments and flimsy costumes, not of fine quality and certainly not of good taste. As Amalie gingerly held up each piece for her companions to examine, she wondered aloud if these items perhaps had belonged to Leopold's father's mistress. The style was outdated but not terribly so.

Annabelle exclaimed in awe, "Yes, I wonder who they could have belonged to! Are there any letters or photographs?"

Amalie continued to delve through the contents, and as she lifted a pile of linens, discolored from age, a large photograph fell to the floor. By this time Amalie's heart was beating faster, and her lady companions had gone silent. Leopold's father had been dead for almost twenty years, and the photograph was most certainly more recent, perhaps just ten years or so old. It clearly had been taken in an artist's studio, and the subject was a woman, dressed quite inappropriately in some sort of Greek or Egyptian costume, with her hair hanging almost to her knees. She didn't look particularly young, perhaps as old as thirty, and as Amalie turned the photograph over, with all the ladies watching over her shoulder, they saw an inscription.

July 1890, Darling Leo, with love, your devoted Violette.

All went quiet, awaiting Amalie's reaction.

Well, she thought, *my darling's past exploits have caught up with him at last.* She finally spoke. "If she's French, then I'm Henry the VIII. Clearly an actress. Must be well past forty by now and clearly never much to look at, even fourteen years ago. How stupid of him to leave this lying around. I've certainly never found anything else from his past, and believe me, I looked thoroughly when first we were married."

The others laughed, relieved that Amalie didn't appear to be upset, overmuch anyway, and Imogen took hold of the photograph. "I know that studio stamped on the back—Edgar Henderson. It's in Covent Garden. It's still there. She's definitely not French, Amalie. More likely, she hails from Spitalfields! Henderson's is well renowned for photographing actresses and other performers; they are certainly not society photographers."

The ladies passed around the photograph, each one proclaiming her disdain for the poor woman. Annabelle mused, "I wonder why she left her things here. I mean, she couldn't have been very well off."

Amalie exclaimed, "Well, perhaps my husband bought her all new things, on his account in Harrods!"

Just then Blanche and Cordelia appeared, and they too perused the photograph. They looked through the meager belongings, and the mood was suddenly lifted when Blanche held up a worn, flimsy piece by her fingertips. "Well," she said, "he certainly wasn't a very generous lover. Amie, sweetie, I hope you're not upset. This was clearly years before you met. He never professed to be a saint, and I doubt he replenished her wardrobe."

Cordelia chimed in, "In point of fact, he was absolutely dreadful before you tamed him. Possibly he threw her out?"

Amalie responded, "Or she ran away! I wonder how long she was here. I intend to get to the bottom of this!"

As the ladies made their way back to the main house, having made no definitive decisions on the disposition of the remaining furniture, Henrietta exclaimed, "Oh dear, I do hope my dinner won't be ruined again this evening!"

Amalie, of course, ran along to Blanche and Cordelia's room, wide-eyed, looking for advice. The ladies were much relieved that their little Amie was not overly upset by her discovery; however, she did seem inclined to make Leopold pay, fourteen years later, for his past misadventures.

Blanche suggested, "I think it would be fun to select stage names for our little play, possibly French ones? Amalie, our names are already French, but I was considering perhaps Violette for you?"

Cordelia and Amalie laughed.

Amalie then surprised them, saying, "A little while ago, Bridgette told Leo about the Russian prince my father was considering marrying me off to. Leo insisted that I show him his photograph, but he can be quite jealous and was so loving that day we spent in the turret that I showed him a photo of Prince Vladimir Mikhailovich Ivanov's father instead. He had a big belly and lascivious lips, and Leo made fun of him. I do have the real photograph, however, so Leo better not vex me tonight!"

Amalie then left them, and Blanche remarked, "Well, this is

a new one on me. Our little Amie never fails to amaze. Dinner will be fun tonight!"

And so it was. Amalie was all sweetness to her husband as they prepared to go down for dinner, and Leopold knew his wife well enough to realize that something was afoot, most especially considering the care she took over her toilette that evening and the donning of her diamond tiara. However, he decided to leave sweet Amalie's latest treachery to unfold in due course—no doubt that night at dinner. Dolores was still gazing at him adoringly, and he regretted his misjudged decision to flirt with her that one night. He had paid for it ever since, and although he longed for the day when he would finally get rid of his visitors, he knew that the worst was yet to come with the play and with Lady Agatha.

The play was the main topic that night at dinner, and having heard Annabelle's story of what had transpired in the afternoon, Harvey Havemeyer was greatly looking forward to the evening's entertainment.

Edward March was, as usual, uninformed. He had joined sides with his nephew years beforehand, with the consequence of never being let in on anything.

Blanche decided to dive right in. "What do you think, ladies? Wouldn't it be fun if we all took stage names for our little play? I think Lady Agatha would enjoy that."

The ladies agreed on what fun that would be, even Dolores, who had no idea what was truly going on.

Leopold wasn't paying too much attention to the conversation, instead competing with his uncle for who could eat the most cockles and mussels. Although Amalie loved oysters, prawns, and langoustines, she detested both these varieties of shellfish and the mess they made of her table linens. Her uncle had had Chef Moreau order them in, and it seemed only he and Leopold were enjoying this particular course at dinner, since even the other men had declined them.

To Blanche, Amalie responded, "Yes, why not? Let's make some suggestions to take our minds off the shellfish at the other end of the table."

Henrietta enthusiastically joined in. "Indeed, my dear, and please accept my apologies for your uncle's table manners!"

Eventually, the offending plates were removed from the table and replaced with more palatable Dover sole and asparagus tips in a delightful béchamel sauce.

Blanche carried on with her conversation. "Amie, what do you think of Violette? Would you like that name? I'm thinking you should still use a French name."

This caught Leopold's attention, and he stated flatly, "Don't be ridiculous, Blanche. You are not, in fact, real actresses. Sounds rather childish to me." He had a questioning glint in his eye. Was this truly a coincidence? It had to be. That unfortunate episode in his life had been a long time ago.

Amalie took it from there. "Oh, I don't know, Blanche. Doesn't that sound like some woman from Spitalfields putting on airs?"

Annabelle couldn't help but burst into laughter, and this caused the other ladies to join her, even as the remainder of those seated looked confused. Something was going on, but what?

Leopold now surmised that this was indeed no coincidence and that his darling wife's jealousy was quite evident. She had clearly found something. A photograph? But where? No point in denying anything if she was about to go for him at his own dining room table. "My sweet, cosseted wife, what could you possibly know about Spitalfields?"

She looked at him, and there it was, that Parisienne superior look he knew and loved so well.

"Absolutely nothing, sir, except that is where men who pretend to be gentlemen roam around at night, seeking out loose women with painted faces and dirty knee-length hair and who wear cotton instead of silk!" Amalie raised her chin majestically, even though inwardly she knew how terrible she sounded. It was just that as the night wore on, she could imagine that man sitting opposite her making love to that awful woman in the photograph, and it was almost too much for her heart to bear.

The others were about to turn the conversation around to something more dinner-worthy until Leopold responded, "Well said, my dear." And to the others at the table, he remarked, "I must apologize for my wife. She was raised as a princess. Never taught to lift a finger. Spoiled beyond belief by her father, who commissioned a new portrait of her every year and who would have married her off to a lascivious prince, had he lived, just so she could be a real princess and live in a palace. She therefore shows her true colors this night, as she looks down her nose at us mere mortals."

Even Blanche was shocked and said, "That's enough, Leo."

Malcolm was glaring at him with naked hatred even as Dolores smiled with admiration, having thoroughly enjoyed Amalie's put-down.

Amalie hid her humiliation as best she could, and as she arose to leave the table, she responded, "He wasn't lascivious. That was his father. Prince Vladimir Mikhailovich Ivanov was exceedingly handsome and a thorough gentleman—after all, he is a prince." To the others, she said, "Excuse me please. I find I've lost my appetite."

She majestically walked out of the dining room, although tears were stinging her eyes. Perhaps she had overstepped herself, but this wasn't the first time Leo had spoken of her being spoiled, and she thought, *I truly believe he hates me.*

The ladies soon joined her, all except Dolores, who chose to remain with the men to finish her dinner until her husband told her to go join the ladies.

"Well, Amie, you certainly got his gander up tonight. I swear, my brother has all the delicacy of a pit bull when you get him started. I would like to see your prince's photograph, however." Blanche had decided to downplay the incident, hoping that Amie wouldn't be too upset by her brother's cruel remarks.

Amalie felt more angry than hurt and ventured, "How dare he? Horrible man! I shan't speak to him ever again! And then he can go back to Spitalfields since he prefers the women who live there! I'm too good for him anyway!"

The others were laughing, even Henrietta. Life was never dull at Blakefield Castle, and in truth, it was always fun for the others when the Blakeleys were fighting.

By the time the gentlemen joined them, the women had moved on to other things, most especially the WSPU meeting that they were planning to attend later that week. Imogen spoke intelligently and enthusiastically, and Blanche and Cordelia especially enjoyed her conversation.

Amalie glanced over at her husband, who awarded her with one of his straight-faced glowers, and she again put her nose in the air and turned away from him to speak to the others—most notably, Malcolm, who had joined her on the sofa.

Annabelle sat down at the pianoforte, with Harvey turning the pages of her sheet music, and the conversation had turned quite congenial until Dolores stated rather loudly, "Gee, Amalie, that was sure embarrassing!"

Amalie, now having fully adopted her French air of superiority, responded, "What was, my dear? Oh, you mean my husband? Don't be taking him too seriously—about anything, actually. And don't say I didn't warn you." She then turned and calmly resumed her conversation with Malcolm.

Leopold was watching this. His wife's claws were definitely out tonight, and although he felt he might have been a little hard on her, he knew that he was in for a rough night ahead, since clearly, she had found a photograph of this woman from long past—a time in his life that he really didn't care to remember. He shouted over to her, "So, my darling, it seems you have something that doesn't belong to you in your possession. You can give it back to me later."

Amalie stood up and glared at him. "Give it back? Seriously? I think not!" She turned her back to him and walked over to join Blanche and Cordelia. By now she was thoroughly embarrassed as well as angry and whispered to them, "He needn't think I will ever forgive him for tonight's behavior."

Before either lady could answer her, Leopold came striding over to where they stood open-mouthed and, quite unbelievably, lifted Amalie over his shoulder and shouted back as he exited the room, "Please excuse my wife. She has a headache!"

Amalie was shocked and totally mortified, and even as she held on to her tiara, she kicked him with all her might, all the way up the grand staircase.

Blanche turned to the other guests and suggested, "Whist, anyone?"

As Harvey Havemeyer agreed to join her, he thought, *These people are truly crazy. This gets better every evening.*

❧⤳❧

Once they were alone in their room, Amalie was tossed unceremoniously unto her latest lilac coverlet, sweetly adorned with tiny yellow roses. She sat up and glared at her handsome husband, who was actually smiling at her.

A knock at the door produced a concerned Bridgette, who had rushed to her petite's rescue.

"Of course," said Leopold, gesturing toward his wife. "There she is, Bridgette. Your mistress is just fine. However, I'm locking her in her room until she learns table manners. You may return later if you hear screaming, but in the meantime, please have one of the maids bring up a bottle of brandy and two glasses."

Bridgette decided to leave them to it and report to Blanche that her crazy brother was, at the very least, smiling.

"Well, my dear, what do you have to say for yourself, behaving so badly in front of our guests this evening? And I want the photograph or whatever it is you and your ladies in waiting found today. I also want the real photograph of your so-called prince." Leopold spoke in his renowned "let's talk to Amalie like a child" voice as he generously poured himself a large measure of his preferred beverage and his wife a very small one.

Amalie was, of course, completely incensed. "What do I have to say? You crazy, awful, womanizing beast!"

"I'm not sure where the 'womanizing' came from, but I'll admit you have driven me crazy—certifiable, I think. However, what you have in your possession does not belong to you, so give it back." Leopold knew he should be angry, but his wife's passion, both the good and the bad, always kept him coming back for more. Her beauty still amazed him, and even though he couldn't quite comprehend her complete adoration of him, sometimes resulting in her extreme jealousy, he thanked God for her every day of his life. He would be nothing without her, and if she ever turned away from him, he would surely die.

Amalie, still embarrassed about being unceremoniously carried out of the drawing room, spat back, "Your castle, your dining room, your horses, your motorcars, your land, all your possessions! Greedy man! Who's the spoiled one, really? Not me!" Amalie stood up and started to undress, first taking off her diamond tiara and pulling down her hair. She was somewhat relieved that her husband wasn't really very angry, so she went about the business of removing her dress and stockings, well aware that he was watching her. She made the most of these tasks, performing them in her most alluring manner.

Leopold knew she was performing for him. She knew how

much he desired her, and as he watched her, entranced, he said hoarsely, "You forgot 'my wife.'"

With her little saucy smile, she responded, "I never forget that, my husband, and you better not either." She then proceeded to help him undress, and he decided to take up the matter of the photographs after his seduction.

CHAPTER 13
Just Another Day at Blakefield Castle

The next morning, Amalie breezed into Blanche and Cordelia's suite carrying both photographs, of Violette and the prince, concealed inside a periodical.

"Blanche, will you keep these? Your brother has gone to his river and has 'commanded' me to produce them upon his return. However, I cannot produce what I do not have. I'm supposed to stay in my room. Can you seriously believe that? He tells me I've driven him crazy, and he is certifiable, or something like that. Well, he is crazy, but that surely isn't my fault! Can you believe he carried me upstairs last night? I managed to avoid the lecture. I seduced him instead."

The ladies laughed; how adorable their little Amie was. They thought that possibly she had driven Leopold crazy, but he was much the better for it. They excitedly perused the photograph of Prince Vladimir. He was in uniform and standing very arrogantly, posing for the photographer. He was fair like Amalie and very good-looking.

Blanche unexpectedly felt a little sorry for her brother. This photograph would certainly bother him. She alone knew his insecurities, for all his bravado.

"Amie, it seems that you might have married a prince. Indeed, you probably would have done so if your father had lived longer. Any regrets? Leo will be—well, you know him—a little crushed by this."

Cordelia concurred, and Amalie sat down, crestfallen. "Oh, I do hope he isn't. Why should he be? My Leo is the handsomest man alive. That's a photograph of a mere boy, no doubt spoiled and petulant, just like me." She took the photograph and began pointing out the subject's assumed deficiencies. "There, see, a weak chin, thin lips, and he's far too skinny. My Leo's a real man, virile and strong. He could knock this man out with one punch! Oh, why did I bring this up anyway?"

Blanche took the photograph back and locked both it and the image of the woman in the room's desk drawer. "Because you were jealous of some old actress in an old photograph," Blanche said. "I know how much you love my brother, sweetie."

Blanche embraced Amalie warmly, aware that this little French girl had brought such wonderful joy to her brother.

Cordelia commented thoughtfully, "Well, we'll need a plan, because I know he won't let up about it, and Amie, your job is to keep up your role as his seductress. Now let's go down to breakfast. I, for one, am starving since I missed most of my dinner last night."

As they made to walk down together, Amalie said, "I put an old blanket on top of the bed in case he decides to dirty my new lilac coverlet when he realizes I didn't stay in my room. Do you think he really meant it? I think he intends to interrogate me!"

Everyone looked up as Amalie entered the breakfast room,

and Malcolm jumped up to pull back her chair. She too was very hungry, and once she had generously loaded up her plate, she realized that her guests were expecting some sort of explanation for the previous evening's bizarre behavior. She was about to make an amusing remark, to ease their various levels of discomfort, when she looked up and saw Leopold enter the breakfast room. He looked completely disheveled with his shirttails hanging out and his hair divinely messy, and Amalie fully realized how she loved him this way, even as she expected a caustic comment. But had he seriously expected her to remain in her room all morning?

He greeted everyone pleasantly, filled his plate, and sat down. After he had almost emptied his plate, he turned to Amalie. "Amalie, would you mind joining me in my study?"

Amalie turned wide-eyed to Blanche, who ventured to say, "I hope you won't be long, Leo. Amalie and I have made plans."

Of course, no such plans had been made, and well Leopold knew it. "That depends," he said. "I shouldn't imagine we will be long, although I am surprised that my wife has made any plans today."

He helped a wide-eyed Amalie from her chair. She was holding back a giggle, which finally escaped her in the great hall.

She said nothing, and neither did he, until he motioned for her to sit in his old worn leather chair, which held such sweet memories for her. He sat behind his desk, and she suddenly felt ten years old. She would let him say his piece and then tell him to go to hell. Was he seriously trying to intimidate her?

"Have you brought the photographs, Amalie?"

"No, I don't have them. Blanche does. You need a bath. And why are we in here? This conversation surely could have taken place upstairs in our bedroom." Amalie got up, but he asked her if she would stay awhile.

She really couldn't figure out this mood and sat down again, waiting for him to speak. He almost seemed at a loss for words, almost as if he didn't know where to begin. He didn't seem angry. He seemed sad. And suddenly, Amalie wondered if he was okay.

They sat in silence for a bit, Amalie watching his face as he appeared to look through paperwork on his desk. Finally, she could take it no more. "Leo, do you have something you need to discuss, or is it your intention that I sit here as you go about your business?"

He finally looked up. "You're always talking to McFadden. What do you talk about? I suppose you find him very amusing?"

That came out of nowhere, she thought. *I thought he was going to talk about the photograph.* "I don't know, Leo. Many things. He likes to talk about Texas and his ranch. He asks about me, my family, and Paris. He has suggestions for my folly too. I'd like to fix it up. Why are you asking me this?"

"Your folly? First I've heard of it. If you mean my folly, it's dangerous. I'm going to have it pulled down. What else do you discuss? Me? My shortcomings as a husband? Intimate details of our relationship?"

Amalie was not at all comfortable with the way this conversation was turning, and she stood up. "Leo, you're acting very strange. Of course, I would never discuss what is personal to us. As for the folly, of course it is yours. Everything at Blakefield Castle is yours, except a few sticks of furniture and a few old paintings. The children, the rose garden, the dress I'm wearing, even my new lilac coverlet—all yours. And so it seems you intend to take away the folly that I mistakenly thought of as mine. So be it. Oh, and your actress's photograph and her cheap worn undergarments that are still in the oak armoire. Have McBride show you where to find them since these things are yours too. Is that all? Is that what you brought me here to tell me? To remind me that everything is yours?"

Amalie was now on a roll, hurt and confused after the previous night's lovemaking. "I can tell you one thing, however—if I am yours, it's through choice. That is unless I choose otherwise. Think carefully before you make Blanche give you that photograph, however, because it's Violette or your spoiled little wife. I'm sure you know exactly where to find her, and women like her, who have your profound sympathy. My God, Leopold, your parents truly did a number on you! Excuse me!"

Amalie was angry and about to leave the study, which suddenly felt dark and stuffy and not cozy and romantic as she had always considered it.

Leopold said, "Please sit down. I'm not very good at conversation. Isn't that why you always surround yourself with others?"

"No, Leo," she responded. "I do that because you're not very good at spending time with me. I would be happy just walking with you, doing little things, I suppose, but you really don't have time for me, do you? Well, except, of course, for the obvious, and I'm always available for that, aren't I? How convenient for you. After Cornwall, everything was so wonderful, but difficult to keep that up, isn't it? The loving husband? Leo, I don't know what this is about, but you're making me feel very uncomfortable."

Amalie sat and stared at him, waiting for some sort of response. It was a while in coming.

"When I was younger, much younger, I found little interest in young ladies of my social class—all giggles and silly conversation, no substance or depth. For a while I sought companionship with women such as Violette, women who had experienced life, and then I didn't. In the end they disgusted me. She disgusted me. I told her so. She came here uninvited. I was angry, and when I discovered her here, I threw her out. I had McBride take her to the station, and I don't know what happened to her after that. I never sought to find out. It's shameful, I know. You possibly believe there were many such women in my life. There were a few, not many. I suppose I was socially inept like my father.

Whatever it was, I felt nothing noble inside of me, and yet women pursued me—women like Lydia, young women like Dolores. There was nothing, that is, until I saw you, perfect in every way. I knew right away you would be mine, yet I couldn't understand it, why you loved me. Amalie, I thought at first it was just my manly attributes, the way you looked at me. But it's more than that, I think, but I'm not sure what. I'm not sure why."

Leopold stood up, almost as if the interview was over, but to Amalie, it was far from over. All this over a photograph? Her complicated man had just become even more complicated. She'd spent six years loving him, never ceasing to do so, no matter what his moods. And he could be funny too, making her laugh at his antics, and above all, he was thrilling—always the most interesting and enigmatic man in the room. Others paled in comparison. Is this what the lack of a mother's love could do to a young man, so that even as he approached forty, he was still so insecure, even after six years of her praising him, loving him, adoring him?

Amalie stood up too. She walked to the door. Leopold watched her, expecting her to leave, having said nothing about what he'd just told her. Why he had said all this, he wasn't sure. Everyone told him she was too good for him, and she was. What type of man would humiliate such an angel at dinner? She was simply jealous of an old photograph—probably didn't even know what or where Spitalfields was. But he hadn't been able to let it go. Leopold Blakeley, on the attack as usual. And his punishment? She loved him, as she always did. She would surely grow tired of it in the end.

Amalie didn't leave. She locked the door and turned to him. "Leo, I don't know what you expect me to say to all that. I'm your wife, and I love you with all my heart. If that's not enough for you, my body, my love, my passion, even compassion, I don't know what else to say to you. I've given my whole life, my whole soul, to you."

Leopold just stood there. Initially, Amalie had planned to go to him, to make it all better, as she always did, but she was quite suddenly depressed and exhausted. She stood and stared at him for a moment and said, "Tell your sister to give you the photographs." She then turned away, unlocked the door, and walked out.

Bridgette was awaiting her upstairs since Cordelia had told her that her mistress had been more or less summoned to the monsieur's study. Amalie's new riding ensemble had just been delivered by the Harrods delivery van, and Bridgette had laid it out on the bed. Hoping to make light of whatever had occurred in the master's study, she exclaimed, "Mon Dieu, petite, riding britches! Why did you purchase such an item? The design is beautiful, but wouldn't a skirt be more appropriate for a lady? Who ever heard of such a thing? Do you seriously intend to go outside in these things? The monsieur won't be very happy, to say the least!"

Amalie responded while examining and holding the ensemble up to herself in front of her full-length mirror. "Oh, Bridgette, don't worry about him. He probably won't care. I actually believe that he is missing his old life, sulking in his study. I can no longer get through to him, and I'm tired of trying. He tells me that he is going to have my—sorry, *his*—folly torn down, probably because I wanted to fix it up. I've been far too giving to that man, and he can go to hell! Not only am I wearing this today; I intend to ride Louis-Alphonse, and not sidesaddle either. Will you help me get this damn corset off? I'm starting a new fashion—comfortable clothes suitable for ladies who don't give a damn!" Chuckling, she continued, "Also, Louis-Alphonse is one creature who doesn't actually belong to the master of this mausoleum."

Bridgette was laughing, relieved that her mistress was not tearful following whatever exchange had taken place in the master's study that morning, and she helped her to don her newly created, if somewhat scandalous, fashion.

Before going down to the stables, Amalie stopped by to see Blanche and Cordelia. They already knew about the britches since they too had acquired similar apparel when they all had gone shopping together. Amalie, of course, was first to wear them.

"I cannot tell you how different I feel wearing these! They make me want to swagger. Perhaps I can adopt Leo's 'master of the castle' walk. Anyway, you can give him back his photo of 'Violette,' but let me see it first."

Amalie again perused the woman in the photograph. She found herself feeling guilty about how she had made fun of her, this poor, desperate woman taken to the station by McBride all those years ago. She told the ladies about her interview with "the master," which she was now calling him, and added, "Soon I will be able to call him Sir Leopold; that suits him, doesn't it? Master of all he surveys, including apparently me."

Cordelia responded, "I have to admit, that always somewhat irritated me—how he always refers to everything being his."

Blanche agreed, adding, "Off you go, Amie sweetie, and we'll watch you from the window. Are you sure you will be able to manage that stallion without breaking your neck? Oh, and what about the photo of the prince?"

"I have little choice on my mount, since the others all belong to him. Don't let him have Prince Vladimir's photo. It does not belong to him. Okay, I better hurry. Yes, will you watch me from your window? I've never ridden astride before, or in britches."

Amalie ran downstairs, narrowly missing running into her husband, who was about to make his way upstairs.

Blanche and Cordelia both agreed that Amalie looked stunning as they watched her from their window. She waved up at them. Her hair was loose, and she looked so much at ease as she sat confidently astride the beautiful black stallion, who it seemed belonged to no one.

They were soon disturbed by a knock at the door, which produced a straight-faced Leopold. "Where's Amalie? I think I may have upset her." He then noticed that both women were standing guiltily with their backs to the window, and he approached them in order to look out.

Blanche attempted to lead him away, but it was too late; he had seen her.

Shocked, he said, "What the devil! I specifically forbade her to ride that horse. She is far too small for it!" And then he added, "What in hell's name is she wearing?" He made to leave them, and both ladies hoped that little Amie would take a different pathway than usual so that she could, for a while at least, avoid the inevitable confrontation and enjoy her ride on the beautiful stallion.

Amalie did indeed decide upon a different route. She had been a little nervous at first, even as she insisted that McBride saddle the stallion up, but surprisingly McBride had given her little resistance, as had the stallion, and now off she rode feeling young and alive. Whatever was wrong with her husband, he would need to get over it. He had humiliated her at dinner the previous night and embarrassed her at breakfast that morning. She had had just about enough of him for the present time.

Leopold soon was saddled up and riding off in search of his willful wife. He knew his land well, having surveyed it all his life, and soon he spotted her up ahead. As improperly dressed as she was, she nevertheless looked magnificent astride the great beast. He was angry, though, more at himself than with her after his ridiculous dialogue in his study, and soon he was upon her.

Amalie heard a horse approach from behind and knew before she turned around that it would be her husband. She considered galloping off away from him, but she was a little nervous upon the fine animal; he was so much larger than she was used to, and it seemed a long way down to the ground should she fall off. So instead she turned toward him, ignoring his murderous expression.

"This is most vexing!" she declared. "Why are you following me? I thought you would be gazing at your lady friend's photograph. I told Blanche to give it to you! And anyway, this is not your horse. Please go away and allow me to enjoy what is left of my morning! And don't bother saying that you are better and faster than me. Who cares? Go away!"

Leopold rode up and calmly took hold of her reins. "I thought I forbade you to ride this horse. And why are you seated and dressed like a man? Is this to prove some point? You need to go back to the house and change before anyone else sees you."

After Amalie's morning in her husband's office, she was livid. "Go to hell! I will do what I please and wear what I please. Now go away!"

Leopold didn't answer her at first. He was about to lead her back to the stables, but she was biting her lip as she looked at him, and somehow that always got to him. And she was so lovely, magnificent really, even in britches, and he felt suddenly so immensely proud that she belonged only to him. This he was sure of, even as she was by now looking as if she might try to punch him again as she once had two years before, and he said, "Come on, I'm taking you to the Black Raven for a tankard of ale. You once offered one to me, so now I am returning the favor. Besides, if my wife prefers to dress like a man, she best learn to drink like one."

Amalie's stare turned from angry indignation to awestruck amazement. "But Leo, I'm wearing britches—what will your tenants think of me? I can't!" But she was laughing.

"Might buy you a pork pie. Mrs. Tottle makes a delectable pork pie." Leopold dismounted to help Amalie off the stallion. "I'll pay a boy to take the horse back to Blakefield. For half a crown and a ride on a stallion, there will be many who will volunteer, I'm sure." He then silenced Amalie's expected protest with a kiss. "The horse is too big for you, Amalie. I don't want you to fall and hurt yourself. You can sit astride with me and hold on tight. I'll give you a good gallop, and next week we'll be picking up the filly. You can think of a name for her—French, of course."

Amalie didn't argue. She enjoyed riding with Leo, though never before astride, and as she held him close, she felt so happy and thrilled to be with the man who never failed to thrill her.

When they reached the tavern, sure enough, there were several volunteers to take the black stallion back to Blakefield. Leopold picked the most reliable in appearance but gave him a strong warning and a message to alert the household that Mrs. Blakeley was safe and sound.

Everyone had turned in shock to see the squire appear with his wife, so strangely attired, and Amalie enjoyed how each man tipped his cap and called her "my lady," although she wasn't quite that yet. Leopold ordered a tankard and a glass of ale and three pies, two for him and one for Amalie. He then told the landlady that he would stand a tankard for all that afternoon, and Amalie giggled at how quickly the old-fashioned tavern filled up. It was the first time she had ever been inside, and she felt very special to be seated with her husband, the squire, proudly holding her hand.

The village folks seemed very interested that their squire's wife had deigned to join them since she had never done so before, and yet he often stopped in for a pie and a cool tankard. Amalie hadn't quite realized that the "princess" theory was an actual belief among her husband's tenants, and this somewhat surprised her. She visited the cottages now and again, bringing children's clothing, blankets, and such—after all, wasn't that how she contracted measles? *No*, she thought, *that's not good enough*. She could see the ease in her husband's interactions with the men in the tavern. He knew their names, and even in their deference to him, they seemed to very much like and respect him.

Amalie did not know their names or those of their wives

and children. Leo had never encouraged her in that regard, and it was not as if she ever had taken any special interest. She fully understood the whole princess rumor, but the truth was that she had never been taught or shown how to interact with those who were not of her social class. She left that to Bridgette. Even when she helped her chosen women to achieve their God-given potential, she was behaving like lady bountiful. Lady Agatha, Amalie's family, and Bridgette all loved her no matter what, but she realized that other than within her very close circle, she had no idea how to be likable. Leo had been the first person to see through her vain and aloof behavior. He had done so from the very start, and he loved her in spite of her flaws.

She sat with him that afternoon, quite proud to be his lady, but she realized that although she tried, she had no idea what to say, and the words she did speak were stilted and bland. Bridgette knew everyone in the village by name, as did Leopold, but she knew not a one.

Eventually, they made their way quietly back to Blakefield Castle. Amalie held tight to her husband, grateful for his love and protectiveness.

As they dismounted, she asked him shyly, "Leo, will you show me how to be, you know, interesting and comfortable with strangers, so that the townsfolk might like me a little?"

This request thoroughly flummoxed Leopold. That very morning, he had been telling Amalie that he was socially inept, and now she was basically telling him the same thing about herself. He all at once felt so very protective toward her. All of her airs and aloofness hid a shyness she felt with strangers. He could feel it that day in the tavern. There she had sat, looking so magnificent even while wearing those ridiculous britches, so that the farmers and tradesmen actually blushed when she graced them with a smile, yet all along, he could feel the palm of her hand sweating in her discomfort as she tightly held on to his.

He laughed gently and said, "I wonder what my sister would make of you asking me, of all people, how to be more amiable, when I understand I am universally known as a most unpleasant man. Those folks you met today are hardworking men and women. They need to be, in order to put bread on their table and provide for their families. I respect them, so much more than many of the so-called ladies and gentlemen in our social class— idle people who have never had to lift a finger or do a day's work."

Leopold realized that his wife was looking at him in confusion, thinking he might be describing her. He explained, "Amalie, my tenants love you, and the servants adore you. Everyone you touch adores you. You are kind and thoughtful and so beautiful that even strangers are entranced when you grace them with one of your little smiles."

They had reached the house, and Leopold led his wife back into his study, but this time he sat upon his old leather chair, pulling her onto his knee. "I was cruel last night, the way I spoke to you at dinner. You now know why. You brought back memories of a very dark time—I'm sorry to say one of many. I treated that poor woman very badly."

Amalie responded, "Oh, Leo, I'm so ashamed of the things I said about Violette. I don't know where she came from. And I've never even heard of Spitalfields. It was Imogen who first said it. Her clothes are old now, but I think you should recompense her somehow. But I would like to do it. I'm afraid if you see her again, you might love her. You've no idea how she turned out after all."

Leopold thoughtfully responded, "That's my kind and generous wife, willing to make amends for her husband's misdeeds in an ill-spent youth. Seriously, Amalie, she must be close to fifty, maybe even dead. That was a long time ago, and why would I love anyone else when I have my very own Venus? Just let it go, please."

Leopold was hoping that for once, sweet Amalie would listen

to him, and after all, she didn't even know the woman's real name. He decided to lighten the mood. "So, beloved, will you be donning a white tie and cutaway for dinner tonight or a pair of britches? Really, my darling, I live in constant trepidation of what you next have in store for me."

Leopold lifted Amalie off his lap as he spoke, and she had the feeling of being dismissed. She responded, "I suppose you will have to wait and see." As she walked out of the room, she saw her uncle March descending the stairs and thought, *Ah, it seems that I was indeed being dismissed.*

❧

Amalie called a meeting in the east turret to set the plan in motion for the next day.

Leopold and Edward were taking the eight o'clock train to London. Everyone else would be on the nine o'clock, even Malcolm and Harvey. The ladies would be attending a WSPU assembly in the St. Ignatius church hall. Imogen had arranged for them all to go, even Henrietta, and although Malcolm would have preferred that they not include Dolores, they had no choice but to allow her to accompany them as well. This somewhat worried the others, who were concerned that she would deliberately blurt it all out to Leopold, but Amalie insisted that she didn't care. The gentlemen had insisted on going with them to provide protection, since the hall was located in a dodgy part of the city, as Imogen referred to it.

With the arrangements all made, the group disbursed to go about their day, but Blanche and Cordelia were somewhat surprised that little Amie had no dramatic tale to tell with regard to Leo's reaction to the britches and the black stallion.

"So, Amie, please do tell. What happened?" Blanche said while taking Amalie's arm and leading her along to their suite.

"Well, he was really quite kind. He said if I wanted to dress like a man, I should drink ale, and he took me to the Black Raven, where he also purchased pork pies. There were all men inside except the landlady, and once he announced that the drinks were on him, all sorts of folks piled in, even women. The men were courteous, but the women just stared at me—well, except for the old women. Leo tells me his tenants love me, but I don't believe that is true. I didn't know what to say to them, and I was a little nervous. Leo seems to prefer their company to ours. I think he goes there quite a lot, although I have never been there before."

Cordelia remarked, "Not to speak out of turn, but we all expected some sort of drama, and he didn't come back about the photographs either. Blanche, your brother is behaving quite strangely, and in his case that means downright weird, since his behavior is always a bit off the beaten track."

Amalie quickly answered, "It's guilt. Not about me, but about Violette. I intend to find her, and you ladies can help me. Malcolm will come with us. We can start at the photographers in Covent Garden. The others can go to the Victoria and Albert Museum as we originally planned, and Malcolm will be more than willing to shake off Dolores for a while, and not a word to her! Oh, and the photograph—change of plans. Don't give it to him, Blanche—if he asks, that is. We will need it for identification purposes."

Blanche and Cordelia were all for the plan, since they thrived on mischief. As Amalie was about to leave them, she said, "I do wish I could wear my britches, but I suppose I can't—although Leo suggested a white tie and cutaway for dinner tonight. Wouldn't it be fun if we purchased them too and called his bluff?"

As their little Amie danced happily out of the room, the ladies both agreed on how much they just adored her.

CHAPTER 14
An Unfortunate Coincidence

As the train left the station at Hertford, Amalie found herself more excited at the prospect of potentially tracking down Violette than about the actual suffragist meeting. The plan was that Annabelle and Harvey would look after Henrietta and Dolores while Malcolm and Imogen accompanied Amalie, Blanche, and Cordelia to Covent Garden, after which they would join the others at the museum.

The meeting hall was busy with women excitedly chatting among themselves. Imogen was one of the founding members, and as such, she explained the two American men to her fellow members, all women, and since it was unlikely that either man knew anyone of consequence in London, they were allowed to remain with their female companions.

There were several speakers, all very articulate and passionate about their cause. Imogen excitedly explained that the final speaker was an Englishwoman who had just returned to England, having spent the last ten years or so in South Carolina, where she had developed quite a southern drawl. She was a widow who had been left comfortably off by her late husband and was to be the keynote speaker at the day's gathering.

Mrs. Moira Mungavin held the room spellbound. She was passionate in her opinions and was disdainful of men, making several satirical remarks at their expense—even as she smiled over at Harvey and Malcolm. She spoke of her own humble beginnings in Birmingham and how, after making many mistakes along the way, she finally had found a good man, one who had treated her kindly and looked after her well. Everyone laughed when she said the late Mr. Mungavin had been nothing much to look at, but at forty years of age, she had quite had her fill of pretty men with empty pockets. She then grew serious and stated that it shouldn't be that way for women in 1904, reliant on finding a good husband for the very bread on their table.

She shouted, "All of that is about to change, ladies! Our time has finally come!" and there was a rousing cheer in response.

Amalie was mesmerized—they all were. Even the two men who had accompanied them were captivated by her speech. Imogen offered to introduce her party to Mrs. Mungavin, and all thoughts of Violette were swept aside as the woman approached them. She had dark, piercing eyes and beautiful salt-and-pepper hair, worn up in an elegant chignon. Amalie thought her to be close to fifty and suspected that she must have been lovely in her youth. She whispered to Blanche and Cordelia, "I wonder about the mistakes she referred to. She must have led a fascinating life!"

However, Blanche didn't answer her, nor did Cordelia. They had nudged one another as the woman was speaking. They had studied the photograph of Leopold's former companion very carefully. Amalie had merely taken a superficial look at it, knowing that this woman had at one time been her husband's lover. This woman was certainly much older and clearly had come up in the world, but Blanche and Cordelia's suspicions were fully confirmed when Amalie introduced herself to Mrs. Mungavin.

Amalie held out her hand and said, with much enthusiasm, "I'm so happy to meet you, Mrs. Mungavin. I'm Mrs. Leopold Blakeley—Amalie."

The woman's whole demeanor changed, and the color drained from her cheeks. At first Amalie didn't understand what had just happened, until the woman said, "Well, that's a name I'd hoped never to hear of again. So he married you? Of course, he did. So sweet and so wholesome."

Amalie, speechless, turned to Blanche, and Mrs. Mungavin also turned her attention to her. "You're Blanche," said the woman. "My, my, what a coincidence. I saw your photograph. Of course, you were considerably younger in it, but you haven't changed overmuch. He hated you, as I recall."

If Amalie had hoped there was some misunderstanding, she knew now that there was not.

Blanche replied, "Violette, indeed, quite a coincidence. I have your photograph too. You are dressed very differently in it, if that is the correct word—dressed, I mean. You left some of your clothing at Blakefield Castle. We just came upon it, strangely enough, while clearing out some old furniture. My brother had no idea you'd left it there. Perhaps you were hoping to be invited back. Hardly likely, of course."

Blanche, when angered, was formidable, and this woman, whom they all so recently had been admiring, was suddenly diminished in all of their eyes, even as she attempted to maintain her composure.

Imogen, feeling stupid and irresponsible and thinking, *How could I have not seen the likeness?* suggested they go outside or around the corner for a cup of tea in a little tea shop she often frequented. "Ladies, I don't think we want to carry this conversation on here," she practically pleaded.

It was agreed, and the rest of the party carried on to the museum, leaving Amalie, Cordelia, Imogen, and Blanche to take tea with Mrs. Mungavin, a.k.a. Violette.

Malcolm McFadden slipped away unnoticed. He saw the embarrassment and confusion on Amalie's face, and she hadn't spoken a word. He knew where Blakeley's office was located and made a quick decision that he was the one who needed to go there to clear up this mess.

The ladies sat down and ordered tea and cakes. Moira Mungavin noticed that Imogen was holding the young woman's hand. They were all protecting her, like a murder of crows, as she sat there quietly, almost serenely. Moira Mungavin felt all the closed-up, forgotten feelings of hate and betrayal tumbling back. She recalled the pain and humiliation. She had been in love with Leopold Blakeley, and he had used her badly, broken every promise he'd ever made to her, and in the end had his servants throw her out. And here she was, sitting with a wide-eyed young beauty, his wife. He no doubt treated her like a piece of fine Dresden china.

Amalie was not feeling at all serene. She was studying this woman, her hands, her hair, her posture. She knew that if she tried to speak, she would cry, and she didn't want to cry in front of this woman, the woman who had owned the indecent costumes left behind in an old armoire. *Did she ever wear those things for Leo?* Amalie mused wretchedly. *Of course, she must have done so. That would explain his reluctance about me dressing provocatively for him, even when we are quite alone. Then there is his obsession about my hair—"I love it worn down, but only for me."* Amalie wished she had never found that photograph. Without it, the costumes would have been less relevant. She wished Bridgette were here with her. Bridgette had always protected her from any unpleasantness, and this meeting was beyond unpleasant. She wanted to run away and never look back. Bridgette would have seen to everything, but she hadn't wanted to come that day, although she had on many other occasions. Amalie knew that she would never go to another meeting. Perhaps the room was filled with his ex-lovers. *Oh, why didn't I beg Bridgette to come?* Still, she remained silent, her face expressionless, staring at the awful woman.

Blanche broke the awkward silence, smiling condescendingly. "So, Mrs. Mungavin, what brings you back to England, after all those years away? There is quite a strong movement in New York. Really, no need to travel so far in order to arouse your audience—unless, of course, New Yorkers were not taken in by your phony southern accent."

Imogen and Cordelia visibly cringed. Blanche could be ruthless.

However, Moira Mungavin had spent most of her life living by her wits, and as such, she wasn't slow to respond. "Mrs. …? Sorry, I don't know your husband's name. I have some unfinished business to attend to, although it may now be dealt with more quickly than I thought." She then seemed to become irritated by Amalie's silence and turned to her. "Don't you speak? That must suit Leo very well. I wonder what it is that you do that's so special—I mean, to have caught a rat? Of course, catching and keeping are two different matters. I'm sure he'll soon grow bored with having you in his bed, if he hasn't done so already, or maybe you are not quite as dull as you look. I recall him to be a very proficient lover. Has that been your experience? Or are you just on board to provide heirs for all his money?"

Amalie felt sick. She had had enough of this. To be spoken to this way was a nightmare. Soon the proprietor was asking them to leave. She was about to ask Imogen to take her to join the others at the museum, just to get away from this awful woman, when suddenly Leopold appeared with Malcolm, who must have fetched him. Amalie stood, ready to go to him or leave, she wasn't sure which, until she heard him say, "Violette?"

Hearing that name on his lips crushed her, and Amalie decided that leaving would be the best option. On her way out of the tea room door, she shouted back, "Moira—her name is Moira!" She then stopped to watch the exchange between this vile woman and her husband, before quickly making her way away from them.

Leopold Blakeley hadn't been able to hide his surprise when Malcolm McFadden walked into his office unannounced that afternoon. Malcolm had gotten right to the point. "Amalie is with Violette. The others are with her, but she is no match for that bitch. You need to come with me now."

Leopold had thrown on his coat and followed his archenemy without question. He learned that they all had attended a WSPU meeting at St. Ignatius church hall and that Malcolm and Harvey had accompanied the women to make sure they were safe.

"It turned out that one of the speakers was your past mistress, who hates men. Understandable, it seems, due to her past experience with you. You never seem to be available to look after your wife, but this is your mess to clean up. God alone knows your history with this woman, but I imagine she's giving our innocent Amalie a full account of it."

Leopold was too concerned to take offense at McFadden's tone. "I forbade her to attend these meetings. She never listens to me! Is Blanche with her? Bridgette?"

Malcolm reassured him that Blanche had been taking care of the matter when he left them there. Finally, they were dropped off at the little tea shop where the whole abhorrent scene was being enacted.

Leopold was almost as shocked to see Violette as she him. He thought she looked old and unrefined, as sour as Amalie was sweet. He wondered how he ever could have touched her, although she had been different back then. The last fourteen years had done little to improve her countenance or her manners.

Moira Mungavin, on the other hand, felt her heart leap at the sight of Leopold Blakeley. The years had been very generous to him. He was devastatingly handsome and dressed immaculately in the finest-quality attire. There was murder in his eyes, but that only served to render him more attractive in hers. She knew in that moment that she had never stopped loving him, in fourteen years, in spite of all of his past ill treatment of her. She also knew that he was the real reason for her return to England following her divorce. Mr. Mungavin had been a kind and giving man. He had been most generous with regard to her divorce settlement and had even paid for her first-class ticket back to England, allowing her to return as an upper-middle-class, respectable widow. Leopold Blakeley possessed neither of these qualities, but wasn't that a part of his allure? She had planned all along to meet with him. She had imagined him older but still unmarried. Hadn't he told her that he had little intention of ever seeking a respectable wife? Yet here she was—his little respectable wife—afraid to open her mouth. Moira Mungavin knew she would readily resume her love affair with Leopold Blakeley, even with his little wife pining away in his big castle.

He was first to speak, flatly, cruelly. "What are you doing here? How dare you address my wife?"

Moira turned to the young woman, who, wide-eyed, appeared to be backing away from them. She was very lovely, and Moira had noticed her in the church hall, admiringly so until she found out who she was. She responded, "Oh, Leo, you can't seriously be telling me that little nitwit is enough for a man like you?"

Amalie had had enough. She turned to run off, but Malcolm, Cordelia, and Imogen caught up with her quickly. Blanche had refused to leave her brother alone with that trollop, as she referred to her.

The trio decided to take Amalie home. Harvey could take care of the rest of the women, including Dolores, to whom Malcolm hadn't given a second thought.

The train journey felt endless to Amalie. In their first-class compartment she finally allowed her tears to fall. "Oh, why did I sit there like a dummy? Why didn't I defend myself? Because everything she said was true. I am a little, boring, stupid nitwit, and could that be the real reason he married me? For heirs? I brought all this upon myself. I brought Leo and that horrible woman back together."

Cordelia held and shushed her. Malcolm wanted to do so, very badly, but as always, he knew he couldn't, so he consoled her instead by saying, "Amalie, that was hate and disgust on your husband's face, and for all I think of Blakeley, his one concern today was you. Whatever she said to you was just jealous, vindictive nonsense."

Imogen added, "Yes, that's what I saw, and this is really my fault, although she seemed so different from the woman in the photograph."

Amalie remembered that they'd brought the photo with them. "Who has the photograph? Blanche?"

Cordelia said, "Yes, and God help the woman who tries to mess with her brother or her little Amie!"

Amalie laughed at this, slightly cheered, but she still felt small. She still felt stupid to have run away and left her man with that awful woman. *Thank God Blanche stayed with him*, she thought.

Finally, they arrived at Blakefield Castle. None of the others were there as yet, and Amalie was glad. She ran upstairs to Bridgette, followed by Cordelia and Imogen.

Bridgette held her petite lovingly as Cordelia and Imogen

explained what had happened. They both marveled at the love between Bridgette and her mistress, and as Amalie wept in her arms, Bridgette murmured reassurances to her in French.

Bridgette then stood and announced, "I am going to run ma petite a lovely, warm, rose-scented bath. Would you like that, petite?"

Amalie nodded gratefully, and Cordelia and Imogen, both exhausted, were happy to leave them to it.

ᥫᦉᥬ

Malcolm had, of course, been excluded from the feminine chat in Amalie's bedroom. He so wanted to console her. She was the most magnificent woman he had ever beheld and with a heart as pure as it was loving. He noticed that the turret door was very slightly ajar. It was usually kept locked, but there had been such chaos the past couple of days. He looked around, and since no one appeared to be about, he took a chance and crept up the narrow winding stairs.

There it was: the painting. It was covered with a canvas cloth, but he had come this far, so he gently removed the cover. There she was—a goddess. He felt tears in his eyes, the eyes that had adored her for two long, yearning years. Her beauty was beyond compare—her breasts, her legs, those eyes that seemed to be looking back at him with a welcoming smile. He sat down on the bench and couldn't hold back his tears. Unrequited love, the very worst love of all.

Suddenly, he was startled by footsteps on the stairs. He looked up expectantly. Blakeley had to still be in London, and he didn't care who it was otherwise. His emotions were at a pitch.

It was Imogen, and she didn't appear surprised to see him there, staring at her beautiful work. "I thought I'd find you here," she said. "She's very lovely, isn't she? Even my painting does not fully do her justice. I worked much harder on this one than on the other. I know you love her. I love her too. She's in her bath, crying that she is stupid and boring, when we both know she's magnificent. I have something for you."

Imogen opened up the old oak chest for which Amalie had given her the key. She then lovingly produced a much smaller version of the painting that now stood exposed before them. The detail was amazing, even though it was not much bigger than Violette's photograph, and Malcolm was stunned.

"You're giving this to me? Truly? Does Amalie know about it? I want to pay you for it, anything—name your price."

Imogen handed him the painting. "I don't want payment. I've already been paid handsomely for those that were commissioned by Leo. But where will you keep it? And what about your wife? How will you hide it? I doubt Dolores will be pleased, and she would tell Leo. This is just between us."

Malcolm insisted, "No, I must pay you. I can't accept it otherwise. What about Amalie? I don't want to upset her. Does she know?"

Imogen answered thoughtfully, "Yes, I suppose I should require payment for such an exquisite piece. What do you think? One hundred guineas? Amalie might find out after you sail. She won't be upset. We talked about it, but although I think she wanted you to have it, she was afraid to say yes. I don't want to make money from my friend's kindness, however. I love her too, and it doesn't feel right. Leo's never asked to see it. Amalie asked me if he had, and I wouldn't lie. I think she was a little hurt."

With a sad smile Malcolm responded, "Maybe he snuck up like me."

"Perhaps," Imogen said. In that moment they heard voices coming from the great hall, and Malcolm had to make a quick exit.

"Please keep it just now," he said. "Two hundred guineas.

And that's a bargain for such a prize. Give me a couple of days, and don't mention it until I am gone. I have no wish to embarrass her. However, please when you do tell her, make sure she understands it's the most beautiful and wonderful painting that I have ever beheld and that I will treasure it all my life."

And he was gone, back to Dolores. Back to the stark reality that was his life.

❧

Henrietta and Annabelle immediately ran up to see Amalie. Cordelia forestalled them first to explain what had occurred since they were last together. Blanche and Leopold still had not returned, and they all wondered what was taking so long. He, at the very least, should have been in a hurry to come home and reassure and comfort his wife.

Amalie was lying atop her bed. Her room, as always, smelled of roses, and she had changed out of the sophisticated suit she had chosen to wear to London. Her hair was down, tied with a blue ribbon, and she was wearing a simple white lawn dress, and as such she looked like a little girl.

Henrietta exclaimed, "Despicable woman! A harlot! No one you need concern your pretty head with, my dear, although I wonder what's keeping them. I hope Blanche hasn't been arrested! She had murder in her eyes!"

Everyone laughed, as they usually did at Henrietta's singular way of thinking, even Amalie, although a little sadly.

Cordelia surprisingly added, "Henrietta, for once I agree with you, but I'm glad she stayed with Leo. She refused to leave him."

Amalie spoke up now. "That's what I should have done, instead of running away like a little coward. What must he think of me? What do you all think of me? And Harvey too and Annabelle, not to mention stupid Dolores. She must have enjoyed it all immensely!"

Annabelle responded, "Harvey thinks you're a dear, sweet girl. We all do. And Dolores was livid at Malcolm. I can see those two getting divorced when they get back to the States."

Henrietta was about to reprimand her daughter for such a comment but reconsidered. "Actually, my dear, that might be for the best. He clearly still loves our Amalie and demonstrated that fully today!"

Amalie said, "You have no idea, Annabelle! She told Leo that I'm a nitwit and not enough for a man like him—that he only married me for heirs for his money. She called him a proficient lover, and she made fun of me as a wife, and I didn't stand up for myself—I ran away. Oh, how could he ever have touched such a woman? And if that is indeed his preference, then he must be very bored with me. Perhaps he has a new mistress? Perhaps more than one?"

Henrietta silenced her. "Stuff and nonsense, Amalie, all of it—sheer jealousy. The man's devoted to you, and well you know it! Now tonight we will dine casually in the conservatory. No need for fine gowns, and Amalie, you look lovely as you are, fresh and sweet and such a comparison to that woman today—I will not say her name. When brother and sister come home, they will take us as they find us, and as usual Mr. March is uninformed. If Leopold wishes to bring him up-to-date, so be it!"

So it was decided. All of the women chose fresh and simple attire that evening—all except Dolores, who was overdressed and uninformed—and Cordelia and Amalie joined arms as they proceeded down to the conservatory. It was a beautiful sunny evening. Amalie kissed Malcolm's cheek and thanked him for all he had done for her that day. He almost seemed to blush, which somewhat surprised Amalie, although she was not surprised by the murderous look she received from Dolores.

No sooner were they seated than they heard voices in the great hall.

Cordelia announced, "It seems the prodigal siblings have returned at last."

Amalie's heart skipped a beat when Mr. Carmichael came in to announce that the master and his sister were freshening up before dinner.

When Amalie asked Cordelia what this could mean, Cordelia kissed her hand and said, "Perhaps it means they want to freshen up, Amie?"

The others laughed—well, all but the McFaddens, who also were clearly not speaking to one another.

A short while later, Blanche and Leopold finally joined the others. Leopold was wearing a freshly starched white shirt, which was his usual attire, but he had forgone a tie and dinner jacket. Amalie was staring at him, wide-eyed and breathless. This was what he had expected, of course. In so many ways she was like a child, in so many other ways a sensuous and incredible woman. He could have punched that other woman when she'd attempted to make fun of his beloved wife, a vile creature from a dissolute time in his life that he wished his pure and sweet Amalie had never borne witness to.

⤮

He and Blanche had gotten rid of her fairly quickly, in the middle of the street. He fervently hoped that no one had seen them, and he and his sister had laughed later about how dangerous his road to a knighthood had become.

He had told Moira Mungavin that she repulsed him, and Blanche had followed up by viciously threatening to make public the clothing and the photograph should Moira ever attempt to contact Blanche's brother or sister-in-law at any time in the future. They both knew that their behavior toward this poor woman was merciless and cruel, but they needed to get their point across. This was a side to both of them that Amalie had never witnessed; not even Cordelia had really—or not to this extent.

Brother and sister had gone to grab a late lunch or an early dinner and had polished off a bottle of red wine between them. Neither had felt ready to face their respective and respectable partners. Leopold loved sweet Amalie more than his life. Blanche loved her too and was angry at herself for exposing the sweet girl to such wickedness.

Leopold told his sister that she couldn't possibly have known that "Violette" would be the keynote speaker, but Blanche guiltily confessed the whole Covent Garden plan to him.

"Amalie can be very persuasive, Blanche. We both know that. I've had six years of her often outrageous yet always adorable schemes and revelations. You've borne witness to many of them too. I wouldn't want her any other way, and I fervently hope she took nothing of what that woman said to heart. I'm ashamed and embarrassed by it all, but for Christ's sake, Blanche, look at the example we had to follow from our parents. And I was thirty-two when first I met Amalie. It was like she stepped out of a dream or down from heaven. I never presented myself as a saint, yet she loved me in spite of everything. She changed me—made me a better man. She brought you and me together too, for I doubt it would have happened otherwise—which would have been a tragedy. I hope she doesn't think the worst of me for today's treachery. I pray she doesn't."

Blanche responded easily, "Leo, you know little Amie better than anyone. She probably did take what that evil woman said to heart. She'll be thinking she's boring and stupid and that you have at least half a dozen mistresses. You'll soon convince her otherwise, and she'll love you with all she's got. The girl is crazy about you—has been from the start." She added playfully, "God alone knows why, however, little brother!"

Leopold knew that this was probably true, and he rejoiced

in it as they eventually made their way to King's Cross station, hand in hand.

⁂

Edward March was at a loss about what was going on, and when Leopold joined him in a large brandy, he said he would tell Edward about it the next day over lunch at the club, but at the present time he needed to go to Amalie.

Cordelia moved over so Leopold could sit beside his wife. He took her hand, at a loss for what to say since everyone appeared to be looking at him. The decision was taken away from him, however, when Amalie, after staring at him wide-eyed, even as he smiled warmly at her, suddenly leapt up and sprang from the room. It was as he'd expected, and he excused himself by saying, "I believe that's my cue to follow." He picked up a bottle of brandy and two glasses and followed her slowly from the room.

Malcolm watched him with jealousy, Dolores with envy, and the rest of those gathered with amusement, as they turned the conversation toward the play and Lady Agatha's arrival the following day.

⁂

"Amalie, open the door," Leopold said calmly, standing outside his wife's locked bedroom door.

Bridgette had told him that her petite was calling herself a nitwit. "Mon Dieu, Monsieur, this is all your doing, and you must put it right."

Eventually, Amalie opened the door, slowly and with a petted lip. "I'm sorry. I ran away. I'm a nitwit, and I'm boring, and you have every right to be angry!"

Leopold put down the bottle and glasses. "Amalie, seriously? I know you don't believe that. And I have no right to be angry unless you mean because you attended one of those damn meetings when I told you not to do so."

Amalie just stared up at him, saying nothing.

"Aren't you going to speak to me, my darling? Do you think I'm a monster? This is very unfortunate, Amalie—an unfortunate coincidence—although I understand your plan was to seek her out anyway. Why? What did you think you'd achieve? It seems Mrs. Mungavin has arisen from the gutter, but her mind will always remain there. I'm ashamed of it, Amalie. But it's long past. Can we move on now? You have your play this week and Lady Agatha's visit."

Amalie felt he was speaking to her like a child, which was no more than she deserved, so she proceeded to act like one. "I don't think I want to be in the play. I'm not a real actress, as you said before. Nor do I want to be one, now that I've met one. I just want to hide in my room and never come out. It's too embarrassing. Why haven't you asked to see the painting? I'm sorry I did it now. I'm not alluring. I'm not enough for you. You only married me for heirs."

Exasperated, Leopold pulled his delightfully spoiled and cosseted wife onto his lap. "Aren't you going to look at me? Or is the pattern on the carpet more interesting? It might be. I do need a shave."

Amalie smiled unwillingly but kept her eyes on her sumptuous lilac and yellow flooring. He lifted her chin and kissed her. Of course, she responded; she always did. But the woman's face and her words came back to Amalie, and she jumped up.

"What about what she said? What about my stupid painting? Why didn't I defend myself? Why did you really marry me? Why were you such a proficient lover—that's what she said! What did you and Blanche talk to her about?"

She was working herself up again. *My princess*, thought Leopold, *jealous of an old witch*. "Okay, Amalie. First of all, I confess, I've watched your painting go from a mere outline to the magnificent piece of art that now stands in the east turret. It is too beautiful for my dressing room, yet I don't want others to see it. Perplexing. I have the master key. Remember, I'm the master. I thought you'd be angry with me if I told you I was watching it through the stages of its creation, but really I couldn't help myself from doing so."

Amalie was elated. She had been somewhat hurt that he appeared to have no interest in the painting's creation. "Do you think it looks like me? I haven't seen it yet. I'm kind of scared to look at it, actually."

Leopold easily responded, "Do you want to see it now? With me?"

Amalie blushed. "Oh, I don't know. It's embarrassing, especially after what Mrs. Mungavin said about me."

Leopold stood and took her hand. "I married the most beautiful girl in the world—a true lady, in every sense of the word. Too much of a lady to have a cat fight in the middle of the street, unlike her sister-in-law, who took care of the matter on her behalf—mercilessly, as I recall, but you know Blanche. And Blanche loves her little Amie. Oh, and it seems she loves me too."

If that was meant to console Amalie, it didn't. "Now I really sound like a boring nitwit! And what about what she said?"

Leopold finally got the message. Amalie was the most sensuous woman he ever could have imagined, even in his youth, when he had dared to imagine that such a woman could exist. How could she not know this? "Amalie, you're not a nitwit; you're intelligent and creative. You're never, ever boring, and this is a little embarrassing, but I'll try. You want me to reassure you? As a lover? Amalie, how could you ever doubt that? As for heirs—well, Amalie, that part is ridiculous, and you know it."

Amalie had to admit to herself that she was feeling decidedly better, and it seemed after six years, she could still embarrass her Englishman with her frankness. Therefore, after her awful day courtesy of his old mistress, she thought to turn the tables on him and his confident, smug expression. Amalie knew she satisfied her husband. How could a woman not know such a thing? And their lovemaking was beyond what she could have imagined as a girl, or at least until that very first kiss. So she asked him straight out, unable to hold back her little smile, although she tried, "Leo, do I fully satisfy your desire in bed? That is my question. Your old lady friend thought I could not possibly do so—you being so proficient and everything."

Amalie thought she noticed a slight blush, but all he said was "More to the point, do I satisfy my saucy French siren?" He was laughing now, as was she.

"Is that the only answer I am to receive from my buttoned-up Englishman?"

"Yep," he said. "After today's escapade? Anyway, too much of a gentleman to say more. Now let's to the turret, madam."

Amalie slapped his arm playfully. "I will make you answer that question a bit later!"

"I'm sure you will try," he laughingly responded, "and I might even answer you at that time."

❧

Amalie was gazing at her naked, tastefully draped self with a furrowed brow. Leopold had removed the covering and was watching Amalie's reaction, since it seemed this was the first time she had viewed the painting.

"Is that really me? I mean, is that what I look like to you? Is it accurate, do you think? I think possibly Imogen has been too kind to me in her rendition."

"Ah," said Leo, "you find fault? I think it's an excellent

likeness of my beautiful wife, and I am the best judge of that. The painting is exquisite, as are you."

"Truly?" she said. "I was concerned about my curves, you know, having given birth to two children—your heirs—but if you think that's what my body looks like, you should know."

The painting portrayed Amalie lying partially on her side, completely naked with the exception of a sapphire-blue silk scarf draped tastefully for a little modesty. She was smiling seductively, and her hair was somewhat tussled. Amalie loved the painting. She was studying it with a little smile upon her lips, examining the curvature of her waist and hips, her legs and breasts, even her hair and eyes.

Leopold was watching her. "Is that a smug little smile that I see upon your face, my love? You are quite pleased with yourself, aren't you? I wonder what thoughts are being stirred up in that brain of yours."

Amalie was feeling a little smug, most certainly after her humiliating afternoon, being called names by his past mistress. "I was thinking if that is truly how you see me, no wonder you pursued me so vehemently when first we met—I mean, compared to what you were used to, that is."

"Ouch!" he said with mock severity. "Actually, I thought it was you who pursued me? However, I do admit that you were a slight improvement."

Leopold covered up the canvas, and as Amalie was about to take offense at the word "slight," he started working at the buttons on her dress, saying that he wanted to compare the painting with the real thing.

Amalie ran away laughing, followed by her handsome husband, who was also laughing, with every intention of carefully examining the subject of the painting. Once they both reached the lilac and sunshine-yellow bedroom, all thoughts of Moira Mungavin were forgotten—at least for the time being.

CHAPTER 15
Dueling Pistols

"I feel I've spent the entire summer making discoveries about my husband and his deplorable family and then being told to forget I ever made them. And now this?"

Amalie had taken Imogen up into the attics to view all the paintings that Amalie had unceremoniously placed there, gradually, during the first years of her marriage. She felt the need to confess that she and Leopold had viewed Imogen's painting of her the previous night, and it turned out he had been following the painting's progress without ever mentioning it to her.

Imogen wasn't totally surprised and asked what she should do with the painting. They laughed about how to get it down the stairs without asking for assistance. Amalie wanted to place it in her husband's dressing room so he could figure out where to put it. It clearly couldn't remain where it was, yet it seemed sinful to hide it away. It was beautiful and showcased the artist's talent every bit as much as the subject's beauty. Amalie thanked Imogen profusely for such a flattering rendition, and Imogen insisted that it was exactly how Amalie appeared in her eyes.

The subject of hiding paintings away was what had decided them upon the tour of the attics. While Imogen perused the paintings, Amalie was digging through an old wardrobe, seeking out more buried treasure, similar to the caftans. Leopold's family history still fascinated her, most especially because he very rarely spoke of it, or at least he seemed to know very little about it. Many old English families like his were only too proud to discuss their heritage, but not he, and certainly not Blanche.

This was when she made yet another discovery. "Imogen, look! How fascinating! These are old dueling pistols. What a beautiful wooden case, so dirty and uncared for. I wonder why it's hidden in this old wardrobe under old costumes. I wonder about the story of the costumes too. Stage costumes, I would think. What a secretive and mysterious family. These must be the costumes he had in mind for the Castilian fancy dress ball in 1898. It was forestalled in favor of regular evening attire, thank God! First that horrid armoire downstairs and now this? I wonder if there is a connection."

Amalie was intrigued. Her imagination was fully engaged. Leopold was in London with her uncle. They would be bringing Lady Agatha back later that day, and Amalie considered this a perfect opportunity for further investigation, without delay.

"We need to fetch Malcolm to examine the pistols," she said with drama. "He must know about guns. And Blanche—she might know about the costumes." Both women ran downstairs to fetch Malcolm for his assistance.

Shortly afterwards, Blanche and Cordelia joined the group in the attic, where they found Imogen and Malcolm sitting on the floor beside Amalie, who was holding a wooden box containing a very old set of dueling pistols, her eyes wide like saucers.

"Blanche, who is MWB? The initials on the case?" Amalie handed the pistol she was holding to Malcolm. "Malcolm, you must know about guns. What do you make of these? They're not in very nice condition. My father had a set, Jean Le Page. They are very beautiful and rumored to have been owned by Napoleon. I keep them hidden away. I've never shown them to Leo, though I always intended to give them to him one day, actually. Somehow, I never have."

Malcolm examined each one. "The condition is very poor. Wogdon and Barton, 1797. Fine gunsmiths. They're old for sure, but the mechanism on this one isn't right. It appears to have been tampered with. They have not been taken care of anyway."

Blanche sat down on the floor, as did Cordelia, and they both examined the guns. "Amie dearest? You never fail to amaze! Where do you keep your father's hidden?"

"In my closet. Leo would never dare go in there. I will show you them later."

Everyone looked at Amalie with some surprise.

Blanche shook her head. "I have no idea about these, Amie. It seems you have uncovered another mystery." She looked to Malcolm. "What do you mean, tampered with? Deliberately? As in a cheat?" Before he could answer, she continued, "I don't know those initials, Amie, but clearly a Blakeley. Where exactly did you find them?"

"In that wardrobe under those moth-eaten costumes. Do you think there was a murder committed at Blakefield? If there was a duel and someone cheated, that's murder! Oh, we must investigate this! Oh, how confounding!"

Blanche approached the wardrobe and suddenly grew thoughtful. She all of a sudden remembered this wardrobe and the costumes inside it. It all came flooding back. She and Leopold used to play in the attics as children, dressing up in the elaborate costumes. She also remembered the day Leopold discovered the gun case. They used to play with the pistols, pretending to be soldiers, until one day Leo fell and broke his by accident. He was so little at the time. The mechanism had been so old and delicate, and it hadn't been deliberate. Their father had discovered it, however, and her brother had received such a thrashing that the siblings had never gone up again. She didn't want to share her memories of that awful day, not even with Cordelia and Amie. She had almost forgotten the incident, one of many from their abusive childhood, and wondered that her brother still kept the pistols. Did he even know they were up here?

Just then Bridgette came to seek out Amalie. This cut short any further speculation. Bridgette quickly dismissed the guns and exclaimed, "You must make haste, ma petite. You are filthy! McBride will be back soon with Lady Agatha and the master. Mon Dieu! What next in this household?"

As all stood up to go downstairs, Blanche said, "Perhaps no one should mention the pistols just yet, until we find out who the initials belong to."

Everyone agreed. However, Amalie wasn't really listening to her, too absorbed in wondering about yet another strange discovery.

Soon afterwards, Lady Agatha was settled in her suite, and Amalie, already dressed for dinner, rushed along the hallway to sit with her. She poured out her story about Moira Mungavin and the pistols and the Castilian costumes. She even told her about the black stallion and Leopold's intention of tearing down the folly.

"Child, it seems I have been missing much activity at Blakefield Castle! It's so good to be back among it again! But you really mustn't be putting it about with regard to your husband's past. All men have a past, but you are his present and his future."

Amalie looked shamefaced until the duchess added mischievously, "Still, I am curious about the photograph. You must have Blanche show it to me later. As for the initials, they can be easily identified. Isn't there a family Bible?"

Just then Bridgette appeared to fix Lady Agatha's hair. It had become the duchess's habit not to bring O'Rourke to carry out the task, and so it fell to Bridgette to take care of her.

When Amalie said that she had never seen a Bible at Blakefield, Bridgette stated quite flatly, "The monsieur keeps it in his safe. It was open one day when I went to see him about something or other, and I briefly saw inside the safe before he closed it. I think it was a Bible. It looked like one anyway."

Amalie was shocked. "Oh, Bridgette, why didn't you tell me? Did you see anything else? He has never allowed me to look inside the safe. I wish I knew the combination! What a bizarre creature my husband turns out to be! I mean, who keeps the family Bible in a safe? I wonder what he is hiding."

Lady Agatha laughed, "Oh, dearest Amalie, how dull my life would be had never I found you! It seems that we shall soon need to find out!"

Leopold finally appeared to take the ladies down to dinner and said, "Dare I ask, Duchess, what my wife is conjuring up for me now?"

"No, you certainly may not," she responded with a smile to Amalie. "Or you may ask, but I shall not tell you!"

By the time they went into dinner, the duchess on Leopold's arm and Amalie on Malcolm's, with Dolores walking behind, as had become usual when Lady Agatha was in residence, Leopold was convinced there was again some treachery afoot in his home. And it seemed that everyone was in on it, except, of course, Edward and Dolores. There were all sorts of looks and smiles going back and forth between his wife and visitors, yet his sister looked uncomfortable. He was impatiently waiting to confront his wife about it later. He was well aware that she was not about to let the subject of Violette drop as yet, but was there also another matter causing her wide-eyed drama?

Once seated and served, Lady Agatha asked, conversationally, "Leopold dear, you must allow me to peruse your family Bible.

Have you added your wife and children's names to it? Where do you keep it?"

Amalie had to cover up a giggle with a cough, most especially when Blanche added, "Come to think of it, Leo, where is it? I haven't seen it in years."

Amalie, of course, had shared Bridgette's knowledge with Blanche and Cordelia, who both seemed as mystified as Amalie.

Leopold looked uncomfortable as he answered, "I will need to look it out, Duchess. It is somewhere about."

Amalie couldn't prevent the giggle that escaped her, and Leopold stated calmly, "I know there is some conspiracy afoot, yet again, in my home. Am I to find out during dinner or later this evening, beloved?"

Amalie thought, *Your home, your Bible, your dinner, but whose pistols?*' She responded, "Well, actually, I came across the initials MWB on something and wondered who it could be. Blanche doesn't know, so we thought we could look it up in the family Bible, which I've never been shown."

"I can save you the trouble of looking, Amalie. There were several Blakeleys named Mortimer. Possibly my great-grandfather or great-great-grandfather. Where did you find these initials, dearest?"

Amalie was wide-eyed. This was easier than she had expected. "And the W?"

"William, I imagine. I'm not sure. Are you going to tell me, my love?" Leopold seemed to be growing impatient with her.

Amalie knew she was headed for another put-down at dinner, so she just said, "Nowhere important, Leo. Never mind." She wondered if he had the combination of the safe written down.

Lady Agatha took the matter up from there. "Mr. Havemeyer, as you may well imagine, we English have many skeletons in our proverbial closets. Some of us quite literally, it seems."

Harvey Havemeyer just smiled pleasantly at the duchess.

Amalie had informed Annabelle and Henrietta of their unusual discovery, and since Annabelle had told him, the only uninformed people were, as usual, Leopold, Edward, and of course, Dolores, who had been dropped from the inner circle in favor of her husband. Harvey was looking forward to seeing how this latest distraction would play out.

The conversation felt a bit stilted after that, until Amalie decided to announce, "My father owned a magnificent set of Napoleonic dueling pistols of the highest quality and condition, and they have never been fired. He used to show them to me as a girl, and I found that fact quite comforting. I'm not sure what made me think of them."

Leopold had known nothing of these pistols—another of his wife's revelations—and he would have loved to have owned such a pair. "How fortunate for you, my dear. I would like to have seen these mysterious pistols. But tell me, how can firearms be comforting? I am intrigued. And for that matter, where are they now? With the count?"

Amalie smiled serenely. "Oh, there's no mystery surrounding them. My father bought them from a reputable dealer in Paris. And of course, I found it comforting to know that they had never been used to murder someone in cold blood. I'm not sure where they are, actually."

Since most knew the reason for Amalie's evocative comments, they sat quietly, silently enjoying the dialogue between their hosts, a couple who could never resist challenging one another, possibly due to the passion between them, which appeared to have grown rather than lessened after six years of marriage. Lady Agatha never failed to marvel at this when in their company, having never experienced any such passion with her late husband, the duke. She always so very much enjoyed her time with the Blakeleys.

Leopold did not believe that his wife knew nothing of the

whereabouts of such sought-after and highly expensive items, but he let that pass with everyone seated around them and instead said, "My dear, in days of old, duels were considered a matter of honor. If a man fell, it was not particularly perceived as cold-blooded murder, as you describe it."

Amalie felt she had the advantage. "Well, I suppose if all was equal and aboveboard between the two participants."

"Meaning?" Leopold was quite certain that once again, he was being set up. However, never having participated in a duel himself, he waited for sweet Amalie to trip herself up.

"Well, dear husband, I am sure there were cheats—cowardly men who turned too soon or perhaps tampered with the pistols?"

"That is why gentlemen chose their own seconds, whose duty it was to ensure that the duel was carried out honorably and with equal weaponry." He stood up. "Ladies?"

"Ah," said Amalie, "my apologies, ladies. I seem to have neglected my duties as hostess so that my husband is forced to inform us that it is time to withdraw. He is always the honorable gentleman after all."

Once the ladies had left them, Edward exclaimed, "What was that all about, Leo? Felt she was goading you into some admission. My niece is such a caution, what? Keeps you on your toes, I'll warrant."

Leopold responded, "God alone knows, Edward. Yesterday I was a womanizer, and today I apparently cheated in a duel, although I have never actually participated in one. McFadden, I'm sure you are well aware of what is going on. I'd be most appreciative if you would let me in on the matter."

Malcolm felt he had no option but to tell his host of the discovery. He almost felt sorry for Blakeley as the women conspired against him—almost.

Leopold grew thoughtful, remembering, but said lightly, "Ah, what next? Where did she hide these murderous weapons? Never mind. I fully intend to find out."

The conversation turned to other matters, including the upcoming cricket match against the village. Blakefield Castle had to come up with eleven competent players to avoid being beaten for the third year in a row by the village team. Malcolm had played two years previously and was looking forward to it. Harvey was willing to try, and the rest of the team would be made up of Freddie Allsop, possibly his brothers, McBride, and several of the more able-bodied servants. Coming up with eleven competent players was never an easy task.

When the men joined the ladies, the cricket match was still being discussed, and Dolores opined, "Oh, I wish I could take part in it!"

Leopold smiled indulgently at Dolores as Amalie responded, "Oh, Dolores, you must realize the humiliation for the gentlemen should we ladies be permitted to form a team and then very soundly beat them!"

All laughed at the absurdity of such a notion until Leopold said, "I am quite certain that some ladies could certainly challenge the gentlemen, given half a chance. However, I don't see my wife as a possible contender. You are far too little, ma petite. By the way, I heard about the pistols you discovered. Where did you hide them?"

Amalie looked at Malcolm questioningly, just as Lady Agatha interrupted with a change of topic. "So are the performers all prepared for tomorrow night's performance?"

The conversation turned to the play and how well everyone knew their lines, and Leopold was forced to wait for his answer until they all retired for the night, when he could get Amalie alone. He was always forced to behave himself when Lady Agatha was a guest in his home.

Meanwhile, Amalie confided quietly to Lady Agatha, "Would

you mind terribly if I changed the ending of the play, just a little bit? I have just decided that perhaps Miss Mabel should turn Lord Goring down. After all, he is such a cad!"

The duchess laughed. "Oh, my dear, just look at Lord Goring scowling at you. I don't think I would accept him either!"

It was soon time for Amalie to assist the grand dame up to her suite, where Bridgette was waiting to attend her.

Before saying good night, Amalie said, "Lady Agatha, I don't think Leo likes me much—as a person, I mean. He is always making fun of me. And now thanks to Malcolm, I will be interrogated later about the pistols. I still have my father's, by the way. I was going to give them to him a long time ago. I just never did. I don't think I ever will. He can have his old broken ones and his photograph of Violette. They belong to him, after all, like everything else in this mausoleum."

Lady Agatha called Amalie to sit with her, and Bridgette poured them both a glass of sherry, which was the duchess's preference to a cup of warm milk and honey, and gratefully bid them both good night.

The duchess took Amalie's hand. "I have decided that you must call me Aunt Agatha, my dear, a privilege I will allow no others, not even my great-niece. I am so very fond of you and of Leopold, so heed me well. Your husband loves you so very much. However, he has built up a defense, I believe to protect himself. Why do you confide so much in Mr. McFadden? I can see you like him, and he is most definitely in love with you. Is he so much easier to talk to than Leopold? I think you worry overmuch about your husband's moodiness. If you don't take him on so, he might improve somewhat. He always seems pleasant enough to me. I think sometimes you bring out the worst in him. But that is because he loves you so very much yet feels he doesn't deserve you."

There was a knock at the door, which produced Blanche and

Cordelia. Lady Agatha asked them to join them and then shared the thoughts she had confided to Amalie.

Amalie said, "Lady Agatha has graciously allowed me to call her Aunt, and I am so much honored." She then continued, "I talk to Malcolm because he is always kind. He never belittles or makes fun of me, but I could never love him as I do Leo, and yet Leo always does these things to me. Well, not always, but he does it a lot. Perhaps there is something wrong with me." Amalie was clearly feeling sorry for herself. "I don't think he finds me exciting like Violette."

Blanche groaned, "Oh, Amie! Utter nonsense! I have to tell you something before you get yourself into any more bother. But first"—she handed the old photograph to Lady Agatha—"what do you think, Duchess?"

The duchess studied the subject carefully with her monocle and a very critical eye. She then exclaimed, "Oh, Amalie, how can you even compare yourself to her? She's just plain awful, with legs like tree trunks. Young men often seek out these types of women, and then they grow up and settle down with respectable maidens. It is a terrible shame you found it. Leopold should have destroyed it years ago, along with these costumes and undergarments. Have they been destroyed now?"

Amalie said peevishly, "I don't believe so. They are not mine to destroy. That's up to him, I suppose. Now I sound really exciting. So he already had his fun, in other words, and then settled for me? He did say he could tell that I had never been kissed. And there was that day with Mrs. Sutton. It is all too much! What did you need to tell me, Blanche?"

But Blanche had changed her mind. If anything, it was Leo's place to tell the story and not hers, so she said, "Never mind. It wasn't important. But Amie, I have to say this—are you not mistress of this house? It is time you made my brother aware of that. Blakefield Castle is beautiful because you made it so, and you are much more fun than either one of those old hags and more beautiful than anyone Leo has ever known or deserved. He was thrilled, I'm sure, to be the first man ever to kiss you. So stop this."

Lady Agatha said, "That is exactly what I was trying to say. It seems it came out all wrong. Your husband isn't belittling you, my dear girl. You are doing it to yourself. Now I must to bed. Tomorrow is a new day, and he will be here with you because that is where he wants to be. I have never seen such love and devotion in any man. Now off to bed!"

Amalie found Leopold waiting for her in her bedroom. He looked cross, and she threw the offensive photograph at him and said, "Your lady friend," before grabbing her chemise and proceeding into the bathroom to get undressed, slamming the door behind her.

When she came out, he was still sitting on the bed, the photograph lying beside him. She grabbed it and threw it into his dressing room, closing the door upon it. "I'm going to bed," she said petulantly, pulling back the covers.

Leopold said, "Can we talk?"

"Tons of opportunity earlier when you were too busy belittling me, as usual. What have I done now, or what am I being commanded to do?" Amalie wasn't sure whether she was angry or hurt, or perhaps a combination of both, but she felt stupid and sick inside.

"Is that how you see me? Not much of a gentleman then. Not like McFadden or perhaps your prince. I need to ask you where you found the pistols, where you put them, and to say no more on the subject to others."

Amalie exclaimed, "The attic, which means I'm banned from there in the future! They are in your girlfriend's bedroom in the chest with her moth-eaten clothes, and okay, I will do as you command and never speak of it again. Perhaps I should just remain quiet like the nitwit I am. You can draw me a map of where I'm allowed to go. I understand not the folly, which is yours and which you're tearing down. I should stay out of the back wing also, in case I find anything else terrible back there. And please have my painting put up in the attic so I can enjoy the east turret if I'm still allowed up there, and I suppose I should stay out of the gardens and the conservatory too. Have I got all that right?"

Leopold just stared at her throughout all of this. He loved her so very much, and he was supposed to be her hero. Yet he brought her down in front of others, even as she loved him when they were alone. He knew it was time to be truthful and confide in her, as one should with a wife. Perhaps that was what a real hero would do, rather than hide his insecurities behind caustic and belittling remarks, made to such an angel who was his wife.

"Amalie, please sit down."

She did breathlessly and on the verge of tears, desperately trying to hold them back. She waited.

"I will attempt to address all of that. Do you remember when I told you I was forbidden to go up to the attic? My father was angry about it, and I got a thrashing? It was me who broke the pistol. That was the real reason for the beating. I was just a child, and Blanche and I were playing soldiers. The place scared me after that day. It was quite a thrashing. I thought he was going to kill me. I looked for the pistols the day you and I were up there. Being with you that day, I felt better, and in my mother's room too. You chased the demons away. You did that the first time I ever saw you. I would ask that Bridgette clear out that chest with the tatty old rags. I don't want to see them ever again, nor do I want to tell the servants. I'm having plans drawn up to fix up your folly, to make it safe because you are so precious to me. I've never thought myself worthy of you, and I really don't mean to belittle you in front of others. I just hope you can love me with all my weaknesses. I fear one day you might stop doing so. As for the painting, I'm putting it in my gallery, which will be locked and shown to very few by appointment only. You are my Venus and not something to be hidden. Finally, the Bible—one night long before I knew you, I got drunk and ripped out all the names. How could I leave that out for anyone to see?"

Amalie was stunned by her husband's frankness and so ashamed of herself for making him peel back all the layers he had built up for himself over the years.

She went to him. "Leo, you will always be my hero. I am a jealous, stupid woman who doesn't deserve you. Can we please forget all of this now and be as one? We just had certain people come into our lives this past summer who had no right to be there. One made me afraid, the other jealous. But Leo, I am too little to ride a stallion, and I was terrible at athletics at school. You are correct. My best friend Beatrice always beat me at tennis and badminton, and I can't even swim. I'm amazed I can ride a horse! But I love to watch you swim and play cricket, even chop wood. I suppose perhaps we are each everything the other isn't. I love that you are so strong and can throw me over your shoulder. I love that you're so smart, and I love that you're so handsome and manly."

Leopold took Amalie into his arms. "And I love that you're little and that I can still throw you over my shoulder. I love how beautiful you've made our homes. I love that you are sweet and gentle and so funny when you are angry at me. Many things, my love. Let us enjoy our good fortune instead of rallying against it. Let's also agree to make sport for our visitors without ever really hurting one another."

They shook hands playfully, and Amalie chanced a question. "Leo, can I sit next to you at dinner? I mean when we have guests. I hate sitting so far away, especially after I've missed you all day. I usually just want to throw my brussels sprouts at you when we are seated so far apart."

He said, "I thought you would want your rightful place, my

darling. It took you six years to ask me that? Does that mean I have to have my sister staring down at me every night, watching my table manners?"

"Yes," said Amalie, getting up and walking over to her enormous closet. As she knelt down to rummage through, she said, "Go ahead, my handsome husband, say what you always say."

Leo responded, putting on a mock serious face, "I think I spoil you overmuch, madam!"

"Ah," she said, standing up, holding a beautiful hand-carved burred-walnut box. "I was waiting for the right time to give you this. I almost did on several occasions, but I'm glad I waited since this is the right time."

Leopold reverently opened the exquisite case, which revealed a perfect set of Napoleonic walnut pistols, pristine and with all the accompanying accoutrements. They appeared reverently cared for, in mint condition, and there inside the case was displayed the Napoleonic crest.

Leopold was speechless. Other than his wife, he had never handled anything quite as well-crafted and exquisite. And it was she who was giving it to him.

"Do you like them, Leo? They need to be cared for. My papa showed me how, but I often forget. They are yours if you would like them. Leo, what? Say something! Are they nice? I've never shown them to anyone but you. My father was a little extravagant. Well, anyway, they are yours now—even though you haven't said a word. You can always keep them in the safe with the Bible." She laughed.

"My love, do you know how valuable these are? They can be ours, surely; they are too fine to be given as a gift. You are really the most amazing girl."

Amalie's heart was so full to have given such prized specimens to the little boy who had had but a few toy soldiers and who had been thrashed so badly for breaking a much lesser item. Leopold

Blakeley was a man who had everything a man could ask for, yet the awe with which he received the walnut box quite amazed Amalie, and she had never loved him more than she did in that moment.

"No," she said, "they are all yours, for I take no further responsibility for their safekeeping."

He seemed almost childlike when he said, "Can we go show them to Blanche?"

"Of course, as you wish. They are yours."

Moments later, they knocked on Blanche's door together. The ladies marveled at the beauty of such an exquisite set and congratulated Leopold on his gift.

Amalie had never felt so proud. Blanche embraced her and whispered, "You have no idea what these mean to my brother."

Amalie responded, "I think I do," and she kissed Blanche's cheek and took her husband's arm to leave. They walked back to their lilac and yellow rose—covered bedroom together, the walnut case held carefully in both of his hands.

CHAPTER 16
An Ideal Husband

"Leo's given me the family Bible! And look, also the pages he ripped out. I've found Mortimer William Blakeley, his great-grandfather, but that's unimportant now. I think he needed to make room in his safe for his new toys. He and my uncle March have shut themselves in his study with the pistols. I hope they're not plotting a duel!"

Amalie had burst into Lady Agatha's suite in order to take her down to breakfast. She was excited since not only was it the day of the play, but also Leopold was finally taking her for her new filly.

"Of course, he's refusing to do a dress rehearsal for tonight, and quite frankly, Aunt Agatha, I doubt he even knows his lines because he has attended only two rehearsals when the rest of us have done six! Cordelia had to stand in for him most of the time!"

Lady Agatha was delighted at how everything had worked out. Amalie exclaimed, "Still, I'm a bit disappointed that there is no murder to investigate!" and Lady Agatha laughed.

The two women were still laughing as they entered the

breakfast room, where they found Leopold and his guests already seated.

"Leo, Aunt Agatha has generously agreed to rewrite your ancestors' names in her beautiful hand, all of them right up from Vlad the Impaler to Leon and Cosette! Isn't that wonderful? Leo, where are your pistols? I thought you would be showing them off."

Everyone was in jolly spirits that morning, even Leopold, who merrily responded, "They are locked away safely in my safe, dearest. I was hoping you wouldn't find out about Great-Uncle Vlad, but it's out now, I suppose."

Everyone laughed at the remark until Dolores asked, in all innocence, "Leo, you have an ancestor called Vlad the Impaler?"

All looked astonishingly at her and then ignored her. Cordelia said, "You know, Amalie, you have just provided your husband with yet another item that he can claim as his!"

"Oh dear, I didn't think of that," laughed Amalie.

Leopold lightly responded, "I had already thought about that, Cordelia, so I've made an important decision. Amalie, you may lay claim to your bedroom, the folly, and the conservatory."

"What about my east turret room?" she asked with mock severity.

"No," he said lightly, "I'm keeping that."

Amalie displayed her petted lip and threw a sausage at her husband, saying, "No, you're not—it's mine!"

Leopold laughingly threw it back, along with another, as the others decided to go about their day and avoid taking part in a threatened food fight.

Blanche asked as she arose from her chair, "Leo, do you know any of your lines for this evening? You've attended only one rehearsal."

"Two," he said, "and probably not."

Leopold was taking Amalie for her filly that morning. She

was happy and excited and so very much in love with him. It shone in her eyes. He could clearly see it since her eyes displayed her every emotion. He loved when she was happy. Her happiness was childlike and pure. Leopold was happy too, because she belonged to him, and the sun was shining, and she had awakened him so sweetly that morning.

"Okay, Amalie, let's go! Do you want to ride with me? If so, you can wear your riding britches. We will walk the horse back. It's not far, but you will need to get to know one another first. She's only three."

Amalie quickly donned her britches and climbed up to sit astride with Leopold. This was the second time he had asked her to do so, and she happily pondered how kind he could be when he had half a mind to be so.

Sir Archibald came out to lead them to the stables. It seemed he was practically a neighbor, and he was very nice. Amalie made a mental note that she must try to get to know some of their neighbors as well as her husband's tenants. It felt like a tall task, especially since she had already lived in Hertfordshire for six years.

The filly was pure white and very lovely. Amalie decided upon Tulip for her name, and Leopold was surprised that she hadn't picked a French name. She laughed happily as she confessed, "Leo, it can be either, only in French one adds an *e* at the end."

He laughed too. He never did employ a French tutor, even with a household that spoke the language fluently, including his children. He had asked if Amalie would teach him, and she had reminded him playfully that he'd hated French class, and that was as far as any further thought about lessons was to get.

Sir Archibald told her that the filly would be small for a mare, at just fourteen hands, and he laughed when she responded that her husband would have chosen the filly deliberately for that reason, since he was always telling her she too was little.

Sir Archibald invited them to dinner and was impressed when Amalie referred to her special guest as Aunt Agatha. He said, "Bring the duchess along with you!"

Amalie shyly agreed and set a date the evening before the duchess was to return to London, providing the duchess was agreeable, of course.

While Amalie was petting Tulip and feeding the filly carrots that Cook had given her that morning, Sir Archibald said quietly to Leopold, "Blakeley, where have you been hiding your wife? She's delightful! My wife will like her very much." He added thoughtfully, "Bit nervous about the duchess, however. Fancy your wife calling her Aunt."

On the ride home, and after thanking her husband profusely for her new filly, Amalie said, "I hope the duchess doesn't mind. I'm a little nervous to meet Lady Beaton. I hope she likes me. Leo, do you think people generally find me aloof? I don't mean to be."

Leopold realized that over the years he had done very little to broaden his wife's horizons, keeping her mostly to himself, and he mentally vowed to do better in the future. "Possibly, my love. Only those closest to you know that you're a little shy. I knew you were shy that first night at dinner at Blakefield—the night my sister sat you at the other end of the table. Others, including Blanche, thought you to be vain and aloof. Well, I suppose you are a little of each, but mostly you're polite and kind. Blanche knows that now, of course, and she looks out for you, as does Bridgette and as do I. That's why you have the loveliest yet smallest mare that my money could buy. You've been near death four times, and I lost you twice, once in London and once in the sea. Do you wonder why I worry so much about keeping you safe?"

They had stopped to allow the horses to drink at the river. "That night at dinner, you hardly looked at me," said Amalie. "I remember it well. I was hoping those seated around me thought me aloof rather than boring. I could barely understand their dialect amid all the conversation at the table that night, and I wished that I had been seated near you. I didn't understand why you had placed me there and thought it was because of the skirt incident in your woods and that possibly you thought me a bit stupid. That was so humiliating!"

He laughed. "No indeed. I found it charming, and when I caught you as you jumped off the tree stump, you took my breath away. I was in turmoil that night at dinner. I had never thought to be married, yet I suddenly knew I wanted you as my bride. But I thought you to be too good for me. I did come to your room—saw you brushing your beautiful hair. I wanted so much to walk inside that room, although I knew I couldn't do so. I'm grateful that you allow me now—well, except, of course, when you lock me out."

Amalie was smiling, enjoying her husband's wonderful romantic mood and thinking, *All this because of dueling pistols?* She whispered, "Leo, thank you so much for everything. For taking care of me and for our beautiful children. I love you so much more than I can even describe to you."

Leopold kissed his wife gently, feeling so peaceful inside. Then he lightened the mood when he admitted, "I don't have a damn clue about my lines for tonight's grand performance."

Amalie responded, "That's what I feared! You are an awful man! I'm in love with a truly crazy man!"

Leopold laughed and simply said, "Yes, madam, but who was it that made me so?"

✑⟶⟲✎

Imogen had done a delightful job of setting up the conservatory for the evening's performance. It seemed that for the most part the drawing room had been abandoned in the evenings in favor of the conservatory except for in the dead of winter.

Imogen would be leaving Blakefield after the cricket match the following week, having no good reason to extend her stay any longer, and she was a little sad to go. She and Amalie had become close after the significant time they had spent together for her sittings, and Amalie now referred to Imogen as her best friend. She had received an open invitation from Amalie to return anytime she wanted to do so, since Amalie had not yet learned of Leo's surprise. He had commissioned a painting of his entire family, including Blanche and Cordelia, as a special Christmas present for her. Consequently, Imogen would be back again in early November, to stay for the whole holiday season.

Blanche and Cordelia knew about the plan and had already decided to remain through to the New Year, most especially since Leopold was planning yet another renewal of his vows on Christmas Eve, to make up for the last time that hadn't quite gone as he'd planned. Everyone, it seemed, delayed their departures from Blakefield Castle for as long as possible. It was a magical place full of fun and drama and most especially love. No one ever felt that they outstayed their welcome, since Amalie always begged them to stay longer—Leopold, not so much, but that was all part of the fun.

The following week, all but Blanche and Cordelia were disappearing for a while, which made Leopold deliriously happy. The McFaddens were going to Scotland, and the others back to London. Soon afterwards would be the accolade and the surprise ball being given by Lady Agatha, which everyone knew about except Amalie. It was to be her surprise after all, and Leopold had sworn them all to secrecy.

The stage was set, and act one was announced by Imogen. She had set everything up so professionally, and the duchess was truly delighted.

Leopold had a vague idea of his lines, and those he improvised drew laughter from their small audience, which included Leon in his country squire suit, Bridgette, and some of the senior staff. Malcolm thought, *The idiot didn't even learn his lines, and now he's stealing the show!'*

Blanche was brilliant as Mrs. Cheveley, since being mean and treacherous came naturally to her, and everyone else at the very least knew their lines.

Amalie tried to play her part to perfection, but it seemed she was also in charge of feeding her husband his lines. This tended to be quite a distraction since Leopold was determined to be ridiculous. He was, however, aware of the play's ending. He was to propose as Lord Goring to the lovely Amalie, who was Miss Mabel. He had known from the start that he intended to exasperate his beloved wife, and if he did it well enough, this would be the first and last play he would ever be asked to perform in.

The final scene was upon them, and Leopold was trying his best to keep a straight face as his wife whispered through clenched teeth, "Propose. You need to propose to me. Oh, Leo, how could you forget that part?"

"Propose what?" he said out loud, feigning ignorance.

"Marriage, you idiot!" By now she was laughing, and so was everyone else. The couple's son was in a fit of giggles.

He finally declared, "Oh, I get it now! You are going to propose to me! Okay, I'm ready."

Amalie stood tapping her foot in mock annoyance until Leopold finally grew serious and got down on one knee. "Amalie, will you marry me again on Christmas Eve? This time I will make the evening's entertainment a little more fun. I promise you."

It took her a moment to realize that he was being serious, and for the third time she happily accepted. She turned to Blanche, who had left the stage, and Blanche said, "What the heck? It's out now. Cordelia and I have to stay through Christmas since my crazy brother is including us in the family portrait."

Amalie looked over to Imogen, who just shrugged her shoulders. Amalie said ecstatically, "Was everyone in on this but me?"

Of course, Dolores shouted, "I wasn't, as usual!"

The performers took their bow, and the audience clapped heartily. It seemed that Leopold indeed had stolen the show, though that certainly had not been his intention.

Lady Agatha said, "Leopold dear, you will have to do better than that in the Christmas pantomime you're putting on for the children. What do you think, Amalie? Would your husband make a pretty Cinderella?"

Leopold said in shock, "But Lady Agatha, that wasn't my intention in messing up my lines!"

The grand dame responded, "Don't I know it, my boy!"

Amalie happily responded, "Absolutely, Aunt Agatha! He will be quite extraordinary in the role!"

Cordelia's martinis were flowing, and there was merriment all around. Even Bridgette joined in the fun.

Amalie did notice that the McFaddens looked a little sad, and she felt sorry for them—but what could she do about it? The day had been one of her happiest ever, and at Blakefield Castle, who could tell what the next day would bring?

CHAPTER 17
Amalie Revealed

The following days were idyllic for the ladies, who took tea in the garden in the late summer sun. Cosette often joined them and behaved like such a little angel that even Lady Agatha was impressed. She often remarked, "Who ever could have imagined the sweetness of this child, given her method of entering the world!" Cosette would sit quite adorably like a little lady, clutching her doll baby and drinking cool sweet tea from a china cup.

Leon was, of course, with the men those fine mornings, watching them practice as he fetched the balls, dressed in cricket whites and whining all the while that his papa was mean, since he wouldn't allow him to play. Leon, at five, knew that he was still too little to play, but that did not prevent him from deliberately giving his father a hard time, much to the amusement of the other men practicing on the field, less so to his father's.

One day, as he walked backed to the house accompanied by Harvey, Leopold said, with a little annoyance, "I understand that Leon wants to join us in practice, but Amalie has him so spoiled. I can't even imagine most boys getting away with half of what he does, and so effortlessly too, without any reprimand from his mother, yet I hesitate to reprimand him, remembering my own father."

Harvey replied thoughtfully, "Leo, there is quite a difference between a good telling-off and a beating. Yes, I see how his mother dotes on him—it's apparent to all—and he knows it full well, I think, and takes full advantage. He looks so very much like you, however—quite uncanny, actually. Possibly, that's why she is so benevolent, since she dotes on you also. When is he off to boarding school? Age eight, as I recall."

"Yes." Leopold was a little embarrassed by the doting remark—he had never thought of it in that manner—but said resignedly, "Three years. I'll have gray hair by then, and his mother will be begging me not to send him. Fatherhood! Still, at one time I never dreamed I'd be a father, a traditional family man. Yet here I am at the mercy of them all."

Harvey laughed. His host was a very lucky man. One just had to look at McFadden to fully comprehend that. He said, "And yet here I am at this age, about to be a father again, after more than twenty years. However, I know it is all worth it, most especially when I gaze upon my wife's happy countenance."

Leopold volunteered, "Harvey, your wife is a true English rose, and probably the nicest of the whole clan."

Harvey responded, "Don't I know it, Leo! Don't think I ever could have kept up with your Amalie, although there's just a year between them. So beautiful and willful. Everyone, it seems, falls in love with her, even the servants. Still, I know you wouldn't have her any other way."

Leopold heartily agreed, since he knew it was the truth of the matter.

The two men found the other men already seated with the ladies, in the process of being served fresh tea and sandwiches. Leopold immediately noticed his daughter sitting happily, feeding pretend food to her dolly, and his son whispering something in his mother's ear.

He lovingly took his baby girl onto his lap, and Amalie smiled over at him. "Papa, can't Leon have just one turn at bat? Or whatever you call it? He so wants to."

Leopold looked over to where his wife and son were both watching him with petted lips and gave a resounding response. "The answer is no! Where's Eloise?"

As if by magic, the children's nanny appeared. Leopold kissed his baby girl before she was led away, and he returned the truculent look given him by his son.

The others wondered how Amalie would react, but she was used to such behavior. "My husband and son are so much alike," she said. "I feel quite in the middle of a battle scene at times. However, Leo, it's only a game, and I believe Blakefield has won only one in the five I have witnessed."

Leopold responded, "Two, actually, madam, and if we win on Saturday, it will be evens! Leon is not playing and furthermore is not coming to practice tomorrow. It's the final one, and Freddie is bringing some fellows he knows who are damn near professional!"

Even as Henrietta was about to admonish Leopold for his language, Amalie interrupted, "But dear heart, isn't that cheating? I'm surprised at you. Are you all really that bad?"

The ladies laughed, and Blanche chimed in, "My brother used to be an excellent batsman, according to him anyway. Perhaps he's just getting a bit soft."

Malcolm also added cheerfully, "Amalie, I remember you once telling us that your husband was excellent in all his athletic pursuits!"

By now even Leopold was laughing. "Well, gentlemen, I can hardly win the game on my own, so whatever it takes! Billiards, anyone?"

Edward March readily agreed, saying, "About that time of day, son."

Henrietta said, "You know that's their new signal for a cognac. Disgraceful, the pair of them, and I am uncertain as to who is leading who astray!"

As the other two gentlemen drifted off behind them, Amalie confided in the remaining ladies, "Blanche, you were in New York last year and missed Blakefield getting hammered by the village men. Your brother was like a bear for days. The truth be told, I prefer the village lads to win—our men all dressed up like dandies and those poor lads working all day long and then practicing at night. Now he's bringing in near professionals. I'm really very surprised at him. I hope he loses."

Cordelia responded, "Actually, I feel the same way. It's all such nonsense and bravado! But that won't get all the catering done. It's such a huge undertaking. Presumably, Bridgette has it all in order. Let's call her down and see what's been going on below stairs. I'm sure I heard shouting and banging in the early morning."

Amalie remarked, "Well, that's nothing unusual at Blakefield, but let me go find her."

Amalie happily walked into the house to seek out Bridgette and was suddenly stopped cold in her tracks. There it stood in the great hall, for all the world to see, or all the household at any rate—the very personal painting, the very one that had so perplexed her husband as to where to put it that it had remained covered up in the east turret.

She stood for a moment in indecision. How had it gotten there? It was heavy, too heavy for one person to have brought down on their own. But who would do such a thing? And why? Dolores? But who had helped her? Who had borne witness? Who had viewed the painting?

Amalie just stood there, at a loss for what to do, until suddenly Bridgette appeared. "Mon Dieu!" she shouted. "Whose work is this? Amalie, petite, are you all right? I will have it covered up and removed at once!"

Bridgette immediately went out to fetch Blanche. However, all the ladies came inside to find out what calamity had befallen Bridgette's mistress—all except Dolores, who had remained in her room that morning, claiming a headache.

Bridgette ran to fetch the monsieur as Lady Agatha and Henrietta were taking Amalie upstairs. She almost seemed in a state of shock. She hadn't spoken a word. Lady Agatha took charge and barked at a nearby maid, "Bring tea and a bottle of your master's fine cognac to my rooms at once!"

The maid ran off quickly to carry out her errand. The whole household below stairs was in an uproar, and one particular sturdy young man, newly employed, sat terrified of losing his situation. Mrs. McFadden had said it was to be a surprise, and the painting had been well wrapped as he carried it all the way down from the turret—that was, until she had him remove the wrapping. He had never seen such a beautiful painting. He had known, of course, that his mistress was beautiful; her beauty was legendary in Hertfordshire. But to see her thus?

Bridgette barged into the billiards room, where the men were laughing and drinking. Her master looked up with a furrowed brow before seeing her worried expression. He said just one word. "Amalie?"

He excused himself and hurried from the room, followed by a concerned Malcolm McFadden.

By then the ladies had gone upstairs, all except Blanche, and both men stared at the beautiful painting, somehow more exposed in the sunlight filtering through the vast windows, the ones Amalie had replaced to freshen and brighten up the once dark and dreary hall.

Leopold instinctively knew that this was not the first time McFadden had viewed it. Had their positions been reversed, he would have done the same thing. So there they stood, neither speaking to the other, one man who had loved the woman there portrayed so many times, the other who would long for her for so many years to come.

Blanche broke in finally. "Leo, please take care of this outrage! Why don't both of you carry it upstairs? *Now!*"

Leopold seemed to finally come to his senses. He turned to Bridgette, who was awaiting further instructions, and said quite simply, to the amazement of Blanche and Malcolm, "Find out who did this and have them carry it up to the attics, where it will remain. I will speak to the responsible party later on, after dinner, and get to the bottom of this calamity."

He spoke calmly, strangely, and Blanche and Bridgette watched in quiet amazement as he led his arch-rival, who had just stood entranced, staring at a nude painting of his wife, back into the billiards room to finish his game.

When Blanche finally joined the others upstairs, all five women were sitting in Lady Agatha's private sitting room, sipping a glass of Leopold's best brandy. The brandy had been procured by Mr. Carmichael, who felt terrible for his mistress and also for the young lad, Thistlewaite, who'd had no idea of the contents of the huge painting that had been wrapped up so well, until he was told to unwrap it in the great hall.

Thistlewaite's heart had swelled at the image of such a beautiful woman, even as his stomach had lurched at the certainty of his imminent dismissal without a reference. He could see full well that it was his mistress and knew the painting was probably very personal to his master. The sneer he had noticed on Mrs. McFadden's lips confirmed that he had been duped and badly used for the amusement of a most unpleasant young woman.

Amalie had been crying but was quite calmed down when she spoke. "Blanche, was Leo very angry? I was too afraid to listen. It's his own fault really. He should have taken it down to his private quarters as he said he would do. He's been too wrapped up in this cricket game and before that, the French pistols. I did tell him many times to take it downstairs. Is he now finally locking it up in his gallery? Of course, why bother? I suppose the whole household has seen it by now."

Blanche hesitated before awkwardly responding, "He is having it taken up to the attics. I'm sorry, Amie. This is quite low, even for my brother."

Amalie was stunned. "The attics? With all of his wretched ancestors? Your mother and father? I don't understand. Does he somehow blame me? Is my buttoned-up Englishman ashamed? Of me? It is my naked body laid bare for all to see. I am not ashamed! Why should I be? It is art and damn fine art! I know Dolores is behind this, and this will not do her much good at all with her husband!"

All sat silently until suddenly Amalie stood up. "Leopold Blakeley can go to hell! My painting is not going up in the attic with those dreadful people. It will be brought to my room until *I* decide upon its final resting place. He can put himself in the attic, for he will no longer be allowed entry into my chamber. You all heard him! That room has now been declared officially mine, while the rest of the house is, of course, his!"

Amalie had worked herself up to a pitch. She felt so hurt. Her beautiful painting, destined to live out its life with the dysfunctional Blakeleys in the attic—how could he even consider such a thing? "I will stop him!" she shouted.

Amalie was about to go downstairs when Lady Agatha called Amalie to sit with her, handing her the glass of amber liquid that had remained untouched. "My dearest one, right now your husband is angry and embarrassed. I do not visualize that your painting will be left to languish in Blakefield's attics for the years to come. If indeed that were to be the case, I would have it removed to Pengallon House."

At last, the artist herself spoke up. "Well, I painted it, and the subject is my dearest friend. I have no written contract, Amalie; he can have his money back. I will have it brought to the museum where they allow me to store my work. Who knows? One day it might be discovered, and you will be proudly displayed in the British Museum. You have no reason whatsoever to be embarrassed, but he does, for not immediately coming to you!"

As the ladies prepared to retire to their respective rooms, they silently agreed with Imogen, who walked Amalie to hers, followed by a much-concerned Bridgette, who held back to make Her Ladyship comfortable before leaving her to rest.

Blanche and Cordelia couldn't help but notice that little Amie did not seek them out. She was far too hurt by the whole ordeal, not particularly due to the public display of such a private painting but more particularly due to her husband's reaction to it. Blanche was tired of making excuses for him and said so, and she and Cordelia agreed to allow Amalie her privacy, locked up as she was in her pretty lilac and yellow-rose bedroom.

Amalie awakened and realized that she must have been asleep for several hours. It was almost time to prepare for dinner, but no one had come for her. The house was so quiet. No sign of Leopold, no knocking and begging for entry. All very odd.

Amalie made a decision. She would forgo dining with the others that evening. She felt certain that Lady Agatha would understand. She would send her a note explaining that she would come by her room later in the evening. Amalie needed a little time to work through her hurt and embarrassment, and now that she had decided upon this course of action, she already felt the better for it.

She ran herself a warm bath, infused with an ample helping of *huile de rose.* Usually, Bridgette helped her with her bath, but on this particular evening, she was enjoying her solitude. Bridgette had promised to keep her husband away, although it did not appear that he had even attempted to come to her.

Amalie laid out her softest creamy silk evening gown. It was plainer and more modest than many she owned, but it was one of her favorites. No need to dress her hair either, since an aquamarine ribbon would suffice. While Amalie was sleeping, Bridgette had thoughtfully left a plate containing pâté and cheese with a fresh baguette and a bottle of fine French white wine, and she nibbled on some before pouring herself a generous glass and carrying it with her as she stepped into her rose-scented bath.

She had made Bridgette promise to see to it that no one was let go due to Dolores's treachery, and Bridgette had promised profusely. The young man was innocent after all.

Amalie found herself reflecting on her life, her marriage, and even the display of her intimate portrait. She would have expected to be mortified, but somehow, she wasn't. She felt amazingly serene. In her vanity, she fully realized the beauty of her painting, and if her husband was embarrassed by it being revealed, well, that was his shame, not hers. She luxuriated in her bath until the water began to cool and until she felt ready to again face the others. Perhaps she could join them for dessert.

Meanwhile, dinner downstairs began as quite a somber affair. Imogen had stayed in her room, as had Dolores, but no one cared about Dolores, certainly not Malcolm. He hadn't argued with her following her cruel and callous act. He actually hadn't spoken to her at all. His disgust by now was visible to all, most especially to his ill-chosen wife.

Amalie's chair, the one now beside her husband's, sat empty, and there wasn't one person present, especially Leopold, who didn't dearly miss her presence. There was conversation but none of Amalie's idiosyncrasies and none of her outrageous remarks, not even her petted and pouting lip, usually displayed quite frequently and teasingly at her husband.

Finally, Lady Agatha spoke up. "Well, I have to say, Leopold dear, if this is dinner at Blakefield Castle without my sweetest girl, I find it very dull indeed."

Since everyone had been made aware of the attic remark, they all soon joined in with the duchess, even Edward, who said wistfully, "It was a wet summer's night in 1897 when she first came to us in London, and nothing was the same after that. She changed us forever. She is indeed beautiful, inside and out!"

Henrietta added, "So very lovely and yet so kind! She built me a wonderful conservatory, for goodness sake! My dearest wish! And one that Mr. March never would have seen to. I've never before known such sweetness!"

Annabelle was next to speak up, with her husband smiling and looking on. "She gave Judith and me our choice of her pretty French ball gowns when she first came from Paris, and she seemed to glow in the giving of them. She has been giving ever since. She even helped persuade my parents to allow me to go to America! Her beauty is only surpassed by her kind and generous heart, and I love her dearly."

Next up was Cordelia. "She gave me a dollhouse and beautiful French dolls. We sat for hours, carefully wrapping up each piece of exquisite tiny furniture for the dollhouse. Yes, Annabelle is correct—she did seem to glow in the giving of these, her personal belongings." She laughingly added, "She somehow also made my Blanche a much nicer person to be around!"

Blanche joined in, remarking, "She brought sunshine to this old mausoleum and made it beautiful. She gave me my brother back after thirty years of hatred and brought peace and contentment into both of our lives."

Malcolm was last to speak up and surprised everyone with his comment. "She is the most magnificent woman that I have ever beheld or ever will behold, and Blakeley, you are the luckiest man alive to have her as your wife."

Amalie had been outside the door, about to enter, when she overheard these remarks. She knew that each person was talking about her, and her heart was full to bursting. Was she really so very special? To each of them? She couldn't fully comprehend why. But she was so very grateful for their love. She waited, however, to hear if her husband would speak up—if he too had such kind and generous words to share—and finally, it seemed that he did, with great sincerity.

"Okay! All right! The painting is not in the attic. It's in my gallery. Why in God's name would I do such a thing? My beautiful wife? Well, she has been revealed to all at Blakefield, probably even the servants, and I'm immensely proud. Just embarrassed, as usual, about my initial reaction. I always seem to get it wrong. I know I'm the luckiest man alive—and yet a most unworthy one. To be truthful, I don't know why she puts up with me! Although I would die without her."

Amalie had to compose herself after such a speech and then decided it was time she made her entrance. Everyone turned as Leopold jumped up to welcome her.

Amalie said, "I think it's your dark curls, my love—well, that and your smoldering brown eyes. Your muscles too—they play a part—and the way you hold a cricket bat or an axe. Or the way you like to command me to do your bidding, knowing full well I never will. Oh, and your lectures about money. I'm very fond of those too. I could stand here for hours and extol my man's virtues, some of which are really rather personal, yet I know it is just too easy for me to embarrass my stuffy Englishman, so I must leave it at that."

Leopold Blakeley's face was bright red when his wife finally showed him a little mercy and happily asked, "Did I miss dessert?"

That night, the Victor Victrola was put to very good use

in the great hall, and even Leopold danced happily to the latest American popular music. All was well at Blakefield Castle once again, even as on this occasion, Dolores felt she had no choice but to remain upstairs and miss all the fun. She would not be dancing with her husband that night or even with her handsome host. And how she hated Amalie Blakeley, who she knew would be dancing with each man in turns.

CHAPTER 18
Anyone for Cricket?

In the end Leopold had decided against bringing in his professional players. After Amalie accused him of cheating, he had thought better of it. Better to lose respectably than to win with an unfair advantage. And when Freddie appeared with his hapless older brother, Bertie, Leo fully expected that his team would be soundly defeated once again.

Leopold called Thistlewaite to his study the day after the incident with the painting, and he actually felt quite sorry for the lad, who anxiously awaited his fate as he stood nervously before Leopold. He had been recently employed as a footman, but there was a quiet intelligence about the young man that had drawn Leopold's notice even before this incident, as he waited at table. He was well spoken, and his countenance was pleasing, his bearing distinguished. Leopold made a surprising and spontaneous decision. Amalie had Bridgette; perhaps it was time for him to have a valet. He had never considered the idea before, but now that he was approaching forty, why not? In a few weeks he would be knighted, after all, assuming no further calamities or impediments presented themselves beforehand.

He began, "So, Thistlewaite, it seems you were duped by my guest, Mrs. McFadden. You aren't the first, nor will you be the last, to be so ill used by a woman. Let's put that behind us now. I'm sure you've learned a valuable lesson. I find myself in need of a valet, a gentleman's gentleman as they call it. Never had one before, but it might be nice to have someone on my team, so to speak. You would be answerable only to me—well, of course, Mr. Carmichael must be shown proper respect as well. And speaking of teams, are you any good at cricket?"

The young man stood stunned, incredulous that his stupidity had somehow earned him a promotion and an enviable one at that. He was well aware that the master had never before employed a valet, and he also was aware of the seniority among the household staff that he would possess. He was determined to be the very best. He already had educated himself on the duties of a valet, having aspired to the position even in his youth. He was interested in men's fashion and in fabric as well as what to wear and when to wear it. He was discreet, and since joining the household, he had maintained a certain distance from his fellow footmen and from the maids, some of whom would often make eyes at him, but to no avail. He finally found his voice. "I can play well enough! I think we will beat them this year, sir. Thank you, sir! I won't let you down." Thistlewaite then paused and tentatively asked, "Sir, Madame Bridgette?"

Leopold laughed heartily. "Mrs. Blakeley will inform her, and hopefully she will grow to like you well enough."

The young man blushed at the mention of Mrs. Blakeley's name, a fact that did not go unnoticed by his master even as he explained about the practice the next day and the match the following one.

"You can get started with your new duties with immediate effect. Once you begin sorting through my personal belongings, you might regret your decision, since I've never paid much attention in that department. Who knows what treasures you may find? I like my shirts brilliant white and well starched, but Mrs. Mowbray can fill you in on all that. Right now the cricket match is the most important issue. Oh, and Thistlewaite, I've no need to tell you that your new position will require the utmost loyalty and discretion."

The young man soon returned to the servants' hall, where all were awaiting his tale of woe, but he was grinning from ear to ear, and they all listened in utter amazement as he told them his good news. He had reassured his master that he would be his eyes and ears, above and below stairs, and he meant every word of it.

⁂

"I really can't believe it, Leo! I wonder how that will sit with Bridgette. I'm not really sure how it sits with me, actually. Why? I mean, you never bothered before. It's quite a personal position. He'll know everything about you—us. Well, I suppose he has already seen quite a bit of me. New horizons now with the knighthood and everything." Amalie found herself feeling a little put out at not having been involved in what she felt was a major decision. Leopold had never seemed the type of man to want a valet, and now suddenly he had one. She had a feeling of things beginning to shift around her. It was as if the impending knighthood would do more than just elevate their status. This worried her a little, but not as much as his next words did.

"I'm thinking of selling the house in Belgravia. You prefer life at Blakefield anyway, and the house often lies empty. It's just an hour or so away, and if on occasion, you want to go shopping or visiting, I can take you."

Amalie spun around in her chair. "On occasion? Really? I'm not a child, Leo, to be *taken* anywhere. The house in Belgravia is mine, remember? Joint twenty-first birthday and wedding present? I am not selling it. I need to use it as a base when I am working, and it is close to Aunt Agatha and Aunt Henrietta—Imogen and Judith even. I am absolutely amazed that you would even suggest such a thing!"

Leopold responded, "Not so much of a suggestion, more of a decision. I know I said that at the time, Amalie, but the house is in my name, and I really don't relish the thought of you gadding about in London anymore, not after the last scenario we had—the last couple, actually. I'm not sure that I want you to continue with your design thing either. It's quite unnecessary."

Amalie wasn't sure if he was serious. Was this a joke? Like the last time? She stared at him wide-eyed and watched as he climbed into bed and put an arm out for her to follow. This was really too much! She was incensed and said as she pulled back the covers, "Kindly, get out of my bed and my room! I have decided that your further admittance into my bedchamber will be by invitation only. And tonight no such invitation has been given. As to the other matters, feel free to sell my house if you so choose. However, I will be consulting with a lawyer before I leave for New York—permanently!"

Leopold sat up and said, "Amalie, don't be ridiculous. I suppose I may reconsider the matter of the house, if it's so important to you. But I still need to protect you and keep a watchful eye—more so now, I think. I'm too tired for drama tonight, however. Come into bed, Amalie."

Amalie stood her ground. "You didn't mean a word of what I overheard last night. You are not immensely proud. You are immensely embarrassed. You just said all that nonsense to be upsides with Malcolm! Please get out of my room. I don't want you here."

Amazingly, Leopold complied. He stomped angrily out of the bedroom, and Amalie sat down, stunned at what had just occurred.

That's it, she thought. *I embarrass him. He's embarrassed by me. That's why he wants to hide me away. Protect me? From what? Him perhaps! Dolores, it seems you have hit your mark after all.*

Amalie was no longer angry. She was hurt, badly hurt. And instead of running along to see Blanche and Cordelia, as she had so often done before, she got into bed, where she was soon asleep. Her heart was so heavy, she couldn't even weep. She had become an embarrassment to her husband, just as the last Mrs. Blakeley had become to Leopold's father. Different reasons but the same end result.

Leopold did not drift off so quickly. He was ashamed of how he had just treated his wife. The truth of it was that he was indeed embarrassed. When Thistlewaite had blushed upon mention of Amalie's name, Leo had wondered about the gossip in the servants' hall. Amalie was, after all, his secret treasure, his wife, and now she had been exposed to all. He found that he suddenly regretted the painting's very existence.

The men were all off practicing for the following day's cricket match, and it had gone noon. Blanche and Cordelia wondered what had become of Amalie. Lady Agatha was seated with Henrietta in the rose garden and would soon be looking for her.

Blanche and Cordelia found her in her bedroom with Imogen and Bridgette. When Amalie explained what had occurred, Blanche said, "This makes no sense, Amie. He said he was 'immensely proud'—his very own words. What a stupid man. I never thought I would call my brother stupid. Ill-tempered and moody perhaps, but he has really hurt you, Amie. I'm so ashamed of him."

Amalie smiled sadly. "I will go down to see Lady Agatha now, and I suppose I must attend tomorrow's match. After that I must decide what to do. One can't un-embarrass a person once one has become an embarrassment. I'm not ashamed. It's only a painting, after all—and, I think, a very beautiful one. At any rate, I can't possibly stay with him now. He thinks he can lock me up and hide me away from the world. That clearly is not going to happen."

Amalie appeared disinclined to discuss the matter any further, and the ladies all went about their day. Amalie sought and found a book to read to Lady Agatha. She chose a murder mystery novel on this occasion since she found she was in no mood for romance.

Somehow Amalie made it through that day, and Leopold did not attempt to come to her at night.

On the day of the match, the sun was blazing in the cloudless sky, heralding a blistering hot day ahead. Leopold knocked before entering his wife's bedchamber. He knew he had behaved badly but was confident of her perpetual forgiveness. He had been embarrassed—wouldn't any man be under the circumstances? But this was an important day, and Amalie wasn't even dressed as yet. She was drinking coffee and writing a letter, and he wondered who it was to, since everyone was already at Blakefield.

"Amalie, we need to talk. I was just a bit, well … try to understand, from a husband's perspective. I won't sell the London house, but I do need to make changes, for your own protection. Aren't you getting dressed? Remember, you are to award the trophy today to the winning team, unless, of course, you prefer not to do so this year. I would probably agree to that, given the circumstances. Who are you writing to?"

He seemed very nervous, and Amalie thought, *Ah, too much of an embarrassment for me to give it out this year. He would probably agree to that. Who is this man anyway?'* She answered him sweetly, "Why not ask Dolores?"

Leopold responded, "Seriously, Amalie, perhaps I should ask Blanche? I asked you who the letter is for."

Amalie responded serenely, in spite of the fact that she wanted to hurl her coffee cup at his bright white sporting attire. "Oh, no one you know. Please excuse me. I have to get dressed. Yes, go ask Blanche. Close the door behind you."

Leopold hesitated. He wanted to know who the letter was for and thought that possibly he shouldn't have suggested that she not give out the cup. He knew he had hurt her, even though he was thinking to protect her. That was always his intention, yet he never got it right.

Blanche didn't hesitate. "Seriously?" Her eyes were flashing mad. "You know what, brother dear? You are an idiot! The answer is no. Go ask Dolores."

Leopold tried to explain that he was trying to save Amalie from further embarrassment, but his sister interrupted him.

"Leo, Amalie has nothing to be embarrassed about, but you do. You've hurt her very badly this time. Go play your game. We might stop by later on."

He went back to his dressing room to pick up his duffel bag and ran down the stairs, knowing full well that once again, he had made quite a mess of things.

Downstairs, the house was abuzz with foods and refreshments of every description being carried out for all the attendees' consumption, including roast pork and mutton pies, even a side of beef, along with fresh summer fruits and vegetables. There were cakes, pies, and puddings and bowls of bright red punch. Barrels of cool ale were retrieved from the Blakefield cellars, where they had been stored for the day's big event. This was an annual tradition at Blakefield, and there was always enough food left over for the townsfolk to take home to feed their families for at least the next few days. Amalie had graced the lawns at Blakefield for the past five summers since her marriage and had shyly awarded the trophy to, most frequently, the captain of the village team.

Amalie sat and watched as folks made their way to the lawn that had been carefully prepared for the occasion, where all the good things to eat were being tastefully laid out, and she fell broken-hearted into Bridgette's arms. Eloise had taken the children, and the house felt quite empty, or so she thought, until all of her favorite ladies knocked and came into her room, one by one. First came Blanche and Cordelia, followed soon by Imogen and Annabelle, Judith, and finally, Henrietta and Lady Agatha.

Blanche remarked, "Well, at least Dolores will be there to show her support, since none of the rest of us are going, unless you are, Amie sweetheart."

Amalie's heart cheered at the sight of all her beloved ladies in waiting, as Leo had referred to them in better times, but she said sadly, "No, I can't go. Leo is embarrassed because of the painting and who all may have seen it. But you must all go. Annabelle, Judith, you must go support your husbands!"

Judith exclaimed, "Well, Amalie, you know that Freddie gives his full support to our cause, given his usual opinion of Leo."

Annabelle added, "Harvey does too! And Malcolm wishes he was playing on the other side so he could give Leo a good thrashing!"

Amalie started laughing. Such wonderful friends and family they were to hold back to support her.

Lady Agatha said, "Bridgette, let's dress up our princess. Where's the aquamarine silk? I have just the thing for that dress."

Amalie still hesitated. "Ladies, I am quite certain that Leo doesn't want me there, princess or not!"

But she was given little choice, as she was undressed and dressed and as her hair was piled high and adorned with her diamond tiara.

Lady Agatha then announced, "Amalie, you have the most elegant swanlike neck. However, I think you should put this on. It was going to be a birthday present, but I'm thinking that the time is right now. I had it specially designed just for you, by Cartier."

She then produced an unmistakable red box. Inside, Amalie found a magnificent diamond and aquamarine necklace. The setting was delicate and intricately designed, as stunningly beautiful as the woman for whom it had been created, and Blanche asked to do the honors and fasten it about Amalie's neck. In the center there was a large aquamarine stone set in platinum and diamonds that dropped to just above Amalie's décolleté. Amalie thanked the grand dame profusely. Never had she seen such a beautiful thing.

She stood surrounded by the ladies and said, "I feel like Cinderella, going to the ball. Oh, ladies, isn't this too much? I mean, I'm very grateful, but I don't think Leo wants me there. I'm an embarrassment to him now, after the whole painting fiasco. I know he said otherwise at the start. I really don't know what to do. At first I thought I should leave him—go away." At this point she started to cry again. "But I can't leave him. I wrote him a letter. I put it in his duffel bag."

All at once, a man's voice interrupted them. It was Leopold. It seemed he'd found the letter. "It was me you were writing to, when I asked you this morning. It was me, wasn't it?"

Amalie wasn't sure what to expect. She hesitated, holding her breath, and then said, "Leo, the cricket match."

"I read your letter. It didn't matter anymore. They're playing a man short. Will you forgive me, Amalie? Again?"

Amalie leapt into his arms just as Blanche said, "Jesus' sakes. Come on, ladies. Let's go watch the match."

By now Amalie was beaming. "Leo, you must hurry, or your team will surely lose!"

Leopold kissed her and ran downstairs, shouting, "We need

to win if you're going to present me with the cup—dressed up like a fairy princess?" He paused before adding, "For whatever the reason!"

As the ladies made their way to watch the match, Cordelia mused, "I never knew anyone who could jump from deep despair to ecstasy in a matter of seconds."

Blanche responded, "And for the life of me, I'll never understand how my brother could have such a resounding effect on another human being!"

Lady Agatha joined in, "She's an angel, I'm sure of it! And she loves him so very much. Now let's go watch this match before it's over!"

The play stopped as Leopold re-entered the game to a round of applause from the spectators. Of course, a player shouldn't actually leave during the middle of an over, but after all, he was the squire, and the food and beverages were especially generous on that hot summer day, so his temporary lapse in gamesmanship was easily forgiven, except perhaps by his fellow teammates.

Malcolm shouted out, "Local hero, Blakeley!" And he was awarded a wide grin as Leopold tonked the ball away out into left field, scoring two runs immediately upon re-entering the game.

They were playing a twenty20 match as opposed to a full 50 overs, for which the ladies were grateful that hot summer's day, as they finally took their seats at the Blakefield Castle side of the lawn. Lady Agatha and Henrietta ordered tea and cucumber sandwiches, and Amalie and her cousins Annabelle and Judith giggled at how incongruous this seemed compared to the feasting and drinking at the other side of the lawn.

Amalie was aware that she was completely overdressed and wished she had insisted upon wearing white muslin, but it was too late now to worry about that. There was a break between innings, and the men ran over for water. Amalie dipped her handkerchief in a glass of water and offered it to her husband to wipe his brow, since he, like the others, was sweating profusely in the intense summer sun. However, to her amusement, he took the glass instead of the handkerchief and poured it on top of his head. Soon his teammates were doing the same, and McBride directed a couple of the stable lads, who were too young to play, to bring over several buckets of ice water.

The Blakefield gentlemen returned to the game in soaking wet shirtsleeves, ready to do whatever it might take to overtake the village lads. Leopold's team had lost two years in a row, and seeing the determination on her husband's face, Amalie was soon shouting encouragement, as were the other ladies, most especially Blanche and Cordelia.

"It's as if he has something to prove, this year especially," said Amalie, "and I truly believe it all has to do with his thirty-ninth birthday this December, since he has made several comments about 'approaching' forty. Still, I have to say it, ladies—my husband still has the best physique on the playing field."

Amalie spoke with pride, and her companions agreed with her. Soon she and her cousins were rating the other men on the field, with Malcolm coming up as a close second and Judith shocking everyone with her jovial comment: "My poor Freddie, I would say, is a distant last. But he is such a sweetheart, so I'll allow him that!"

Her mother tutted disapprovingly and said, "Ladies, please, some decorum. Pretty is as pretty does!"

Lady Agatha was laughing. She had changed significantly since her friendship with Amalie, whom she considered the daughter she wished she had been given. "Young women these days, Henrietta! Can you countenance such talk! I surely never noticed if my late husband the duke even had a physique, good or bad, although he suffered terribly from gout!"

The day had turned into so much fun, and Amalie was

so very relieved that Leopold seemed to have gotten over his embarrassment about her nude.

The match continued, run by run, innings by innings, and over by over. Blakefield Castle was just one point behind, and it was the final innings, with the squire up to bat. Amalie closed her eyes tight and, crossing her fingers, held her breath, waiting for the sound of wood striking leather—and she heard it so loudly that she dared to open her eyes to the sight of Leopold scoring three runs and Blakefield Castle winning the match! He was declared best batsman, and his teammates carried him on their shoulders before dousing him with a large bucket of ice water.

Amalie ran out to congratulate him, but when she realized he was soaking wet, she laughingly began to back off. However, Leopold wouldn't allow her to do so. He wrapped his hands around her tiny waist and lifted her into the air.

"Leo, my dress is wet!" she cried.

He whispered in her ear, "So take it off! Oops, bad joke after what happened the other day."

He was laughing, but somehow it didn't feel funny to Amalie. The joy of the day left her as she left him to shake hands with the opposing team, as the musicians began to play, and as the punch was making everyone merry.

Bridgette had offered to take Lady Agatha and Henrietta back to Blakefield, but Amalie decided to accompany them. It was easy to make her escape in the middle of such commotion, and as the coachman helped them into the carriage, Amalie heard Dolores, in her distinctive Texan accent, congratulate the winners and commiserate with the losers. As Amalie looked back, she saw Dolores hand the cup to the team captain, Leopold Blakeley, and kiss him brazenly on the lips to the cheer of the spectators, who had no idea who the young girl was, this woman who had been spreading unkind rumors about the squire's wife, the soon-to-be Lady Blakeley.

Leopold approached Blanche. "What the hell is going on, Blanche? Who gave Dolores the cup, and where's Amalie?"

Blanche replied evenly, "If she just witnessed what I did, I would imagine halfway to London by now. I will see where she went—presumably to take Lady Agatha and Henrietta back to the house. Maybe she's getting changed out of her wet dress."

"She could have waited for the presentation and had Bridgette take them back. She should be here to support me. This is really too much!"

Cordelia saw that Leopold was getting angry and jumped in. "Leo, Blanche has no idea what happened. Presumably, something did, however. Go mingle, and we'll find Amalie. Stay away from Dolores."

Leopold strode off without saying another word. He wanted Amalie with him but knew deep inside that the remark he had made had been in very bad taste. However, the celebrations would go on into the night, and he wanted her by his side.

Blanche and Cordelia found Amalie getting changed into a cool, simple white muslin dress. It was still so very hot out, almost peculiarly so, which meant that many of the revelers would be getting quickly inebriated in the intense heat. She was glad to have gotten away but was as disappointed in Leopold as she was angry at Dolores.

"I don't want to go back. I don't care what he wants!" she told Blanche and Cordelia.

Amalie told them what Leopold had said to her, and they finally convinced her that it had been just a stupid, ill-timed joke. Blanche said, "Amie, you know Leo never gets it right, but he begged us to bring you back."

Cordelia raised an eyebrow at this obvious exaggeration, but mostly due to Lady Agatha's still being in residence, they were trying to regain some normalcy at Blakefield.

Eventually, Amalie agreed to return to the festivities with

them, but dressed as she was, in her simple dress and with her hair tied back with a blue ribbon.

❦

Meanwhile, Leopold spotted Freddie and his brother, who appeared to be looking for him.

"Leo, thank goodness," said Freddie. "Dolores has been spreading ugly rumors about Amalie. Something about a nude painting? Malcolm is going to need to take her away from here. And there's a woman looking for you, the one who was talking to Dolores earlier. I don't know who she is."

Leopold's head began to reel. "Where's McFadden? I want his wife gone from my home tonight! What woman?" Leopold turned and saw Malcolm approaching.

"I'm looking for Dolores," Malcolm said. "I'm locking her in our room until I can get her on a ship. I'm so sorry, Leo. She ran into Moira Mungavin, or maybe it was no coincidence, since how did she know about the cricket match? They have both been spreading ugly rumors about Amalie. Nasty bitches. I'm divorcing her. I'm so sorry. Good thing Amalie left. She's not coming back, is she?"

Leopold felt he had stepped into a nightmare. "I asked Blanche to bring her back," he said, almost in a daze. How had a day planned for so long gone so wrong? He thought of sweet Amalie, her name being smeared by two disgusting women. He turned again, and there she was; Moira Mungavin, dressed as a burlesque has-been, quite different from the suffragist he had met with previously in London and a grotesque version of the years-ago Violette. She was followed by Dolores, and just as he was about to explode, he looked up and saw his wife walking toward him with purpose, followed by Blanche, Cordelia, Bridgette, and McBride.

He wasn't sure what to expect, but he could not have imagined

236

what happened next. Amalie, dressed in white, with her hair tied back with a blue ribbon, her beautiful eyes flashing, strode right up to both women.

"Ah, the two pathetic excuses for women have teamed up!" she said, putting her face in theirs. "There are so many names that apply to both of you. What were you hoping to achieve this day? My husband to find you somehow mildly pleasing, instead of the loathsome creatures that you really are? Dolores, you will never be a lady, and you disgust your husband almost as much as you disgust mine. The maids are packing up your things, and McBride will drop you at a moderately priced hotel in London. Malcolm, you are still welcome to stay. You will always be welcome here and deserve so much better than this pathetic creature you married. Still, that's none of my business."

She then turned to Moira Mungavin. "You, I want off my land. I don't care if you have to sleep in a ditch. I could say so much more, but you are such a sad sight that it's unnecessary. It seems McBride will be dumping you at the train station for a second time. Bon voyage."

Amalie was still on a roll. She had had quite enough, and as those who loved her watched in amazement, she said, "And if I ever catch either one of you again within a mile of my husband—well, let's just say you'll come out of the encounter even more grotesque than you went into it!"

Neither woman spoke. What could they say? They were surrounded by people with only disgust in their eyes for them, but love and respect for the woman who was berating and belittling them.

This was not what Moira Mungavin had expected from the quiet, meek woman she'd met in London. She knew, beyond a shadow of a doubt, that no woman stood a chance against her with Leopold Blakeley. As for the silly little nincompoop who had invited her to the match in the first place—well, she still had her youthful good looks. Moira hoped she could make good use of them since she had clearly lost her handsome husband, who would probably ship her back to the States on a third-class ticket. Well, if she was smart, she would receive a decent divorce settlement, just as Moira had gotten from poor Mr. Mungavin, which allowed her to always travel first-class.

Dolores turned to Malcolm, who looked away and walked over to Amalie with tears in his eyes and apologies as he kissed her hand.

Bridgette and McBride went to lead both women away from the spectacle they had created, but it seemed that Mrs. Mungavin had decided to have the final word.

"I wish you *bon chance*, Lady Blakeley. You clearly tamed the devil when others tried and failed miserably. Poor Dolores, how she has suffered. I bet your nude is magnificent, and who knows? One day I may see it in the Louvre." She shrugged off Bridgette's arm and proudly walked away, accompanied by a much-diminished Dolores McFadden, who might have been a lot happier had she not allowed envy to enter her very soul.

Amalie suddenly realized that everyone had gone quiet and had listened to her exchange with these awful women, who had maliciously spread rumors about her while she innocently watched her husband play cricket. *Well*, she thought, *there won't be one person in Hertfordshire who hasn't heard about my nude painting now, a painting that was just meant to be Leo's.* She turned to Leopold hesitantly and was overjoyed to find love and respect in his eyes.

She then heard a man shout out, "Three cheers for Mrs. Blakeley!" And then another voice—"Three cheers for Lady Blakeley!"

The people were actually cheering her! Her, little Amalie Blakeley, née Bouchard, who cried about everything and who loved their squire with all her heart. And of course, she began to cry as her husband whispered in her ear, "See, I told you they loved you. Everyone loves you, Amalie, with or without your clothes. And I'm the lucky man who has the flesh-and-blood version and the scent of roses, the scent of Amalie, the woman."

The master then passionately kissed his mistress for the world—or at the very least his tenants—to see, to the sound of more cheers. He whispered again in her ear. "*Your* land? I don't remember saying that."

Amalie laughed up at him as he took her hand, and they happily joined the others in a reel.

There were several men who might have asked Amalie for a dance that night amid all the gaiety, but she held fast to the squire and he to her, allowing no man to come between them.

CHAPTER 19
Changing and Arranging

"The house will be so quiet with everyone gone!" Amalie said. She was taking tea with Blanche and Cordelia in the rose garden on a late summer's afternoon. "I'm so happy you are both staying till Christmas. That cheers me enormously! Otherwise, I would have decanted to London. Leo is in London most days. He promised to spend more time with me, but it seems that he never will. And to think he was going to sell the house in Belgravia? I'd have gone quite mad here all alone!"

Blanche responded, "Well, soon you will have new neighbors. Perhaps they will turn out to be quite fun."

"Hardly likely around here," responded Amalie despondently.

Lady Agatha had declined the dinner invitation to Sir Archibald and Lady Beaton's home, so the Blakeleys had had to send regrets.

"It's such a shame. He was such a nice man, and I love Tulip. The whole estate is up for sale. It is much smaller than Leo's, but he has made an offer. I told him I would like to buy it, if I have any money left, and he and I could be neighbors! Of course, he just gave me one of his glowers."

The ladies laughed, knowing that little Amie was not speaking completely in jest.

Lady Agatha and Imogen had returned to London. This still left the Marches and Havemeyers, and the McFaddens in the end had not been able to obtain an earlier ticket, so they would be leaving two days after the accolade, along with the Havemeyers.

Amalie begrudgingly allowed Dolores to stay in the meantime. This surprised everyone, most especially Malcolm, who moved his things into another room. The divorce was by now inevitable and a fact clearly understood by both parties. The details would be finalized in New York, and Malcolm had informed Imogen, in the strictest confidence, that he would not be returning to Texas anytime soon, so Dolores would be making her way back alone if she chose to return there. He would, of course, provide her with a decent settlement. He had the grounds for the divorce. There was no problem there. After a disappointing wedding night, Dolores had happily provided him with all he needed, although he hadn't fully known it at the time. He had caught her in the act, so to speak, with the ship's purser. There really had been no going back after that, no matter how Blanche and Cordelia dressed her up.

Sweet Amalie, it was rumored, had never before been kissed when Blakeley found her. Malcolm believed this to be true. She was an angel, after all, with the body of a goddess, and the only item he would be shipping over from the States was her beautiful portrait, painted when she was just sixteen. Imogen was keeping his latest acquisition safe until his return to England. He had confessed it all to her. She had a sympathetic nature, and he found he needed an impartial friend. He had told her about his ill-fated marriage and his ever-enduring love for Amalie, and most importantly, she was the first to know that his offer had been accepted by Sir Archibald Beaton. He would keep the name, Beaton Hall, and the old man was happy about that at the very least. The name had a certain irony that suited Malcolm.

Malcolm's offer had been generous, and in this one thing at least, he had been the victor, not Blakeley, whose offer he had easily outbid.

The ranch in Texas had passed to Malcolm and his brothers, who now cheerfully bought him out, since he hardly spent any time there anyway. His father had passed away quite suddenly, and the terms of the will had given Malcolm, as the oldest, a healthy share. The old man, it turned out, had owned several hefty bank accounts. He had been frugal all his life, a canny Scotsman, and his family were now the beneficiaries of his frugality.

Both of Malcolm's brothers had wives and families and were pleased with the negotiated figure. Malcolm was almost giddy with delight that the world was opening up to him, and he had the money to pursue at least a measure of happiness. He had little intention of ever marrying again, after the disaster with Dolores, and had not much guilt in that matter since she was coming out of the marriage much better off than she'd come into it.

Malcolm had a plan, which he had already set in motion. He knew cattle, and he knew horses, and he didn't much mind the rain. He knew how to work hard, although he hadn't done so in a while, and most importantly, he would be close by—and that would need to be good enough. In his heart he knew that sweet Amalie would always be in love with Blakeley, in life or in death, and as much as he envied the man his good fortune, Malcolm's love for her was such that he could never bear to see her broken-hearted. He knew she loved him as a brother—a dearest friend—and that would need to suffice.

Leopold and Edward arrived at Blakefield Castle later than their usual time. They had spent the greater part of the afternoon attempting to find the identity of the anonymous buyer of Beaton Hall—unsuccessfully, of course—and the result was a very irritated and unhappy Leopold Blakeley that night at dinner.

Amalie would have found the whole situation quite amusing if it weren't for the tragic financial circumstances that had brought it about. "What about the horses, Leo? Will the new owner still breed them? Did he buy them too? Oh, I do hope so. I shall introduce myself to them once they are settled. I intend that we become firm friends. Oh, I do hope they are nice! I wonder why all the mystery?"

Leopold sat silently while his wife excitedly prattled on, the customary frown on his face. Amalie noticed this, of course, as did the others, but she was having fun with it.

"Leo, if you wanted the land that badly, you should have made a more generous offer. I'm sure I would have done so if I were a man. And what about the beautiful house? I'm glad nice people bought it anyway. They must be nice, to have made such a generous offer. Perhaps they are French?"

Leopold threw down his knife and fork. "Amalie, can we please talk about something else? Whoever they are, they are likely not French, and I find the fact of their remaining anonymous, keeping their identity so well guarded, quite disconcerting."

Edward March agreed. "Couldn't find out a damn thing today. Whoever he is, no one seems to know the chap. New money, I'll warrant. Possibly the reason for all the secrecy. I don't believe you should be making plans to call upon them until more is known of their identity, Amalie. Might not be the right sort."

"The right sort," mimicked Henrietta. "Why must we always assume the worst? What's done is done, and let's hope that they are a quiet, refined family who merely wanted to keep their business private at the present time."

Malcolm was sitting quietly, listening to the conversation and conjecture. He was quite certain that the penny would soon drop with Blakeley, and he was patiently awaiting that moment. In the meantime he was enjoying Blakeley's quite evident irritation with regard to the matter.

"I agree, Aunt Henrietta," said Amalie. "And if Leo wanted the land so badly, he shouldn't have been so stingy."

Amalie was about to invite the ladies through for their customary after-dinner coffee when Leopold put his hand upon hers and asked, in a demeaning manner, "So, my love, how much would you have paid for a country home, badly in need of updating, and six hundred acres? I'm fascinated to hear your strategy. Kindly grace us all with your expertise in such matters."

Amalie had expected her customary put-down and was quite prepared for it. Leopold had been in such a foul temper since failing to secure the adjoining land, and she had grown quite fed up with it. "Husband dear, as a mere woman, I have no expertise whatsoever. However, I do have enough good sense that I would have consulted with someone who does know, a well-qualified solicitor, and if I wanted the land badly enough, I would have gone well above the asking price and not attempted to save a few pounds on a measly offer, thereby losing any opportunity of being the successful bidder."

Leopold secretly congratulated his wife on being spot-on in her response but did not intend to tell her so. Instead, he calmly poured himself another glass of wine and said, "Gentlemen, you see how well my wife understands money? Most especially when it comes down to spending it."

As he turned to take a swig of his wine, Amalie stuck her tongue out at him, but when he quickly turned back to her, she sweetly said, knowing she had been caught in the act, "You see, ladies, how well my husband compliments me? Quite ceaselessly too!"

Leopold, by now unsuccessfully trying to keep a serious face, said, "Beloved, did you just stick your tongue out at me?"

Amalie answered him with her wide-eyed innocent expression that he loved so well. "I don't think I did, dear husband. At least I don't quite recall doing so."

As usual, the others were enjoying the verbal taunting between the Blakeleys. By that time Harvey was happily anticipating Malcolm's announcement, since Malcolm had confessed it to him before dinner. Meanwhile, Blanche and Cordelia had set a friendly wager between them, Blanche believing that the buyer would turn out to be Malcolm and Cordelia saying, "Surely not!"

Leopold himself brought about the perfect opportunity for Malcolm's announcement. He and Dolores would be going to London the following day, and she was again dining in her room. He would soon be free of her forever. "McFadden, you're quiet this evening. A sad affair, I suppose. Still, you will both be glad to be rid of one another, one would think anyway. A bit of a scandal in Texas, however, I would imagine. Not quite London or New York."

"No, Blakeley, it's not that, although I will be glad to be free again, as will she. I don't believe she likes England much, and we never did make it up to Scotland. I, however, very much enjoy life in the English countryside. I'm looking forward to my first winter here."

Absolute silence followed this statement, among all assembled around the table, until Leopold said, incredulously, "It was you, McFadden! I can't quite take this in! What do you want with a few acres in this corner of the world? What about the ranch? Your father just died—you're the oldest. I really don't get it. All this for what—or should I say for whom?"

Amalie was absolutely delighted but afraid to express it just yet. Blanche whispered to Cordelia, "You owe me ten shillings."

Everyone wondered what would happen next until Leopold

said pleasantly, although still quite incredulously, "Ladies and gentlemen, will you please excuse Mr. McFadden and me? Malcolm, will you join me in a game of billiards?"

The others watched the two men walk out of the dining room together, both men the same height and build, but one as fair as the other was dark. As Amalie watched them leave, the man she loved body and soul and the one she loved as a favorite brother, she said with all of her wide-eyed drama, "Do you think that Leo intends to kill Malcolm?"

That was not at all Leopold Blakeley's intention, but he did intend to finally have it out and clear the air.

Malcolm told him the truth about Dolores and how he couldn't face going back to Texas. He told him of his father's fortune, more than the family had expected and more than enough for him to start a new life on the other side of the world. He told Leopold that he intended to breed horses and to keep some cattle. He had no intention of marrying again after the last disaster.

Finally, with regard to sweet Amalie, he said, "Leo, I would never try to come between you—I never have—not that I would stand a chance anyway. Amalie loves you more than I ever would have thought was possible in a woman. I would say you're a lucky man, but I know she can be quite a caution, and I also know, no matter how you try to hide it, that you're mad about her. I think we are actually friends, you and I, and I'll always continue to have your back. Losing you would break her heart, and I could never bear to see her heartbroken."

Leopold stood in stunned amazement. It was true that McFadden had saved his neck quite a few times, and he'd had no need to do so. It occurred to Leopold that he had very few friends, none that were close to him anyway, although he had a father in

Edward. Now it seemed he had a brother in Malcolm, since he knew deep inside that he could trust him, not only with Amalie but also with his life.

So finally, he spoke, lightly, though Malcolm could see through the veil and see the emotion that he was keeping in check. "Well, if I'm going to have a new neighbor, why not my greatest arch-rival? A Texan, who's about as crazy as the rest of them inside the conservatory, knocking back Cordelia's martinis. Shall we go put my wife out of her misery? She probably thinks I've killed you and am at present burying your body in the garden. You know how her imagination works, especially with regard to me—and of course, my abominable ancestors."

The men were heartily shaking hands when Edward and Harvey appeared, both having been begged by Amalie to go check on them.

Leopold said, "Actually, let's not put her out of her misery quite yet. That was quite a sensible answer she gave to me at dinner, not that I would ever tell her so. Will you both join my new neighbor and me in a large cognac? The more I think about it, what did I want with another damn house anyway? Congratulations, McFadden, although I suppose I must call you Malcolm now."

Malcolm laughed. "No, Sir Leo, McFadden will do just fine. I'm used to it by now anyway. And of course, you're that bit older than me."

Leopold laughingly slapped his back as the other two men stood in wonderment.

Amalie was becoming quite agitated. "Oh, what's keeping them now? Do you think Uncle March and Harvey came upon some terrible scene? Blanche, maybe you should go check."

Blanche and Cordelia decided to do so, and a short while later, Amalie exclaimed, "Now what is keeping *them*? This is really too much! I'm going to fetch Bridgette."

When Amalie came back downstairs with an exasperated Bridgette in tow, she found her aunt and Annabelle in the great hall.

Henrietta announced, "Right, we shall all go and seek them out! Stuff and nonsense. Where is this billiard room or counting house anyway?"

Bridgette led the way, and soon they could hear voices and laughter coming from within. Bridgette opened the door without knocking, and there everyone was, a glass of cognac in each person's hand.

Amalie stood wide-eyed and open-mouthed as Bridgette exclaimed, "Mon Dieu, I don't know who's crazier, the English or the Americans!"

Bridgette then turned to leave them, to resume packing enough clothes to see her mistress through first the accolade and ensuing ball being given by Lady Agatha, then a week at Lady Agatha's country home in Truro, and finally, another week at the beach at St. Ives. Bridgette was to go too, except of course to St. Ives, which also meant that she had to leave a long list of instructions for Eloise and Miss Buchanan. She was shaking her head yet smiling as she made her way back upstairs. Bridgette decided she might possibly handle calling the monsieur Sir Leopold, now that the time was almost upon them, but her mistress would always be "petite," for as long as her petite sought her out when she was afraid or worried or unwell, and it seemed, after all these years and all they had been through together, that she always would.

Bridgette knew Amalie Bouchard better than anyone—all her moods, her kindness, and her capacity to love. She had known her as a young girl who so adored her father and as the young woman who so adored her husband, with an unwavering love that was as constant as it was extraordinary. Neither man completely deserved such adoration, but she supposed they were deserving enough.

Leopold approached his awestruck wife. "Beloved, come and greet your new neighbor, Malcolm McFadden, better known as simply McFadden to me."

Amalie was thrilled. How could it be so? She had expected moods and recriminations, but this? It seemed that through all that both men had experienced, they had become friends, and she was so blessed to be loved by both of them.

She embraced Malcolm, and Leopold shouted, "That's enough, McFadden!" But he was laughing.

Leopold continued, "I'm giving you Nero to welcome you to the neighborhood. He's yours anyway. You broke him in. But once you get this horse farm of yours going, please ensure that my wife does not persuade you to allow her to ride any of your stallions."

Malcolm responded, much to Amalie's chagrin, "Wouldn't ever allow it, Sir Leo—she's much too little!"

Everyone laughed, and Amalie was happy. After all, she had known that already.

Later that night, when they were finally alone together, Amalie said, "Oh, Leo, I missed you so today. I mean, I miss you every day when you're in London, but some days more than others."

"I know," he responded tenderly. "I can always tell. Those are the nights you chide me the most at dinner. Still, I will have to spend more time at home now, with McFadden living next door, so to speak."

This was the exact outcome that Amalie had been hoping for, but she couldn't help asking how he was taking it so well.

"My darling, if there is one thing I am sure about and one person I trust with all my heart and soul, it is you. And yet people like to tell me what I already know. Even McFadden this evening said as much."

This was not quite the answer that Amalie would have hoped for, and she said, "Oh, how exciting I sound! Good old reliable Amalie. Truthfully? Is that how you see me?"

Leopold knew that he had gotten it all wrong as usual, so he tried to explain. "Try to imagine a man spending his working day knowing that a goddess, his own personal Venus, was looking out for his return every evening—knowing that even after six years of marriage, she still missed him and longed for him every day. Imagine that same man keeping a photograph on his desk that he gazes at, remembering the things she has said, her walk, her pouting petted lip, her beautiful eyes and lustrous hair, her womanly scent, so fresh and clean, and her body of a goddess that yields to him in pleasure so very many nights. I thank God every day that I have you and for the knowledge that I possess deep inside, that you will always be true to me, the most fortunate man in the world, whom you chose to be the only man who would ever kiss you, caress you, make love to you, and bask in your eternal grace and love."

At first Amalie was speechless, a rarity for her, but she did manage to find words eventually. "Leo, that's so beautiful. I don't really know what to say. You know you are my heart and soul, and I'm glad that I was so innocent and naive when first we met, because I think you have always treasured the fact that I was. And then you made me a woman—your woman for the rest of my life and beyond. So I suppose I am glad you know this deep inside, for it is true. I could never want anyone but you."

They had climbed into bed, but it seemed that Leopold had something he wanted to share with her still.

"At first I thought Dolores to be ill used," he said. "I felt sorry for her. But Malcolm told me such things this evening, and as I thought of my chaste, unblemished wife, I felt sorry for him. He discovered on his wedding night that he was not the first. Beyond that, she seemed well versed in the act."

Amalie turned scarlet, and Leopold kissed her. "A man always knows these things, although there are women who will try to conceal the fact. A man knows. But he might have gotten over it if he loved her. But he didn't love her, and as if that wasn't enough, he then caught her with another man—the purser, for God's sake—on the voyage over to England. I tell you this not to shame the man, and I feel heartily sorry for him, but to prevent you from feeling any pity toward Dolores. I know how forgiving you can be. But not this time."

Amalie grew thoughtful. "Poor Malcolm. I suppose he wasn't such a terrible husband after all. I always thought his behavior with her seemed out of character for him."

Amalie yawned; it had been quite a day. She was soon fast asleep in her husband's arms, while Leopold lay awake and watched her, remembering that first night together and the wonderful gift she had given to him.

CHAPTER 20
Escape to Paris

"Blanche, I don't want to hurt Leo's feelings, but don't you think the townsfolk will find it a bit silly—us taking our vows together again on Christmas Eve? It's a bit embarrassing, actually. What should I do? I find I am really not in the mood for all that again. One can't go back, and I would much rather move forward; I am just unsure of how to do so."

Lady Amalie Blakeley stood biting her lip, as was her usual habit, while she awaited Blanche's response. She and Bridgette had sought out the ladies in their new, exquisitely appointed suite in the back wing of the house. Amalie had been worrying about the matter for several weeks, really since they returned from Cornwall, and Bridgette had advised that she talk to Blanche.

The autumn that year had been a whirlwind of activities. First they'd had the accolade, which had been followed by Lady Agatha's surprise ball in celebration of the event and then the journey on to the duchess's country estate in Truro. Sir Leopold and Lady Blakeley had enjoyed their time there, so different from that first occasion, the time when Amalie was initially snubbed by the grand dame, only to become her favorite, with the exalted status of permission to call her "Aunt" given that very summer.

Their week in Cornwall with Marnie and Ned Tremayne had been restful, but Amalie felt it was not quite the same as that first year. Leo had seemed distracted, and she had felt he was just going through the motions of enjoying his time alone with her; still, she had put on a brave face, and when they returned to Pengallon House to escort Lady Agatha back to London again, she had tried her best to appear happy and restored.

Lady Agatha had noticed the difference in her sweet girl and had reassured her that she could find nothing amiss in Leopold's behavior toward his beloved wife, but still Amalie felt it—although she endeavored not to show it.

The Blakeleys had remained in London for a few days to help the duchess settle in before traveling on to Blakefield Castle. Amalie was quiet during that train journey, and when Leopold inquired, she responded that she felt a cold coming on, but it was nothing to be concerned about. She feigned being asleep, and he watched her; he was still somewhat distracted and decided to leave it at that.

c✦⋙⟶✦ᥫ

It was early December, and everyone was beginning to settle in at Blakefield Castle for the season.

Uncle March was again usually ensconced in the study or billiards room with Leopold, and Aunt Henrietta was again complaining about his neglect of her. Amalie could fully sympathize because she felt rather similarly neglected, even as Imogen busily painted the family portrait with the invitation and full intention to remain along with the others through the New Year.

Malcolm had not yet returned from America but had written to Imogen that he expected to be back for Christmas. His divorce was finalized, and Dolores was as relieved as he was for them to be rid of one another. She had a generous settlement and had decided to remain in New York. She had hated England and everyone she met there. In particular, she hated Amalie Blakeley, simply because everyone else seemed to be in love with her.

Blanche thought about it and turned to Cordelia. "What do you think, my love—a break away for our sweet sister? Not with my brother—with us. How about Paris? Imogen could join us too. What's your opinion, Bridgette?"

Amalie clasped her hands to her mouth and turned to Bridgette, as was her usual habit. "Bridgette, do you really think I could? Leo would never agree to it. Actually, I am sick of him and of Thistlewaite, who seems to be lurking around every corner. We mustn't tell him—I mean, just go!" She then grew thoughtful. "Of course, I have no money. I wish I knew the combination to his safe."

Bridgette responded, "Yes, petite, a little time apart is in order. I have thought so this past while. But it will be a surprise for the monsieur; we will need to be secretive until after you have left. What about money, Cordelia?"

Bridgette was now accustomed to calling the ladies by their given names, and in the end, she had decided to continue with "monsieur" for the master. "Sir Leopold" just did not feel right to her when she said it aloud.

Cordelia responded, "I will pay for everything, and Blanche can extract repayment from her brother upon our return. We should round up the other ladies and rally their support for our cause."

The ladies all met in the east turret. Imogen was shocked and elated at this turn of events, stating that the painting was almost completed and could certainly be finished upon her return. Lady Agatha and Henrietta said they would be happy to remain at Blakefield Castle with Bridgette, to maintain order with the children and especially with Edward and Leopold.

Lady Agatha surprised Amalie when she said, "I think it has been a while in coming, and a little time apart is indeed an excellent idea. I felt that your escape to Cornwall this year was not all that it could have been. However, you must all move quickly and with the utmost secrecy, for he will never agree to it."

Henrietta agreed. "It will be easily enough kept from your uncle March, but that Thistlewaite is everywhere. Bridgette, how quickly can this be achieved?"

Bridgette responded, "Is tomorrow morning soon enough?"

With that, the ladies sprang into action.

The escape was made easier than anticipated and even more desirable by the news that the owner of the black stallion had finally made herself known to Sir Leopold, shortly after the accolade.

She had contacted his office and arranged to meet him there upon his return from Cornwall. Her name was Lady Caroline De Genève, and she was a renowned beauty and socialite. She was often written about in the London gossip pages, widowed at the age of twenty-nine and much sought-after in London society.

That night at dinner, Leopold had no choice but to casually mention this turn of events, although he dreaded doing so. He reported that she would have the stallion collected by a man servant sometime before Christmas. He said, "She explained to me that it took her so long to find out about the matter because she was traveling this past summer in Europe." He further said,

"She told me she met Xavier Cortez while she was visiting a mutual acquaintance in Cadiz. He told her of his planned journey to England to visit a long-lost cousin and was surprised to learn that she was acquainted with me, from many years ago. She told him that due to the connection he most certainly could borrow a horse from her stables, although she herself would still be traveling. She also mentioned that there had been some gossip about her and my cousin but that there was no truth to it."

The table sat in silence, stunned by this admission. Lady Caroline's antics were well documented in the gossip columns, and her dark-haired beauty was legendary. Amalie felt she had been stabbed in the heart and thought, *This explains his distracted behavior in Cornwall.*

No one said a word until Amalie asked, really very calmly, as if inquiring about the weather, "So, Sir Leopold, why all the secrecy about this woman from your past? Have you rekindled your relationship with her?"

He responded, "Amalie, there was never any relationship in the past, or certainly in the present—but now you can understand why I didn't tell you about her, since I knew this would be your reaction."

Amalie smiled and stood up, saying, "Oh well, who cares anyway?"

The ladies all followed her into the drawing room, leaving Leopold and Edward March to their brandy and cigars, with shocked expressions on their faces.

Edward said, "I told you, Leo—you shouldn't have acted so secretively with regard to the whole matter. Had you mentioned this when first you knew it, you most likely would have saved yourself from the drama you will no doubt experience when you retire tonight."

Leopold responded, "Of course, you are right, but I didn't want to spoil our holiday in Cornwall, and you know what Amalie can be like. It turns out I spoiled it anyway, and I now feel guilty, although I have nothing to feel guilty about. I have been accused, but I am completely innocent. No one, not even Lady Caroline, can come close to my wife's beauty or could tempt me away from her, but I doubt she believes those are my thoughts tonight."

Amalie was first to retire that evening, but the other ladies soon followed. Leopold surmised that since no one had questioned or indeed said one word about his news that night that the worst was yet to come, and he braced himself for a confrontation as he climbed the stairs to Amalie's bedroom. Surprisingly, the door wasn't locked, but his relief was short-lived.

As he entered, she said, "Leo darling, would you mind terribly sleeping in your own room tonight? I feel rather unwell and would prefer my solitude this evening."

She had spoken calmly, pleasantly even, as she was brushing her beautiful hair, and he felt such relief that he had finally told everyone, her in particular, what had been bothering him that past while. He wanted so badly to hold her and make love to her, the love of his life. However, he had no choice but to allow her the solitude she had requested, and he retired next door, where Thistlewaite was waiting to assist him.

Amalie actually had wanted the same thing that Leo desired and to be reassured by him, and she believed in his fidelity, but she wondered about his prolonged secretiveness and deception and about how well he knew this woman from "many years ago."

After a long and painfully sad and worried night, she arose the next morning ready to face the world and in particular Paris, France.

It was 8:00 p.m. when the exhausted travelers finally arrived at L'hôtel Ritz Paris. Imogen, who had never before left England, was ecstatic and couldn't wait to visit the Louvre, the Palace of Versailles, and all of the wonderful places of interest. The other ladies had visited before, although not for a number of years, and were much more anticipating the shopping. As for Amalie, when she was finally shown to her room to freshen up and change for a late supper, she just thought, *This city was once my home.*

It wouldn't be until the next morning that Blanche would send off a quick telegram to her brother stating that the trip had been a spur-of-the-moment decision and that Amalie was in good spirits, and they would return in plenty of time for Christmas. The ladies hoped that Bridgette wouldn't be too berated about the whole enterprise, but Lady Agatha had told Bridgette to refer her master to her if he became at all troublesome.

❧

Leopold and Edward returned on the London train that night, completely unaware of what was in store, particularly for Leo. They noticed the house seemed quieter than usual but thought nothing of it, and Leopold made his way upstairs with a bouquet of mixed flowers. He felt relieved to have gotten the matter of Lady Caroline off his conscience and wished he had just told sweet Amalie the truth before they left for Cornwall. However, at least it was all out now. He opened the door to her lilac and sunshine-yellow bedroom, where he was met not by his beloved but by Lady Agatha and Bridgette.

His demeanor immediately changed as he questioned, "Where's Amalie? What has happened?"

He looked so worried that Lady Agatha almost regretted her part in the whole enterprise—almost, but not quite. "They left this morning for Paris, she and Blanche, Cordelia, and Imogen. Just a little break away from the daily tedium. It was such a spur-of-the-moment idea, and I suppose she just forgot to mention it to you, following your surprising news last night. Anyway, she is fine. You know Blanche always takes good care of her."

Leopold was as incredulous as he was livid. He had to control his anger due to the presence of Lady Agatha, and Bridgette well knew this; he would not have been as considerate had she been the only person to impart this news to him.

"Lady Agatha, my wife did not and does not have permission to take off on a whim, with or without my sister. This is quite unbelievable! She can bloody well stay there! Forever!"

Lady Agatha calmly tutted at him. "Leopold dear, watch your language, and don't make threats unless you intend to carry them out. If you wish her to remain in Paris forever, you best turn over her money to her solicitors. But I don't believe you mean that, dear. I will leave you now to settle yourself down. I am sure Thistlewaite is about if you need anything."

Bridgette left with Lady Agatha to see her to her room. Henrietta was already there, and the three women held in their laughter until the door was closed behind them. Henrietta asked how Sir Leopold had taken the news, and Lady Agatha laughed as she responded, "Well, let's just say that dinner this evening will be quite a challenge to get through!"

Leopold was stunned. Never in six years had Amalie done such a thing to him. Paris? This was unendurable, and what had he done to deserve such treatment? Nothing! He could have had he wanted to—opportunities certainly were on offer to him—but he didn't want to, and he had been true to Amalie since the first time he ever laid eyes on her. Was this about Lady Caroline or something else? He could no longer blame McFadden; all that was in the past. Then he realized that although he was an indulgent and faithful husband, he was also a neglectful one, and perhaps, just possibly, he was getting the treatment he deserved.

The ladies were enjoying their time in Paris. It was such a spontaneous thing to have done, and each woman in her own way was making the most of their time away from Blakefield Castle. The city was beautifully decorated for Christmas, and Amalie enjoyed showing Imogen the sights, thus allowing Blanche and Cordelia some time to themselves. They dined primarily at the hotel, due to the dark winter nights and having no male companion to escort them to other fine restaurants. Amalie had no intention of letting Count Le Clair know she was in Paris, and she fervently hoped that Leopold hadn't done so. She wondered if she had unwittingly left him in the hands of Lady Caroline De Genève. However, if that was where he chose to be, it was done anyway. She missed Leo terribly, although she didn't at first admit to it, but felt she missed "Sir Leopold" not one bit.

On the fourth day, she confessed this to her companions. "It feels that since receiving the knighthood, he has become a different person, and I think there is much more to me, and I am too special to be the little woman hiding in the background while he gallivants around London. Good old reliable Amalie—he has as good as said this to me, although in a manner that made it somehow sound appealing. It is not in any way appealing, and if I were to suddenly decide to start hanging around at London's social events as does his Lady Caroline, I would have the advantage over her. I have nicer hair and a better figure, and she might have a French name, but she is no more French than Violette." Then she thoughtfully added, "Although perhaps my husband cannot tell the difference. At any rate, this is the new me, and he can go to hell or to any loose woman who takes his fancy, since they appear to be more his type than I am, most especially now with his stupid title."

Amalie's companions laughed because it seemed to them that this sojourn was just the thing to set Amalie's spirited nature back on course.

Blanche said, "Amie dearest, I have not noticed you to be reluctant to introduce yourself as Lady Blakeley. Don't you think perhaps you too are enjoying the title, just a little? I doubt that my brother is doing anything other than moping with you gone, no doubt consumed with self-pity and the injustice of it all. I wouldn't be totally surprised if he turned up at the hotel. I am sure he has wheedled information of our plans and where we are staying out of Bridgette by now."

Cordelia said, "I agree. I almost find myself looking around corners, expecting to see him lurking around."

Amalie laughed wryly. "A year or two ago, possibly, Cordelia—in fact, I am sure of it. But not now, and if he is truly enjoying this time with me gone, I will be happy to make that a permanent situation. Oh, I wish we could attend the hotel Christmas party on Saturday night, but not without a male escort."

The others knew that Amalie was beginning to pine for Leopold, and Blanche and Cordelia especially hoped this would be a new beginning for them both, but first he had to come to Paris to fetch her back. Cordelia had suggested that they tell him to do so, but Blanche had rightfully said that would defeat the whole purpose of their actual enterprise. Amalie was unaware that there had been any such plan or intention afoot, but even Lady Agatha and Henrietta and most particularly Bridgette had considered it an excellent undertaking, partially for this very reason.

It was very early Saturday morning, and six days had passed without one word from Amalie. Leopold knew this was deliberate. What he didn't know was how far she intended to take it, this whole "disappearing without a word" act.

He decided enough was enough. He had Thistlewaite pack a bag, realizing that at one time he would have done so himself, ran downstairs to an early breakfast, and sought out Bridgette, who had been completely avoiding him. "Okay, Bridgette, the truth—where is she? And remember who pays your wages."

Bridgette quite deliberately put on a show of telling him that she would be going against her mistress's wishes, even though her petite had not said anything in this regard, not expecting her husband to care. "I would rather not say, monsieur. I promised, you see, and I am sure she will return, by and by, or at least before Christmas due to the children."

Frustrated, Leopold said, "If I were to say L'hôtel Ritz Paris, would I be correct? I am assuming they have not been in touch with Count Le Clair. I don't know what my wife thought to achieve with her little jaunt to Paris, but it will not be as expected. This will be the last time she goes anywhere!"

Bridgette turned to walk away, saying, "Do you intend to make her a prisoner again, monsieur? Safe journey, and yes, you are correct about the hotel."

It seemed to Leopold that every time he took on an extensive journey, either to America or to France, his heart was heavy. But on this occasion it was anger that was driving him, at least in the beginning. He had done nothing wrong, yet once again everyone but Edward was against him. He almost wished McFadden was already there to commiserate with him. He thought, *Is this really about Lady Caroline, or is she just sick of me?*

Hours passed, and on the last leg of his journey by rail from Calais to Paris, he began to finally blame himself. He truthfully always did expect Amalie to be there at Blakefield Castle, awaiting his arrival, and he had made a mess of their holiday to Cornwall. He had been distracted by his cousin's name being brought up to him again and the thought of that woman coming to his office. She had quite a reputation, and she was of course very beautiful, but she didn't inspire him in the least; no woman ever came close to his Amalie. Then during her visit to his office, she had attempted to flirt with him—women frequently did—and he realized how unfair this was to his lovely young wife, holed up in the country. Soon she would have McFadden for company, which meant that it was time for Sir Leopold Blakeley to mend his ways and begin to spend more time with his wife and family. He was wealthy, and he and Edward had recently hired another clerk, who was showing great aptitude. Leopold realized that he rarely took Amalie anywhere, to a museum, to the opera, on a long weekend away alone together. There were so many things he didn't do. Was he finally getting what he deserved?

Leopold finally arrived at the hotel. There appeared to be a Christmas party or celebration going on in the ballroom. There were couples dancing, and he nervously looked around, desperately hoping not to see Amalie there—and he didn't. He went to the front desk and asked which room she was in, stating he was her husband. Finally, after an expensive cash transaction, he was given the room number. He was nervous as he got into the lift and even more nervous when he walked out. He quickly found her room and stood for a moment before knocking on the door.

Amalie was smiling as she opened the door, expecting to find one of her traveling companions. They had decided to have their own party in Amalie's room since she refused to join the celebrations going on down below, and the champagne she had ordered had arrived moments before.

She froze for a moment when she saw it was Leopold and then

burst into tears as she embraced him. He stepped inside and took her into his arms, placing the "Do Not Disturb" sign on the door.

When he finally released her, he saw the champagne and looked suddenly concerned. "Were you expecting someone else?"

Amalie looked aghast. "Only your sister, Cordelia, and Imogen since I told them I couldn't possibly go downstairs to the party without my husband. Leo, how dare you even suggest such a thing to me? I am not like these women you seem to be attracted to, and if they are more to your taste, then quite clearly there is no future for us. I have never been a woman who wanted to frequent the ballrooms of Paris or of London. I never will be that type of woman, with or without you. However, I am fully aware that if I were, I could not only compete with those women but soundly thrash them. It seems that you are one minute embarrassed by me and the next minute bored. You allowed that woman to ruin our week in Cornwall. You had no reason to meet with her, and yet you did. Please go away. This marriage is clearly over. And make sure you cancel your plans for Christmas Eve, since I will be seeking a lawyer now for a divorce. I no longer trust you. You have abused that trust."

Leopold just stood there. When it seemed that Amalie was dismissing him, perhaps forever, his stomach turned, and he felt sick. He was tired, and none of this was true, but all along, everyone had been right. He was unworthy, undeserving of the angel who had so freely given herself to him, body and soul. He sat down on the bed with his head in his hands. He simply said, "Amalie," and began to silently weep.

Amalie stood stunned and unsure at first what to do. But then she knew; it was the only thing she could or ever would do. She walked over and knelt on the floor in front of him. "Leo," she said softly. "Leo, I love you—I always will—but have you grown tired of me? Tell me now, and I will try to bear it, but I cannot remain with you if that is indeed the case."

Leopold looked at her, shocked. "God, Amalie, you are everything to me. Nothing is anything without you. I know that as I never did before. I can't ever be without you. Please, Amalie, I was afraid to tell you and to bring all that up about my cousin again. No one and nothing compares to you, and if you leave me today, as God is my witness, there will never be another for me. But Amalie, please don't leave me."

Amalie saw it more intensely than she ever had before. Her husband was almost childlike in his pleading for the woman who would never, ever leave his side. This handsome man over whom other women swooned belonged only to her and had since the moment they met, in spite of everything.

He was looking at her with such intensity, and she was still kneeling on the floor. She felt she saw inside his soul, and she knew she would never doubt him again; whatever his antics, whatever secrets he kept, she knew he was true to her. She thought of Blanche and said, "Leo, I think I need to allow you to relax, but first will you please open the champagne? I'm afraid I don't know how to."

He stood and helped his wife up and said, "God, sometimes being in love is sheer hell." And soon they were both laughing. This felt to Amalie like a rebirth of their love, and when she said so to Leopold, he said he felt the same way.

There was a knock at the door, and when the couple opened it, Amalie's three traveling companions were standing there, dressed for the party.

Blanche said, "We saw the sign and knew it was you. Now we need a male escort so we can go to the party downstairs, so my baby brother, you have four ladies to take to the ball. We'll drink the champagne while you change."

Sir Leopold smiled as he looked in his suitcase and said, "Thank God for Thistlewaite—he packed my white tie!"

It was a wonderful night, and Leo had to dance with all four ladies. He did, however, whisper in his wife's ear, "How long do we have to stay with them? I am fairly certain they will be perfectly fine on their own."

Amalie responded, "Leo, would you have wanted me in here on my own?"

He said, "I looked in when I arrived and prayed that I wouldn't see you, but I should have known better. Never one too much for society, correct? Let's go!"

Amalie responded, "Leo, we mustn't," but she was leading him out the door of the ballroom as she spoke.

That night they made passionate love, and Amalie was reminded of the first time they stayed at the same hotel on their honeymoon. The next morning, they both arose late and wondered where the others were, or at least Amalie did; Leo didn't seem to care.

When Sir Leopold and Lady Blakeley finally appeared at the hotel reception desk, they discovered that the others had checked out. There was a note addressed to both of them in Blanche's hand: "We decided to leave you to it. Take a few more days and just be in love!"

The Blakeleys laughed. Amalie was delirious; Sir Leopold then more than made up for his distracted behavior in Cornwall, and Amalie now got to go out in the evening, accompanied by her handsome male escort.

They went Christmas shopping together in Le Bon Marche, and Leo confessed that he had no idea what to buy Amalie for Christmas. At first she suggested, "How about a white tie and cutaway?" This was rejected, and she next suggested, "How about a new silk coverlet?"

Leopold rejected this idea too and said, "You know, my lady, I think I spoil you overmuch since there isn't one damn thing I can buy you that you don't already have."

Amalie agreed and said, "Leo, you have already given me the very best gift ever this year."

Leopold didn't need to ask since he knew what she meant—his attention—and she had finally fully achieved that, since never before had he so feared losing her. His sweet Amalie didn't care about balls and parties, since for all her beauty and poise, she was still a little shy and happiest among those dearest to her, most especially him, and it turned out that was present enough for him also.

Finally, they left Paris behind once again, cheerfully and happily anticipating the Christmas season at Blakefield Castle, which was well underway.

It had been snowing heavily, and the train just made it through, with multiple stops and starts. McBride picked them up at the train station in a horse-driven sleigh, and they cuddled up together under fur blankets, which reminded Leopold of the mink coat he had purchased in London. "Actually, I already bought your Christmas present, in London, after you left me," he said. He refused to tell Amalie what it was, no matter how much she begged to know.

Then she admitted that she had already bought his gift in Paris, after she left him. She smiled to herself about the scarlet waistcoat she had purchased for the holiday season—it was certainly not her husband's usual style, and she wondered if he would even agree to wear it.

McBride shouted back to them, "I picked up Mr. McFadden yesterday at the station."

His master happily replied, "McBride, remember who pays you."

McBride responded, "Aye, Sir Leo, I know that well enough, but it seems young Thompson, your new stable lad, felt a little differently and is now employed by your new neighbor. By the way, they came and took away the black stallion. Sad to see it go—a fine creature."

Amalie said, "I'm not sad about it. Too many bad memories attached to that horse."

Soon they arrived home to a warm greeting and a late supper accompanied by two of Cordelia's famous martinis, and all was right with the world again.

CHAPTER 21
1908—An English Thanksgiving

The past few years, since Amalie's Paris jaunt, had been tranquil and contented years for the Blakeleys, even with so many changes occurring in the outside world and in society in general. It seemed to everyone that change was the only constant in the twentieth century, and along with ever-improving motorcars, men were beginning to take their love of progress to the air. This was a new fascination for Leopold, which Amalie dearly hoped would never go beyond mere fascination, even though he insisted that the first commercial flight would be within the next decade, and he intended to be on it. Amalie prayed that this would never happen and that it was all just a passing fancy, even as she insisted that her husband would be too old by the time such a thing was possible, if indeed it ever was.

As always, the Blakeleys had their usual ups and downs. Amalie's accusations continued along with Sir Leopold's apologies, though he was usually quite unsure of what he was actually apologizing for. However, he had finally learned to follow his uncle's advice, given to him before he was even married, and it really did make his life much easier. Amalie was French, and it seemed to him that she reveled in drama and thereby created her own dramatic events, usually without cause. Leo had long since determined that she did so because she loved his making up to her, and after ten years of marriage, he still very much enjoyed doing so. Theirs was a unique and passionate union, and Leo knew that no matter what the future might bring, he would be in love with his very special wife until the end of his days.

It was late November, and another American invasion was soon to be upon them. Amalie was in her element, planning an American-style Thanksgiving feast in honor of the Havemeyers especially, who were making their first return journey since their little daughter Ruby's birth in the spring of 1905.

Judith now had five daughters ranging in age from two to almost ten, and Cosette, who would turn six on Christmas Day, was busily helping Eloise prepare the nursery wing for all her cousins who would be coming to stay. Ruby would be there through the New Year, but Cosette's Allsop cousins were leaving after the weekend—much to her father's relief. In addition, the children's Thanksgiving feast would be shared earlier in the day, with their nannies taking part in it and their mothers fondly checking in on them. Bridgette would be joining the family for the feast.

Cosette now occupied her aunt Blanche and aunt Cordelia's old bedroom suite in the east wing, which had been completely done over—at great personal expense to her papa—but when visitors with children came, she was sent back to the nursery, where her papa insisted she still should have been at her age. However, Cosette knew exactly how to get around her father with her giant teardrops and pouting lips, and he always gave in. This had resulted in a pug, a poodle, and two cats, including Kitty, the little calico who had been the first of Cosette's pets to take up residence at Blakefield Castle.

Leon, now nine, was in his first year at Eton and loving it; he most particularly enjoyed cricket and advanced French, since he was already completely fluent in the language. He hated mathematics and economics, much to his father's chagrin, and had taken up writing with the ambition of becoming a famous author.

Thanksgiving was not a holiday in England but rather an American tradition, and Leon had no inclination to spend it with his sister and cousins at any rate, since they were all girls, so he was staying on at boarding school. He had asked his father for an automobile for Christmas, and the nine-year-old's request had been soundly turned down. Leon's likeness to his father was so unusual that it was often remarked upon, but this resemblance was in appearance only, and other than that, they continually butted heads. Amalie still always indulged Leon—her pet—except with regard to the motorcar; however, Leon had held no expectation of actually being given one anyway and had asked for it only in order to irritate his father. By this time, he was addressing his father as Pater, and Pater had already been called up to his school for fighting, his adoring maman insisting that it must have been completely the other boy's fault.

Leopold often compared his son's life to his own at that age, and of course it bore no resemblance. He was immensely proud of his son, who had the easy confidence of a boy soon to grow into a young man, with a doting mother and successful father to guide him on his way. The dysfunctional Blakeley family history was long in the past, where it would remain forever buried. Amalie no longer asked her husband about it, and her quips were only that, quips about how his ancestors all had been ugly with very bad taste in household furnishings, and he actually quite agreed with her.

Miss Buchanan had been kept on for Cosette, and it was quite apparent that she had a marked preference for girls. Cosette was so very sweet-tempered and kind, with a gentle disposition and an angelic face that showed the promise of great beauty when she was grown. Cosette was clearly her father's pet, and there were still times when Amalie grew a little impatient about that, although she would never admit it. However, it was visible in Amalie's face when Cosette ran to her papa to shower him with kisses each time she saw him. Amalie would admonish her behavior as unladylike, and Leopold would wonder aloud to his wife how it had been with her and her father years before. She would soundly reply that it had been very different indeed, and what would he know about it anyway?

Malcolm McFadden was a frequent dinner guest, most especially since Amalie felt sorry for him dining alone in the evening, and thus far, he had shown no interest in marrying again. Amalie and Malcolm often went riding the estates together, just the two of them until eventually Leopold and Edward had taken on enough staff for Leo to work in his study at home more often, so that he could accompany them during their morning jaunts. Edward and Henrietta remained frequent visitors at Blakefield Castle too, so much so that Amalie had designed a study for her uncle's exclusive use, and her Aunt Henrietta had more or less taken over the conservatory, which she and Amalie were planning to extensively modernize and enlarge in the coming spring, most especially since it was all of the ladies' favorite room. Leo and Edward still preferred the billiard room, where they were now frequently accompanied by Malcolm and which was more or less off-limits to the ladies.

Amalie at thirty-one was still as lovely as she had been at twenty-one, and her style and poise were such that she was treated as royalty when she was in London. She certainly had the air of it, with the way she carried herself in public, although those who knew her intimately also knew this was to compensate for the shyness that she had never quite gotten over and still felt among strangers.

Leopold, now facing his forty-third birthday, was still devastatingly handsome—and he knew it. Sometimes Amalie thought he was even more so than when first they had met. He had some graying at his temples, a distinguished look in a man. Amalie had Bridgette keep a close eye on her own tresses, since a woman could never be described, nor would want to be described, as "distinguished." Thistlewaite kept his master immaculate in his brilliant white starched shirts, and Sir Leopold wondered how he had ever managed without him.

Bridgette and Thistlewaite were known to bicker from time to time, but the latter knew that the former would always win in the end. She would take the matter to Lady Blakeley, whom she still called "petite," and Sir Leopold usually would take Bridgette's side for a peaceful life, shrugging his shoulders at Thistlewaite. Still, the valet thoroughly enjoyed his position in the Blakeley household. His master was very easily taken care of, as long as his shirts were kept brilliant white and his boots polished. Also, he had purchased a brand-new Cadillac Runabout, shipped over from the United States, and was in such a congenial mood since its arrival that he was allowing McBride to teach his valet how to drive in the old Wolseley—which was by now on its last legs, or wheels at any rate. This particular new addition to the Blakeley garage was royal blue, and Amalie felt that the color was at least a little more refined than the red Daimler.

Malcolm also had brought two new motorcars over from the States, a 1908 Packard Model 30, which had just arrived on the same steamer as the Cadillac, and a 1904 Studebaker that he'd had shipped over when he left the US for his new life in England.

By this time both Blanche and Cordelia could drive and were considering purchasing their own automobile—"If we are ever in the States long enough to have the time to consider it," Cordelia quipped. So they were frequently to be found out driving in the shiny red Daimler—always, of course, without Sir Leopold's permission.

Leopold and Edward had taken Amalie and Henrietta to New York the year of Annabelle's daughter's birth, and both Leon and Cosette had accompanied them. Amalie had declared that she loved New York and had begun teasing her husband that she was considering leasing a penthouse apartment facing Central Park, which of course he could pay for. However, ever since her Paris jaunt that winter in 1904, she had sensed a fear in him about ever letting her out of his sight for long, and she really didn't mind. In fact, it pleased her that he would feel that way after ten years of marriage.

Leopold and Malcolm had shocked everyone with their recent joint purchase of a large warehouse from a bankrupt textile manufacturer. The previous owner had never quite recovered his reputation from his use of deadly arsenic in his colorful green textiles during the last century. This had given Amalie a new enterprise, along with her team of designers, who were designing new fabrics in a spin-off from Madame Bouchard's Interior Designs. The factory employed women in equal number to men, and Amalie insisted that their wages be on the same scale. Since this was a very recent enterprise by the two men, who were by now friendly rivals, it was a matter that was to be discussed during the first Blakefield Castle Thanksgiving dinner, to be held on Thursday, November 26, 1908, and Amalie was saving the question of her not yet having been paid a shilling in wages for when both gentlemen were present.

❧

"Amalie, how many damned people are staying in my home this weekend? It seems wherever I go, I am tripping over someone's offspring or one of Cosette's pets, and there are people everywhere. When are they all leaving?"

It was the night before Thanksgiving, and Amalie knew where this was heading and why. "Leo, I have no idea how many are staying in your home, but including Lady Agatha, Imogen, and all the children, there are just under twenty staying in mine, not counting Leon, who isn't here, or Bridgette, who comes with the castle."

"Since when did Blakefield Castle become your home and not mine, beloved?"

"Since I made it so beautiful and since everyone we know and love enjoys spending time here. After all, ten years ago, or before you met me, not only were you a ghastly and nasty man, but the castle was old-fashioned, and everything in it was burgundy—yuck! And you had ugly old paintings of your nasty ancestors instead of the beautiful paintings we have on our walls now—primarily of me."

Leo said, teasingly, "Ah, those were the days! Before I met that French woman— what's her name—who spends all my money without a thought or word of apology."

Amalie playfully retorted, "Ah, you mean the French woman who is beyond compare and whom you can't seem to keep your hands off of? That French woman—the one whose bed you are always begging entry into?"

"Begging?" Then he laughed. "Well, only sometimes, when absolutely necessary. Shall I beg now, beloved?"

"Possibly," Amalie responded with her little inviting smile. She certainly needed to keep her husband in halfway decent spirits since she indeed might have overdone it with the guest list, and she really did have to tell Eloise to tell Judith's nanny to keep the girls in the west wing as much as possible, at least when Sir Leopold was home.

First thing in the morning, Amalie was awakened by the sound of some fracas in the kitchen, but that was not so unusual, and Bridgette had promised to have one of the maids bring them up breakfast in bed. The less time that Sir Leopold had to be about his house that was groaning with visitors, the better spirits he would be in for dinner, which was being served early at 4:00 p.m., in accordance with tradition—according to Cordelia, at any rate.

Breakfast arrived, and the smell of it soon awakened Leopold, who had slept through all the noise downstairs, most especially because of Amalie's special treatment the previous night. First, she had given him a bath, scented with lavender to soothe his soul, and then she had playfully seduced him. Leo had known this was Amalie's way of manipulating him into a serene state of mind, and he considered that he should really find more ways to deserve such treatment more often.

As she served him up breakfast and fluffed his pillows, he said, "I could easily get used to this treatment. There's a lot to be said for being moody and ill-tempered, or so it appears."

Amalie responded, "Don't push your luck, sir! However, you better not pull any moods today, on a day when we are to give thanks for all of our blessings."

Leopold was actually feeling very content, even with all the visitors. It was like every so often, something Amalie said or did reminded him so much of the early years, and he was remembering the time she'd fed him warm raw eggs and cold tea—made with water from the pot in which the eggs had been not quite cooked—in her effort to be a good wife. That was a sweet memory. He thought also about the way she had pined for him when he'd gone to France that same year or, even worse, during his trip to New York—the year he and Edward had almost ruined themselves with an overly speculative speculation. And of course, there were the dueling pistols she had shocked him with after six years of marriage, his most prized possession next to his wife's nude portrait, which was now safely kept in his locked private gallery, as were the pistols. He said, "You know, my love, I've decided to keep you, in spite of what you cost me. Do you think we should retake our vows again on Christmas Eve?"

This received the expected answer. "Absolutely not! Three times is enough! The first time was my most magical day ever, and I still reminisce about it often; the second, my most agonizing night ever, although at least it produced our sweet daughter—her papa's pet. Then the third time—do we remember that time, sir? How you got drunk and passed out on our bed? No, I don't need to retake my vows again to know you are completely mine."

They both said in unison, "God help me!" and then burst into laughter at their happy life together.

Leopold intended to have fun at dinner. He loved to tease Amalie—she was so easy to rile up—but he would do so only playfully this time since it was Thanksgiving, and the one thing, person actually, that he gave thanks for every day was the French siren who was by this point pulling and throwing dresses out of her huge wardrobe.

"I need several new dresses. I'm getting rid of most of these to my staff. I am going in for a new, modern, sleeker style of clothing, and I'm ditching my corsets too. That can be your Christmas present to me this year—a whole new wardrobe and a black leather briefcase."

Leopold thought that it would be easier than he'd expected, to rile sweet Amalie up, but he wanted to save it for dinner so he just responded, "I will need to think about that."

"Think about it all you like, sir," Amalie called as she made her way in to run her bath.

By this time Blanche and Cordelia were as much in residence in Hertfordshire as they were in New York, and there were even occasions when they would steal Cook and one of the maids and go to the Blakeleys' London house, when the Blakeleys were not themselves in residence. Neither they nor Amalie felt the need to inform Leopold of this, until the time he called the police after going by to check on the house and finding it fully lit up. He never told the ladies that this had been a deliberate stunt, but after that, they usually mentioned their trips to London to him—but only in passing, of course. Leo was also aware of them driving around in his motorcar, but he really didn't mind and enjoyed their subterfuge in so doing. Amalie was always more content when they were in England, and a contented wife meant a peaceful home—usually, at any rate.

Imogen was in charge of the dining room table, and her use of fall foliage and colonial-inspired decorations led Cordelia to exclaim that she could almost feel she was in Upstate New York, and Harvey Havemeyer agreed. He and Annabelle were enjoying their own domestic bliss in those days; however, they still fervently hoped for some shenanigans at the planned Thanksgiving feast.

Actually, everyone was in that frame of mind that November afternoon, even Lady Agatha and Henrietta, who had long since become famous friends. As for Edward, as long as there was brandy about, he just bided his time until the ladies withdrew after dinner.

Bridgette came upon Amalie's bedroom suite, now aquamarine and rose-petal pink, in complete disarray. "Petite, why are your clothes all on the floor? They will be ruined. I hope you are not fighting with the monsieur on today of all days."

"No, honestly, Bridgette, I am not, but I am giving all of these away to the staff. You can decide how to go about it, but I am going in for a brand-new, sleeker look, and I am also doing away with corsets—well, except for grand dinners in London or in case any unexpected past mistresses of my husband turn up again, in which case I had better keep a few, I suppose."

Bridgette responded thoughtfully just as Sir Leopold was coming in to check on his wife's progress. "Petite, you can hardly have your maids running around in your old dresses. No, I will sell them to a dealer in London, and you can donate the money to a worthy cause. What do you think?"

Amalie responded, "Excellent idea, as long as the worthy cause is not Sir Leopold Blakeley's unfortunate old mistresses. Well, perhaps that would be a worthy cause after all."

Hearing this, Sir Leopold abruptly left the room and shouted back, "Dearest, remember, today is a day to be thankful. You should be thankful for all those lovely frocks that you no longer want, since I don't believe I can afford to buy you any new ones."

❧

Eventually, all were assembled at the dinner table, with Leopold at the head of it and his sister at the other end, since Amalie had long ago given up that seat. It was just the middle of the afternoon, but Amalie had required white-tie attire from the gentlemen, and the ladies were splendid in their best ball gowns. Even Bridgette, who was joining them, was dressed for the occasion.

Edward was about to pour himself a glass of wine when Amalie looked at him, appalled, and said, "Uncle March, first Leo has to say a prayer of thanks before anyone can partake in anything, since he is the host of this fine dinner. Leo? Please be creative."

Sir Leopold promptly stood up and recited a prayer he

remembered from his childhood at boarding school, recited each day before meals. Blanche was the first to burst into laughter, followed by all the others except Amalie, who was trying her best not to do so.

"Really, Sir Leo, is that the best you can do?" she said. "Kindly be seated. Harvey, do you mind?"

Leo sat down and began rubbing his leg against Amalie's. She was so serious about this dinner that he couldn't keep himself from trying to sabotage it. She kicked him, and he shouted, "Ouch!" Amalie told him that she was considering sending him upstairs to the nursery.

Leopold finally grew somewhat serious. "Imogen, you have done a wonderful job decorating the table. I almost feel like a pilgrim—well, I suppose a very rich pilgrim. But my darling Amalie, you have us all dressed up and drinking wine at four o'clock in the afternoon. A bit silly perhaps?"

Amalie gave him her meanest look and responded, "No, Sir Leopold, you are the silly one—and very disrespectful to our American guests, as this is their tradition."

Amalie had arranged for her husband to carve the turkey and was now beginning to regret that decision, just as the footman delivered a huge bird along with its stuffing and sat it in front of his master. The vegetables were then placed upon the table in order for the guests to pass them around, as opposed to their normal habit of serving themselves from the trays that were presented to them.

Utter chaos soon ensued. Leo shouted, "I'm taking a leg. Who wants the other one?" This offer was quickly accepted by Malcolm. Plates were being passed back and forth along with serving dishes containing the various side dishes prepared by Chef Moreau, who felt disgust at the way his fine meal was being presented.

Leopold was being quite the gentleman and serving his wife

seated at his right-hand side. He was serving her very small portions and himself very large ones, and when he gave her just two brussels sprouts, she said, "Why are you trying to sabotage dinner? May I please have a few more? You know they are my favorite, most especially with Monsieur Moreau's special sauce."

Leopold then announced, "Corsets, I hear they are going out of fashion. All the more food for us men, I would think now."

Henrietta was appalled and exclaimed, "Sakes, Leopold, please no corsets at the dinner table!"

Quite shockingly, Lady Agatha answered, "Henrietta, I can assure you I am wearing mine!"

After that everyone resumed tucking in, and the food was indeed delicious. Amalie looked around at those she loved best and happily ate her very small meal while she rubbed her stockinged foot up and down her husband's trouser leg. He smiled at her, and she saw the love in his eyes. How she loved this man. He was the best thing that ever had happened to her, even with all of his moods, and she felt inspired to say something once everyone had finished eating their grand dinner and before dessert was served.

"Now I think we all should say a thank-you for something that occurred during the past year. I mean instead of the usual stuff. Leo, you can start, and don't say me because you have me every year." Then she blushed and said, "Oh dear, that didn't come out quite right, but you know what I mean, and don't be silly."

"Okay, my brand-new blue Cadillac."

Malcolm answered next, saying, "In that case I have to say my brand-new black Packard."

Then each in their turn said something, and the remarks became ever sillier. It occurred to Amalie that this was a day she would never forget, all of these silly things and everyone so enjoying themselves.

Lady Agatha said, "O'Rourke up and left to marry some poor man. I am very thankful about that."

Next Bridgette said, "I am thankful that I didn't have to attend any more WSPU meetings with my mistress due to her fear of coming across any further past mistresses of the monsieur."

Everyone laughed at this and then even more when Sir Leopold said, "You see the respect I get from this woman who is so highly paid and still refers to me as 'the monsieur.'"

Amalie said, "I wonder that all my husband's past—oh, I can't even say the word—ended up as militant suffragists."

"Okay," said Leopold, "enough said on that subject!"

And on and on it went around the table, with the remarks becoming sillier and sillier, from Blanche finally finding the perfect shoes for her size nines to Henrietta finally getting rid of her husband's nasty old easy chair to the tally man and Edward having to purchase a new one.

Finally, Harvey said, "I have to be a little serious. Of course, it goes without saying that we are all thankful for our families, even the families we have adopted in one another, but I think this is the most delightful group of people I have ever spent time with. I have so many fun memories of our time here in 1904, and I am sure I will be taking back many more wonderful memories after the kindness of our hosts inviting us here for the entire holiday season."

Amalie said, "Of course, Harvey, you and Annabelle and little Ruby will always be welcome, and you too, Judith and Freddie, and of course, Aunt Agatha and Aunt Henrietta and my dear sisters Blanche and Cordelia, my dearest friends Imogen and Malcolm, and my cranky uncle March. I love you all so very much. However, I want to say something very special to a very special person without whom I never would have survived and whom I love as a mother."

Leopold interrupted, a little embarrassed at being left out of the recitation. "Oh, not me, I hope."

Amalie gave him a look and then continued. "Bridgette, I love you as a daughter loves the dearest mother in the world, and you are my mother, my comfort, my advisor, and the person who has never let me down. I would like to propose a toast to my very dearest Bridgette."

Of course, everyone stood for that, and there was a tear in Bridgette's eye, a most unusual sight, since this had come completely unexpected to her. She said a little shakily, "Petite, I love you as my beloved daughter and a joy to be beside."

There was a pause after this emotional scene until Sir Leopold cleared his throat. "Um, dearest one, I don't recall my name being mentioned in your list of those you love—quite hurtful, actually. However, I agree with you about Bridgette." He looked to Bridgette and said, "I love you too. You both came into my life as a package, and there has never been a dull moment. I hope it always continues that way." He turned toward Lady Agatha and quipped in the way he was now allowed to address her, "Aunt Agatha, don't you even consider trying to steal her."

To this she responded, "Payback for Eloise, my boy."

Amalie dried her eyes and said, "Now, Sir Leopold, I was saving you for last, so here goes. You are very good-looking, and don't you know it. Um, let me see, you can be funny now and again, when you are not in one of your nasty old moods. Um, what else? You are very easily embarrassed, although you pretend not to be. In fact, I think I will finally let everyone in on why I have put up with your quite beastly moods for ten whole years." She then paused and said, "See, he is already turning red, terrified of what I am about to say, so I will just say it. Sir Leopold, you are one hell of a wonderful lover."

Leopold sat with a red face and shocked expression and thought, *Did my wife just say what I think she said?*

It was Lady Agatha who broke the embarrassed silence. "You see why I love my girl! Who else would ever dare to tell the truth to all of us jealous old fogies? Leopold, a sherry for your aunt Henrietta, or smelling salts, whichever is handiest!"

Sir Leo obliged with the sherry and then took the floor. "Okay, now that I have recovered from that quite unexpected remark—or compliment, I'm not sure," he said questioningly, "I would like to say a few words. We are all gathered here together because of Amalie and the love she has for each one of us—well, me especially—but beyond that, Amalie you are so very special, so very beautiful, but that's the obvious part. The thing is, you are funny. You make us all laugh with your antics. You make those dearest to you happy, and you rejoice in so doing. Everyone at this table loves you in their own special way, and I'm mad about you—always have been, always will be. And for what it's worth, my sweetest girl, you never needed a corset in the first place."

Amalie laughed and then began to cry.

Blanche shouted, "Okay, little brother, you just had to make our dear girl cry! She was doing so well too! However, since we are all getting a bit gooey following all of that turkey and stuffing, I too would like to say my piece, after which I believe my dearest Cordelia will be mixing martinis for cocktail hour. Leo, everything you say about our sweetest girl is true, right down to her knockout figure—sorry, Henrietta! Okay, but here's the thing. We all love you too—some of us more than others, of course, but for a conceited, smug, moody, and ill-tempered man, you're not so bad really, and not bad-looking either, and I love both of you so very much. There, I have said it and probably never will again."

The evening proceeded with more fun and frivolity, and the old Victor Victrola was brought out along with Amalie's favorite records. Leo even allowed Malcolm one dance with Amalie.

Amalie did finally say to both men, "You know, gentlemen,

I don't work for nothing, so if you want my designs for this new enterprise, you will need to pay me for them. And I want my own office in the warehouse so that when I stop by, I can act important, just like you gentlemen like to do."

Malcolm said, "Maybe she's right, Leo. Are we expecting her to work for room and board at Blakefield Castle? I should pay her at the very least."

Leo thought about it. "Okay, McFadden, what do you think? Ten shillings a week?"

Malcolm laughed and said, "I'm sorry, Amalie. Even after ten wonderful years, your no-good husband is still afraid to give you any money. You already have a fine mare, and Cosette a new pony, so how about I give you a cow in exchange for your future designs. What do you think, Sir Leo?"

"I'm agreeable to a cow. And furthermore, I will throw in a milking stool."

Amalie was laughing merrily. "Well, it turns out that I would very much like a cow, and if that's the best I can get, okay, but I still want a black briefcase, Leo."

Leopold answered, "McFadden will buy you one for Christmas since I have to buy all these new frocks."

Malcolm said, "Okay, it's a deal. I will also throw in some sketch pads and colored pencils for your designs."

Amalie replied, "Malcolm, I fear you are spending too much time with my husband—you are beginning to sound like him!"

Blanche and Cordelia appeared with Harvey and Annabelle. Blanche said, "Okay, Amie, we all want to know how your negotiations went. How much are they paying you?"

Amalie started giggling. "A cow and a milking stool. Oh, and a black leather briefcase, sketch pads, colored pencils, and some new dresses."

They all laughed, and Blanche said, "Some negotiator, Amie

dearest. We were going to take bets, but I don't believe anyone would have come up with a cow!"

Just then Edward appeared and said, "Billiards?" And all the men cleared out and left the ladies to their martinis—even Freddie, though reluctantly, of course.

By the end of the evening, both Lady Agatha and Henrietta had to be helped to their rooms, but all agreed that it had been a wonderful day, never to be forgotten.

Malcolm made his farewells and promised to be over the next day for leftovers, as Sir Leopold took his lady's hand and led her upstairs. Malcolm still loved Amalie for sure but was content with his role as best friend and riding companion, which meant he saw her every day, more than he once ever could have hoped for.

Once the Blakeleys were alone and lying in their brand-new bed—the springs having given out in the old one—Amalie said, "I hope Cosette will one day find a husband as wonderful as her papa, but I'm not really sure if that's possible. But he has to love her, even if he isn't very rich. He has to love her an awful lot. I will see to that."

Leo responded, "Well, my love, we are a long way away from that, since she is not quite six. Did you intend to embarrass me tonight? I couldn't believe you said such a thing in front of Lady Agatha. I thought your aunt was going to pass out, and Freddie went crimson—not sure why. They have five daughters after all."

Amalie, being Amalie, said, "Well, my buttoned-up Englishman, that doesn't really require technique."

"Any more out of you, my lady, and I might need to wash your mouth out with soap and water."

Amalie just smiled. "You know something? I have come to realize that you aren't so bad after all. You just pretend to be. Ten whole years. I wonder what the next ten years will bring. In 1918, you'll be over fifty, and I over forty—our children almost grown.

I can hardly bear to think about it, although I sometimes wonder how the world will be by then."

She turned over and held on fast to her husband, who had already drifted off to sleep, and thought, *Well, I suppose that's a long way off and a whole different story.* Lady Amalie Blakeley whispered, "Loving Leopold—*amour toujours*," as she too contentedly drifted off to sleep.

Lightning Source UK Ltd.
Milton Keynes UK
UKHW012214190522
403272UK00008B/151/J